Meet

A race of beings all too willing to worship the first men as gods—with hellish consequences.

A lone human being heading for a rendezvous among the stars that will decide the future of mankind.

A handful of space travelers on the far side of the moon who heatedly debate the most effective way of destroying the earth.

A creature who all too successfully attempts to imitate the ways of his human captors—only to learn the fatal secret of his own nature.

Plus five other electrifying stories of

EARTHMEN
and
STRANGERS

EARTHMEN
AND
STRANGERS

NINE STORIES OF SCIENCE FICTION

Edited by Robert Silverberg

A DELL BOOK

ACKNOWLEDGMENTS

Dear Devil, by Eric Frank Russell, copyright © 1950 by Clark Publishing Company. Reprinted by permission of the Scott Meredith Literary Agency from *Other Worlds*.

The Best Policy, by Randall Garrett, copyright © 1957 by Street & Smith Publications, Inc. Reprinted by permission of the Scott Meredith Literary Agency from *Astounding Science Fiction*.

Alaree, by Robert Silverberg, copyright © 1958 by Candar Publishing Company. Reprinted by permission of the Scott Meredith Literary Agency from *Saturn Science Fiction*.

Life Cycle, by Poul Anderson, copyright © 1957 by Fantasy House, Inc. Reprinted by permission of the Scott Meredith Literary Agency from *Fantasy & Science Fiction*.

The Gentle Vultures, by Isaac Asimov, copyright © 1957 by Headline Publications, Inc. Reprinted by permission of the author from *Super-Science Fiction*.

Stranger Station, by Damon Knight, copyright © 1956 by Fantasy House, Inc. Reprinted by permission of Berkley Publishing Corporation from *Fantasy & Science Fiction*.

Lower Than Angels, by Algis Budrys, copyright © 1956 by

CONTENTS

INTRODUCTION

The first thing every child learns is that he is not the entire universe.

It comes as a shock, even though the discovery is gradual. As a baby's awareness grows, he realizes that at least one other human creature exists—his mother, that large, warm, protective object that is always nearby. Later comes the discovery of other relatives: father, sister, brother, uncle. The doctor, grandparents, friends, all become part of the picture for the child, and he realizes that the universe beyond his fingertips is quite a crowded place indeed.

Then he finds out about strangers.

Strangers are those who do not fit into the family circle, people who cannot be recognized, whose existence is an uncomfortable mystery. Until he has met his first stranger, the child has known nothing but love. Now comes a challenge; for the stranger, being a stranger, does not necessarily love the child. Ties of family and friendship do not exist, and some other relationship must be developed.

Most children learn how to get along with strangers well enough. They find out that it is possible to make friends with certain strangers, and that it is wise to keep away from others. And they make the discovery that for the rest of their lives they are going to be encountering strangers every day. Their happiness and success will depend on their skill at dealing with these strangers, who may be different from them in ways of thinking, in color of skin, in outlook. Growing up, then, is a process of collisions with strangers, and a test of maturity is the ability to handle such collisions.

Not only children but whole planets eventually discover that they are not the entire universe. At least, so the science-fiction writers have been saying for many years. They look to the stars for the strangers, people of other worlds, who one day will intrude on the so-far private existence of mankind. We have never yet encountered people of other worlds, of course—

not in any way that can be satisfactorily documented, that is.
But the sky is full of stars, and some of those stars must have
planets, and it seems likely that in an infinity of worlds there
must be intelligent life besides that on Earth.

We are not alone, say the science-fiction writers. Making
that assumption, they go on to examine it. What will it be like
when we encounter the people of other worlds, the alien life
forms that await us in the galaxy? Will we find ourselves
trampled under the heels of conquerors? Or will we be the
conquerors ourselves, destroying other civilizations in space as
we have done on our own planet? What strange emotional experiences will befall the first men who confront alien
creatures? What conflicts will there be, what philosophical
upheavals, what catastrophes and triumphs?

Science fiction attempts to answer these questions. The contact between man and alien has been one of its central themes
since its dawning. The title of a famous early novel by H. G.
Wells indicates one possible outcome of that contact: *The
War of the Worlds*. Other writers have told of more peaceful
meetings, even love, between earthmen and strangers. Nine
stories of contact with extraterrestrial beings are assembled
here, offering nine different approaches to that relationship.

But what if we *are* alone in the universe? What if it turns
out that the other worlds of the galaxy are as lifeless as the
voyage of Mariner IV has indicated Mars to be? Are all the
speculations of science fiction worthless, then?

No. Because the science-fiction writer, in the final analysis,
is never really writing of other worlds and other times. Behind
the futuristic trappings of his stories lies a more earthbound
core. For the science-fiction writer, no matter how vaulting
his imagination may be, is still a man of twentieth-century
Earth. He has never visited another planet nor laid eyes on an
alien being. What he writes about, then, comes from within—
what he himself has seen and thought. He translates his own
experiences and speculations into the soaring wonders of
science fiction, but we can look behind the rockets and the
strange creatures to find the real world of today. Science
fiction, at its best, illuminates our own time by turning a mirror toward the future.

Even if we are unique in creation, then, we can find merit
in stories of other forms of life. The tales of conflict with
beings of the far galaxies, on the most fundamental level, are
really stories dealing with that most basic of human
challenges: how to get along with strangers. In the stories, the

strangers have purple skins and ropy tentacles; in real life, the differences are not so vivid, but the gulf is just as great.

We are born into a world full of strangers. Slowly we carve an island of familiarity for ourselves, learn to overcome fears and suspicions, break down the barriers of strangerhood. So, too, our world may exist in a galaxy of strangers. The stories in this book attempt to show what may happen when and if we meet those strangers. In any case, they tell on a deeper level the story of us all as we reach out to meet others with uncertain hands.

R. S.

DEAR DEVIL

By Eric Frank Russell

Eric Frank Russell is a towering Englishman whose first science-fiction stories were published in 1937. In the decades since then he has written dozens of notable short stories and such classic novels as Sinister Barrier *and* Three to Conquer. *Cheerfully irreverent in person, Russell as a writer is usually breezy and hard-boiled, a teller of tough, fast-paced tales. He has dealt often and excellently with the theme of Earthman versus Alien, generally against a backdrop of an intergalactic war, and his sly spies were performing slick tricks long before James Bond first saw print.*

But there is nothing breezy, hard-boiled, tough, military, or sly about Dear Devil. *Seldom has a being from another world been portrayed in science fiction with such warmth and compassion. Readers are grateful to Eric Frank Russell for his lively stories of action and adventure, but they will cherish him forever for the unique and wonderful Martian "devil" of this unforgettable story.*

The first Martian vessel descended upon Earth with the slow, stately fall of a grounded balloon. It did resemble a large balloon in that it was spherical and had a strange buoyancy out of keeping with its metallic construction. Beyond this superficial appearance all similarity to anything Terrestrial ceased.

There were no rockets, no crimson venturis, no external projections other than several solaradiant distorting grids which boosted the ship in any desired direction through the cosmic field. There were no observation ports. All viewing was done through a transparent band running right around the fat belly of the sphere. The bluish, nightmarish crew was assembled behind that band, surveying the world with great multifaceted eyes.

They gazed through the band in utter silence as they examined this world which was Terra. Even if they had been capable of speech they would have said nothing. But none among them had a talkative faculty in any sonic sense. At this quiet moment none needed it.

The scene outside was one of untrammeled desolation. Scraggy blue-green grass clung to tired ground right away to the horizon scarred by ragged mountains. Dismal bushes struggled for life here and there, some with the pathetic air of striving to become trees as once their ancestors had been. To the right, a long, straight scar through the grass betrayed the sterile lumpiness of rocks at odd places. Too rugged and too narrow ever to have been a road, it suggested no more than the desiccating remnants of a long-gone wall. And over all this loomed a ghastly sky.

Captain Skhiva eyed his crew, spoke to them with his sign-talking tentacle. The alternative was contact-telepathy which required physical touch.

"It is obvious that we are out of luck. We could have done no worse had we landed on the empty satellite. However, it is safe to go out. Anyone who wishes to explore a little while may do so."

One of them gesticulated back at him. "Captain, don't you wish to be the first to step upon this world?"

"It is of no consequence. If anyone deems it an honor, he is welcome to it." He pulled the lever opening both air-lock doors. Thicker, heavier air crowded in and pressure went up a little. "Beware of overexertion," he warned as they went out.

Poet Fander touched him, tentacles tip to tip as he sent his thoughts racing through their nerve ends. "This confirms all that we saw as we approached. A stricken planet far gone in its death throes. What do you suppose caused it?"

"I have not the remotest idea. I would like to know. If it has been smitten by natural forces, what might they do to Mars?" His troubled mind sent its throb of worry up Fander's contacting tentacle. "A pity that this planet had not been farther out instead of closer in; we might then have observed the preceding phenomena from the surface of Mars. It is so difficult properly to view this one against the Sun."

"That applies still more to the next world, the misty one," observed Poet Fander.

"I know it. I am beginning to fear what we may find there. If it proves to be equally dead, then we are stalled until we can make the big jump outward."

"Which won't be in our lifetimes."

"I doubt it," agreed Captain Skhiva. "We might move fast with the help of friends. We shall be slow—alone." He turned to watch his crew writhing in various directions across the grim landscape. "They find it good to be on firm ground. But what is a world without life and beauty? In a short time they will grow tired of it."

Fander said thoughtfully, "Nevertheless, I would like to see more of it. May I take out the lifeboat?"

"You are a songbird, not a pilot," reproved Captain Skhiva. "Your function is to maintain morale by entertaining us, not to roam around in a lifeboat."

"But I know how to handle it. Every one of us was trained to handle it. Let me take it that I may see more."

"Haven't we seen enough, even before we landed? What else is there to see? Cracked and distorted roads about to dissolve into nothingness. Ages-old cities, torn and broken, crumbling into dust. Shattered mountains and charred forests and craters little smaller than those upon the Moon. No sign of any superior lifeform still surviving. Only the grass, the shrubs, and various animals, two- or four-legged, that flee at our approach. Why do you wish to see more?"

"There is poetry even in death," said Fander.

"Even so, it remains repulsive." Skhiva gave a little shiver. "All right. Take the lifeboat. Who am I to question the weird workings of the nontechnical mind?"

"Thank you, Captain."

"It is nothing. See that you are back by dusk." Breaking contact, he went to the lock, curled snakishly on its outer rim and brooded, still without bothering to touch the new world. So much attempted, so much done—for so poor reward.

He was still pondering it when the lifeboat soared out of its lock. Expressionlessly, his multifaceted eyes watched the energized grids change angle as the boat swung into a curve and floated away like a little bubble. Skhiva was sensitive to futility.

The crew came back well before darkness. A few hours were enough. Just grass and shrubs and child-trees straining to grow up. One had discovered a grassless oblong that once might have been the site of a dwelling. He brought back a small piece of its foundation, a lump of perished concrete which Skhiva put by for later analysis.

Another had found a small, brown, six-legged insect, but his nerve ends had heard it crying when he picked it up, so hastily he had put it down and let it go free. Small, clumsily moving animals had been seen hopping in the distance, but all had dived down holes in the ground before any Martian could get near. All the crew were agreed upon one thing: the silence and solemnity of a people's passing was unendurable.

Fander beat the sinking of the sun by half a time-unit. His bubble drifted under a great, black cloud, sank to ship level, came in. The rain started a moment later, roaring down in frenzied torrents while they stood behind the transparent band and marveled at so much water.

After a while, Captain Skhiva told them, "We must accept what we find. We have drawn a blank. The cause of this world's condition is a mystery to be solved by others with more time and better equipment. It is for us to abandon this graveyard and try the misty planet. We will take off early in the morning."

None commented, but Fander followed him to his room, made contact with a tentacle-touch.

"One could live here, Captain."

"I am not so sure of that." Skhiva coiled on his couch, suspending his tentacles on the various limb-rests. The blue sheen of him was reflected by the back wall. "In some places are rocks emitting alpha sparks. They are dangerous."

"Of course, Captain. But I can sense them and avoid them."

"*You?*" Skhiva stared up at him.

"Yes, Captain. I wish to be left here."

"What? In this place of appalling repulsiveness?"

"It has an all-pervading air of ugliness and despair," admitted Poet Fander. "All destruction is ugly. But by accident I have found a little beauty. It heartens me. I would like to seek its source."

"To what beauty do you refer?" Skhiva demanded.

Fander tried to explain the alien in nonalien terms.

"Draw it for me," ordered Skhiva.

Fander drew it, gave him the picture, said, "There!"

Gazing at it for a long time, Skhiva handed it back, mused awhile, then spoke along the other's nerves. "We are individuals with all the rights of individuals. As an individual, I don't think that picture sufficiently beautiful to be worth the tail-tip of a domestic *arlan*. I will admit that it is not ugly, even that it is pleasing."

"But, Captain—"

"As an individual," Skhiva went on, "you have an equal

right to your opinions, strange though they may be. If you really wish to stay I cannot refuse you. I am entitled only to think you a little crazy." He eyed Fander again. "When do you hope to be picked up?"

"This year, next year, sometime, never."

"It may well be never," Skhiva reminded him. "Are you prepared to face that prospect?"

"One must always be prepared to face the consequences of his own actions," Fander pointed out.

"True." Skhiva was reluctant to surrender. "But have you given the matter serious thought?"

"I am a nontechnical component. I am not guided by thought."

"Then by what?"

"By my desires, emotions, instincts. By my inward feelings."

Skhiva said fervently, "The twin moons preserve us!"

"Captain, sing me a song of home and play me the tinkling harp."

"Don't be silly. I have not the ability."

"Captain, if it required no more than careful thought you would be able to do it?"

"Doubtlessly," agreed Skhiva, seeing the trap but unable to avoid it.

"There you are!" said Fander pointedly.

"I give up. I cannot argue with someone who casts aside the accepted rules of logic and invents his own. You are governed by notions that defeat me."

"It is not a matter of logic or illogic," Fander told him. "It is merely a matter of viewpoint. You see certain angles; I see others."

"For example?"

"You won't pin me down that way. I can find examples. For instance, do you remember the formula for determining the phase of a series tuned circuit?"

"Most certainly."

"I felt sure you would. You are a technician. You have registered it for all time as a matter of technical utility." He paused, staring at Skhiva. "I know that formula, too. It was mentioned to me, casually, many years ago. It is of no use to me—yet I have never forgotten it."

"Why?"

"Because it holds the beauty of rhythm. It is a poem," Fander explained.

Skhiva sighed and said, "I don't get it."

"One upon R into omega L minus one upon omega C," recited Fander. "A perfect hexameter." He showed his amusement as the other rocked back.

After a while, Skhiva remarked, "It could be sung. One could dance to it."

"Same with this." Fander exhibited his rough sketch. "This holds beauty. Where there is beauty there once was talent— may still be talent for all we know. Where talent abides is also greatness. In the realms of greatness we may find powerful friends. We *need* such friends."

"You win." Skhiva made a gesture of defeat. "We leave you to your self-chosen fate in the morning."

"Thank you, Captain."

That same streak of stubbornness which made Skhiva a worthy commander induced him to take one final crack at Fander shortly before departure. Summoning him to his room, he eyed the poet calculatingly.

"You are still of the same mind?"

"Yes, Captain."

"Then does it not occur to you as strange that I should be so content to abandon this planet if indeed it does hold the remnants of greatness?"

"No."

"Why not?" Skhiva stiffened slightly.

"Captain, I think you are a little afraid because you suspect what I suspect—that there was no natural disaster. They did it themselves, to themselves."

"We have no proof of it," said Skhiva uneasily.

"No, Captain." Fander paused there without desire to add more.

"If this is their own sad handiwork," Skhiva commented at length, "what are our chances of finding friends among people so much to be feared?"

"Poor," admitted Fander. "But that—being the product of cold thought—means little to me. I am animated by warm hopes."

"There you go again, blatantly discarding reason in favor of an idle dream. Hoping, hoping, hoping—to achieve the impossible."

Fander said, "The difficult can be done at once; the impossible takes a little longer."

"Your thoughts make my orderly mind feel lopsided. Every

remark is a flat denial of something that makes sense." Skhiva transmitted the sensation of a lugubrious chuckle. "Oh, well, we live and learn." He came forward, moving closer to the other. "All your supplies are assembled outside. Nothing remains but to bid you goodby."

They embraced in the Martian manner. Leaving the lock, Poet Fander watched the big sphere shudder and glide up. It soared without sound, shrinking steadily until it was a mere dot entering a cloud. A moment later it had gone.

He remained there, looking at the cloud, for a long, long time. Then he turned his attention to the load-sled holding his supplies. Climbing onto its tiny, exposed front seat, he shifted the control which energized the flotation-grids, let it rise a few feet. The higher the rise the greater the expenditure of power. He wished to conserve power; there was no knowing how long he might need it. So at low altitude and gentle pace he let the sled glide in the general direction of the thing of beauty.

Later, he found a dry cave in the hill on which his objective stood. It took him two days of careful, cautious raying to square its walls, ceiling and floor, plus half a day with a powered fan driving out silicate dust. After that, he stowed his supplies at the back, parked the sled near the front, set up a curtaining force-screen across the entrance. The hole in the hill was now home.

Slumber did not come easily that first night. He lay within the cave, a ropy, knotted thing of glowing blue with enormous, beelike eyes, and found himself listening for harps that played sixty million miles away. His tentacle-ends twitched in involuntary search of the telepathic-contact songs that would go with the harps, and twitched in vain. Darkness grew deep, and all the world a monstrous stillness held. His hearing organs craved for the eventide flip-flop of sand-frogs, but there were no frogs. He wanted the homely drone of night beetles, but none droned. Except for once when something faraway howled its heart at the Moon, there was nothing, nothing.

In the morning he washed, ate, took out the sled and explored the site of a small town. He found little to satisfy his curiosity, no more than mounds of shapeless rubble on ragged, faintly oblong foundations. It was a graveyard of long-dead domiciles, rotting, weedy, near to complete oblivion. A view from five hundred feet up gave him only one piece of information: the orderliness of outlines showed that these people had been tidy, methodical.

But tidiness is not beauty in itself. He came back to the top of his hill and sought solace with the thing that was beauty.

His explorations continued, not systematically as Skhiva would have performed them, but in accordance with his own mercurial whims. At times he saw many animals, singly or in groups, none resembling anything Martian. Some scattered at full gallop when his sled swooped over them. Some dived into groundholes, showing a brief flash of white, absurd tails, Others, four-footed, long-faced, sharp-toothed, hunted in gangs and bayed at him in concert with harsh, defiant voices.

On the seventieth day, in a deep, shadowed glade to the north, he spotted a small group of new shapes slinking along in single file. He recognized them at a glance, knew them so well that his searching eyes sent an immediate thrill of triumph into his mind. They were ragged, dirty, and no more than half grown, but the thing of beauty had told him what they were.

Hugging the ground low, he swept around in a wide curve that brought him to the farther end of the glade. His sled sloped slightly into the drop as it entered the glade. He could see them better now, even the soiled pinkishness of their thin legs. They were moving away from him, with fearful caution, but the silence of his swoop gave them no warning.

The rearmost one of the stealthy file fooled him at the last moment. He was hanging over the side of the sled, tentacles outstretched in readiness to snatch the end one with the wild mop of yellow hair when, responding to some sixth sense, his intended victim threw itself flat. His grasp shot past a couple of feet short, and he got a glimpse of frightened gray eyes two seconds before a dexterous side-tilt of the sled enabled him to make good his loss by grabbing the less wary next in line.

This one was dark haired, a bit bigger, and sturdier. It fought madly at his holding limbs while he gained altitude. Then suddenly, realizing the queer nature of its bonds, it writhed around and looked straight at him. The result was unexpected; it closed its eyes and went completely limp.

It was still limp when he bore it into the cave, but its heart continued to beat and its lungs to draw. Laying it carefully on the softness of his bed, he moved to the cave's entrance and waited for it to recover. Eventually it stirred, sat up, gazed confusedly at the facing wall. Its black eyes moved slowly around, taking in the surroundings. Then they saw Fander. They widened tremendously, and their owner began to make highpitched, unpleasant noises as it tried to back away through the solid wall. It screamed so much, in one rising throb after another, that Fander slithered out of the cave, right out of sight, and sat in the cold winds until the noises had died down.

A couple of hours later he made cautious reappearance to offer it food, but its reaction was so swift, hysterical, and heartrending that he dropped his load and hid himself as though the fear was his own. The food remained untouched for two full days. On the third, a little of it was eaten. Fander ventured within.

Although the Martian did not go near, the boy cowered away, murmuring, "Devil! Devil!" His eyes were red, with dark discoloration beneath them.

"Devil!" thought Fander, totally unable to repeat the alien word, but wondering what it meant. He used his sign-talking tentacle in valiant effort to convey something reassuring. The attempt was wasted. The other watched its writhings half in fear, half with distaste, and showed complete lack of comprehension. He let the tentacle gently slither forward across the floor, hoping to make thought-contact. The other recoiled from it as from a striking snake.

"Patience," he reminded himself. "The impossible takes a little longer."

Periodically he showed himself with food and drink, and nighttimes he slept fitfully on the coarse, damp grass beneath lowering skies—while the prisoner who was his guest enjoyed the softness of the bed, the warmth of the cave, the security of the force-screen.

Time came when Fander betrayed an unpoetic shrewdness by using the other's belly to estimate the ripeness of the moment. When, on the eighth day, he noted that his food-offerings were now being taken regularly, he took a meal of his own at the edge of the cave, within plain sight, and observed that the other's appetite was not spoiled. That night he slept just within the cave, close to the force-screen, and as far from the boy as possible. The boy stayed awake late, watching him, always watching him, but gave way to slumber in the small hours.

A fresh attempt at sign-talking brought no better results than before, and the boy still refused to touch his offered tentacle. All the same, he was gaining ground slowly. His overtures still were rejected, but with less revulsion. Gradually, ever so gradually, the Martian shape was becoming familiar, almost acceptable.

The sweet savor of success was Fander's in the middle of the next day. The boy had displayed several spells of emotional sickness during which he lay on his front with shaking body and emitted low noises while his eyes watered profusely. At such times the Martian felt strangely helpless and inadequate. On this occasion, during another attack, he took advantage of the sufferer's lack of attention and slid near enough to snatch away the box by the bed.

From the box he drew his tiny electroharp, plugged its connectors, switched it on, touched its strings with delicate affection. Slowly he began to play, singing an accompaniment deep inside himself. For he had no voice with which to sing out loud, but the harp sang it for him. The boy ceased his quiverings, sat up, all his attention upon the dexterous play of the tentacles and the music they conjured forth. And when he judged that at last the listener's mind was captured, Fander ceased with easy, quietening strokes, gently offered him the harp. The boy registered interest and reluctance. Careful not to move nearer, not an inch nearer, Fander offered it at full tentacle length. The boy had to take four steps to get it. He took them.

That was the start. They played together, day after day and sometimes a little into the night, while almost imperceptibly the distance between them was reduced. Finally they sat together, side by side, and the boy had not yet learned to laugh but no longer did he show unease. He could now extract a simple tune from the instrument and was pleased with his own aptitude in a solemn sort of way.

One evening as darkness grew, and the things that sometimes howled at the Moon were howling again, Fander offered his tentacle-tip for the hundredth time. Always the gesture had been unmistakable even if its motive was not clear, yet always it had been rebuffed. But now, now, five fingers curled around it in shy desire to please.

With a fervent prayer that human nerves would function just like Martian ones, Fander poured his thoughts through, swiftly, lest the warm grip be loosened too soon.

"Do not fear me. I cannot help my shape any more than you can help yours. I am your friend, your father, your mother. I need you as much as you need me."

The boy let go of him, began quiet, half-stifled whimpering noises. Fander put a tentacle on his shoulder, made little patting motions that he imagined were wholly Martian. For some inexplicable reason, this made matters worse. At his wits' end what to do for the best, what action to take that might be understandable in Terrestrial terms, he gave the problem up, surrendered to his instinct, put a long, ropy limb around the boy and held him close until the noises ceased and slumber came. It was then he realized the child he had taken was much younger than he had estimated. He nursed him through the night.

Much practice was necessary to make conversation. The boy had to learn to put mental drive behind his thoughts, for it was beyond Fander's power to suck them out of him.

"What is your name?"

Fander got a picture of thin legs running rapidly.

He returned it in question form. "Speedy?"

An affirmative.

"What name do you call me?"

An unflattering montage of monsters.

"Devil?"

The picture whirled around, became confused. There was a trace of embarrassment.

"Devil will do," assured Fander. He went on. "Where are your parents?"

More confusion.

"You must have had parents. Everyone has a father and mother, haven't they? Don't you remember yours?"

Muddled ghost-pictures. Grown-ups leaving children. Grown-ups avoiding children, as if they feared them.

"What is the first thing you remember?"

"Big man walking with me. Carried me a bit. Walked again."

"What happened to him?"

"Went away. Said he was sick. Might make me sick too."

"Long ago?"

Confusion.

Fander changed his aim. "What of those other children—have they no parents either?"

"All got nobody."

"But you've got somebody now, haven't you, Speedy?"

Doubtfully. "Yes."

Fander pushed it farther. "Would you rather have me, or those other children?" He let it rest a moment before he added, "Or both?"

"Both," said Speedy with no hesitation. His fingers toyed with the harp.

"Would you like to help me look for them tomorrow and bring them here? And if they are scared of me will you help them not to be afraid?"

"Sure!" said Speedy, licking his lips and sticking his chest out.

"Then," said Fander, "perhaps you would like to go for a walk today? You've been too long in this cave. Will you come for a walk with me?"

"Y'betcha!"

Side by side they went a short walk, one trotting rapidly along, the other slithering. The child's spirits perked up with this trip in the open; it was as if the sight of the sky and the feel of the grass made him realize at last that he was not exactly a prisoner. His formerly solemn features became animated, he made exclamations that Fander could not understand, and once he laughed at nothing for the sheer joy of it. On two occasions he grabbed a tentacle-tip in order to tell Fander something, performing the action as if it were in every way as natural as his own speech.

They got out the load-sled in the morning. Fander took the front seat and the controls; Speedy squatted behind him with hands gripping his harness-belt. With a shallow soar, they headed for the glade. Many small, white-tailed animals bolted down holes as they passed over.

"Good for dinner," remarked Speedy, touching him and speaking through the touch.

Fander felt sickened. Meat-eaters! It was not until a queer feeling of shame and apology came back at him that he knew the other had felt his revulsion. He wished he'd been swift to blanket that reaction before the boy could sense it, but he could not be blamed for the effect of so bald a statement taking him so completely unaware. However, it had produced another step forward in their mutual relationship—Speedy desired his good opinion.

Within fifteen minutes they struck it lucky. At a point half a mile south of the glade Speedy let out a shrill yell and pointed downward. A small, golden-haired figure was standing there on a slight rise, staring fascinatedly upward at the phenomenon in the sky. A second tiny shape, with red but equally long hair, was at the bottom of the slope gazing in similar wonderment. Both came to their senses and turned to flee as the sled tilted toward them.

Ignoring the yelps of excitement close behind him and the pulls upon his belt, Fander swooped, got first one, then the other. This left him with only one limb to right the sled and gain height. If the victims had fought he would have had his work cut out to make it. They did not fight. They shrieked as he snatched them and then relaxed with closed eyes.

The sled climbed, glided a mile at five hundred feet. Fander's attention was divided between his limp prizes, the controls and the horizon when suddenly a thunderous rattling sounded on the metal base on the sled, the entire framework shuddered, a strip of metal flew from its leading edge and things made whining sounds toward the clouds.

"Old Graypate," bawled Speedy, jigging around but keeping away from the rim. "He's shooting at us."

The spoken words meant nothing to the Martian, and he could not spare a limb for the contact the other had forgotten to make. Grimly righting the sled, he gave it full power. Whatever damage it had suffered had not affected its efficiency; it shot forward at a pace that set the red and golden hair of the captives streaming in the wind. Perforce his landing by the cave was clumsy. The sled bumped down and lurched across forty yards of grass.

First things first. Taking the quiet pair into the cave, he made them comfortable on the bed, came out and examined the sled. There were half a dozen deep dents in its flat underside, two bright furrows angling across one rim. He made contact with Speedy.

"What were you trying to tell me?"

"Old Graypate shot at us."

The mind-picture burst upon him vividly and with electrifying effect: a vision of a tall, white-haired, stern-faced old man with a tubular weapon propped upon his shoulder while it spat fire upward. A white-haired old man! An adult!

His grip was tight on the other's arm. "What is this oldster to you?"

"Nothing much. He lives near us in the shelters."

Picture of a long, dusty concrete burrow, badly damaged, its ceiling marked with the scars of a lighting system which had rotted away to nothing. The old man living hermitlike at one end; the children at the other. The old man was sour, taciturn, kept the children at a distance, spoke to them seldom but was quick to respond when they were menaced. He had guns. Once he had killed many wild dogs that had eaten two children.

"People left us near shelters because Old Graypate was there, and had guns," informed Speedy.

"But why does he keep away from children? Doesn't he like children?"

"Don't know." He mused a moment. "Once told us that old people could get very sick and make young ones sick—and then we'd all die. Maybe he's afraid of making us die." Speedy wasn't very sure about it.

So there was some much-feared disease around, something contagious, to which adults were peculiarly susceptible. Without hesitation they abandoned their young at the first onslaught, hoping that at least the children would live. Sacrifice after sacrifice that the remnants of the race might survive. Heartbreak after heartbreak as elders chose death alone rather than death together.

Yet Graypate himself was depicted as very old. Was this an exaggeration of the child-mind?

"I must meet Graypate."

"He will shoot," declared Speedy positively. "He knows by now that you took me. He saw you take the others. He will wait for you and shoot."

"We will find some way to avoid that."

"How?"

"When these two have become my friends, just as you have become my friend, I will take all three of you back to the shelters. You can find Graypate for me and tell him that I am not as ugly as I look."

"I don't think you're ugly," denied Speedy.

The picture Fander got along with that gave him the weirdest sensation of pleasure. It was of a vague, shadowy but distorted body with a clear human face.

The new prisoners were female. Fander knew it without being told because they were daintier than Speedy and had the warm, sweet smell of females. That meant complications. Maybe they were mere children, and maybe they lived together in the shelter, but he was permitting none of that while they were in his charge. Fander might be outlandish by other standards but he had a certain primness. Forthwith he cut another and smaller cave for Speedy and himself.

Neither of the girls saw him for two days. Keeping well out of their sight, he let Speedy take them food, talk to them, prepare them for the shape of the thing to come. On the third day he presented himself for inspection at a distance. Despite forewarnings they went sheet-white, clung together, but uttered no distressing sounds. He played his harp a little while, withdrew, came back in the evening and played for them again.

Encouraged by Speedy's constant and self-assured flow of propaganda, one of them grasped a tentacle-tip next day. What came along the nerves was not a picture so much as an ache, a desire, a childish yearning. Fander backed out of the cave, found wood, spent the whole night using the sleepy Speedy as a model, and fashioned the wood into a tiny, jointed semblance of a human being. He was no sculptor, but he possessed a natural delicacy of touch, and the poet in him ran through his limbs and expressed itself in the model. Making a thorough job of it, he clothed it in Terrestrial fashion, colored its face, fixed upon its features the pleasure-grimace which humans call a smile.

He gave her the doll the moment she awakened in the morning. She took it eagerly, hungrily, with wide, glad eyes. Hugging it to her unformed bosom, she crooned over it—and he knew that the strange emptiness within her was gone.

Though Speedy was openly contemptuous of this manifest waste of effort, Fander set to and made a second mannikin. It did not take quite as long. Practice on the first had made him swifter, more dexterous. He was able to present it to the other child by midafternoon. Her acceptance was made with shy grace, she held the doll close as if it meant more than the whole of her sorry world. In her thrilled concentration upon the gift, she did not notice his nearness, his closeness, and when he offered a tentacle, she took it.

He said, simply, "I love you."

Her mind was too untrained to drive a response, but her great eyes warmed.

Fander sat on the grounded sled at a point a mile east of the glade and watched the three children walk hand in hand toward the hidden shelters. Speedy was the obvious leader, hurrying them onward, bossing them with the noisy assurance of one who has been around and considers himself sophisticated. In spite of this, the girls paused at intervals to turn and wave to the ropy, bee-eyed thing they'd left behind. And Fander dutifully waved back, always using his signal-tentacle because it had not occurred to him that any tentacle would serve.

They sank from sight behind a rise of ground. He remained

on the sled, his multifaceted gaze going over his surroundings or studying the angry sky now threatening rain. The ground was a dull, dead gray-green all the way to the horizon. There was no relief from that drab color, not one shining patch of white, gold, or crimson such as dotted the meadows of Mars. There was only the eternal gray-green and his own brilliant blueness.

Before long a sharp-faced, four-footed thing revealed itself in the grass, raised its head and howled at him. The sound was an eerily urgent wail that ran across the grasses and moaned into the distance. It brought others of its kind, two, ten, twenty. Their defiance increased with their numbers until there was a large band of them edging toward him with lips drawn back, teeth exposed. Then there came a sudden and undetectable flock-command which caused them to cease their slinking and spring forward like one, slavering as they came. They did it with the hungry, red-eyed frenzy of animals motivated by something akin to madness.

Repulsive though it was, the sight of creatures craving for meat—even strange blue meat—did not bother Fander. He slipped a control a notch, the flotation grids radiated, the sled soared twenty feet. So calm and easy an escape so casually performed infuriated the wild dog pack beyond all measure. Arriving beneath the sled, they made futile springs upward, fell back upon one another, bit and slashed each other, leaped again and again. The pandemonium they set up was a compound of snarls, yelps, barks, and growls, the ferocious expressions of extreme hate. They exuded a pungent odor of dry hair and animal sweat.

Reclining on the sled in a maddening pose of disdain, Fander let the insane ones rave below. They raced around in tight circles shrieking insults at him and biting each other. This went on for some time and ended with a spurt of ultra-rapid cracks from the direction of the glade. Eight dogs fell dead. Two flopped and struggled to crawl away. Ten yelped in agony, made off on three legs. The unharmed ones flashed away to some place where they could make a meal of the escaping limpers. Fander lowered the sled.

Speedy stood on the rise with Graypate. The latter restored his weapon to the crook of his arm, rubbed his chin thoughtfully, ambled forward.

Stopping five yards from the Martian, the old Earthman

again massaged his chin whiskers, then said, "It sure is the darnedest thing, just the darnedest thing!"

"No use talking *at* him," advised Speedy. "You've got to touch him, like I told you."

"I know, I know." Graypate betrayed a slight impatience. "All in good time. I'll touch him when I'm ready." He stood there, gazing at Fander with eyes that were very pale and very sharp. "Oh, well, here goes." He offered a hand.

Fander placed a tentacle-end in it.

"Jeepers, he's cold," commented Graypate, closing his grip. "Colder than a snake."

"He isn't a snake," Speedy contradicted fiercely.

"Ease up, ease up—I didn't say he is." Graypate seemed fond of repetitive phrases.

"He doesn't feel like one, either," persisted Speedy, who had never felt a snake and did not wish to.

Fander boosted a thought through. "I come from the fourth planet. Do you know what that means?"

"I ain't ignorant," snapped Graypate aloud.

"No need to reply vocally. I receive your thoughts exactly as you receive mine. Your responses are much stronger than the boy's, and I can understand you easily."

"Humph!" said Graypate to the world at large.

"I have been anxious to find an adult because the children can tell me little. I would like to ask questions. Do you feel inclined to answer questions?"

"It depends," answered Graypate, becoming leery.

"Never mind. Answer them if you wish. My only desire is to help you."

"Why?" asked Graypate, searching around for a percentage.

"We need intelligent friends."

"Why?"

"Our numbers are small, our resources poor. In visiting this world and the misty one we've come near to the limit of our ability. But with assistance we could go farther. I think that if we could help you a time might come when you could help us."

Graypate pondered it cautiously, forgetting that the inward workings of his mind were wide open to the other. Chronic suspicion was the keynote of his thoughts, suspicion based on life experiences and recent history. But inward thoughts ran both ways, and his own mind detected the clear sincerity in Fander's.

So he said. "Fair enough. Say more."

"What caused all this?" inquired Fander, waving a limb at the world.

"War," said Graypate. "The last war we'll ever have. The entire place went nuts."

"How did that come about?"

"You've got me there." Graypate gave the problem grave consideration. "I reckon it wasn't just any one thing; it was a multitude of things sort of piling themselves up."

"Such as?"

"Differences in people. Some were colored differently in their bodies, others in their ideas, and they couldn't get along. Some bred faster than others, wanted more room, more food. There wasn't any more room or more food. The world was full, and nobody could shove in except by pushing another out. My old man told me plenty before he died, and he always maintained that if folk had had the hoss-sense to keep their numbers down, there might not—"

"Your old man?" interjected Fander. "Your father? Didn't all this occur in your own lifetime?"

"It did not. I saw none of it. I am the son of the son of a survivor."

"Let's go back to the cave," put in Speedy, bored with the silent contact-talk. "I want to show him our harp."

They took no notice, and Fander went on, "Do you think there might be a lot of others still living?"

"Who knows?" Graypate was moody about it. "There isn't any way of telling how many are wandering around the other side of the globe, maybe still killing each other, or starving to death, or dying of the sickness."

"What sickness is this?"

"I couldn't tell what it is called." Graypate scratched his head confusedly. "My old man told me a few times, but I've long forgotten. Knowing the name wouldn't do me any good, see? He said his father told him that it was part of the war, it got invented and was spread deliberately—and it's still with us."

"What are its symptoms?"

"You go hot and dizzy. You get black swellings in the arm-pits. In forty-eight hours you're dead. Old ones get it first. The kids then catch it unless you make away from them mighty fast."

"It is nothing familiar to me," said Fander, unable to recognize cultured bubonic. "In any case, I'm not a medical expert." He eyed Graypate. "But you seem to have avoided it."

"Sheer luck," opined Graypate. "Or maybe I can't get it. There was a story going around during the war that some folk might develop immunity to it, durned if I know why. Could be that I'm immune, but I don't count on it."

"So you keep your distance from these children?"

"Sure." He glanced at Speedy. "I shouldn't really have come along with this kid. He's got a lousy chance as it is without me increasing the odds."

"That is thoughtful of you," Fander put over softly. "Especially seeing that you must be lonely."

Graypate bristled and his thought-flow became aggressive. "I ain't grieving for company. I can look after myself, like I have done since my old man went away to curl up by himself. I'm on my own feet. So's every other guy."

"I believe that," said Fander. "You must pardon me—I'm a stranger here myself. I judged you by my own feelings. Now and again I get pretty lonely."

"How come?" demanded Graypate, staring at him. "You ain't telling me they dumped you and left you, on your own?"

"They did."

"Man!" exclaimed Graypate fervently.

Man! It was a picture resembling Speedy's conception, a vision elusive in form but firm and human in face. The oldster was reacting to what he considered a predicament rather than a choice, and the reaction came on a wave of sympathy.

Fander struck promptly and hard. "You see how I'm fixed. The companionship of wild animals is nothing to me. I need someone intelligent enough to like my music and forget my looks, someone intelligent enough to—"

"I ain't so sure we're that smart," Graypate chipped in. He let his gaze swing morbidly around the landscape. "Not when I see this graveyard and think of how it looked in granpop's days."

"Every flower blooms from the dust of a hundred dead ones," answered Fander.

"What are flowers?"

It shocked the Martian. He had projected a mind-picture of a trumpet lily, crimson and shining, and Graypate's brain had juggled it around, uncertain whether is were fish, flesh, or fowl.

"Vegetable growths, like these." Fander plucked half a dozen blades of blue-green grass. "But more colorful, and sweet-scented." He transmitted the brilliant vision of a mile-square field of trumpet lilies, red and glowing.

"Glory be!" said Graypate. "We've nothing like those."

"Not here," agreed Fander. "Not here." He gestured toward the horizon. "Elsewhere may be plenty. If we got together we could be company for each other, we could learn things from each other. We could pool our ideas, our efforts, and search for flowers far away—also for more people."

"Folk just won't get together in large bunches. They stick to each other in family groups until the plague breaks them up. Then they abandon the kids. The bigger the crowd, the bigger the risk of someone contaminating the lot." He leaned on his gun, staring at the other, his thought-forms shaping themselves in dull solemnity. "When a guy gets hit, he goes away and takes it on his own. The end is a personal contract between him and his God, with no witnesses. Death's a pretty private affair these days."

"What, after all these years? Don't you think that by this time the disease may have run its course and exhausted itself?"

"Nobody knows—and nobody's gambling on it."

"I would gamble," said Fander.

"You ain't like us. You mightn't be able to catch it."

"Or I might get it worse, and die more painfully."

"Mebbe," admitted Graypate, doubtfully. "Anyway, you're looking at it from a different angle. You've been dumped on your ownsome. What've you got to lose?"

"My life," said Fander.

Graypate rocked back on his heels, then said, "Yes, sir, that is a gamble. A guy can't bet any heavier than that." He rubbed his chin whiskers as before. "All right, all right, I'll take you up on that. You come right here and live with us." His grip tightened on his gun, his knuckles showing white. "On this understanding: The moment you feel sick you get out fast, and for keeps. If you don't, I'll bump you and drag you away myself, even if that makes me get it too. The kids come first, see?"

The shelters were far roomier than the cave. There were eighteen children living in them, all skinny with their prolonged diet of roots, edible herbs, and an occasional rabbit. The youngest and most sensitive of them ceased to be terrified of Fander after ten days. Within four months his slithering shape of blue ropiness had become a normal adjunct to their small, limited world.

Six of the youngsters were males older than Speedy, one of them much older but not yet adult. He beguiled them with his harp, teaching them to play, and now and again giving them ten-minute rides on the load-sled as a special treat. He made dolls for the girls and queer, cone-shaped little houses for the dolls, and fan-backed chairs of woven grass for the houses. None of these toys were truly Martian in design, and none were Terrestrial. They represented a pathetic compromise within his imagination; the Martian notion of what Terrestrial models might have looked like had there been any in existence.

But surreptitiously, without seeming to give any less attention to the younger ones, he directed his main efforts upon the six older boys and Speedy. To his mind, these were the hope of the world—and of Mars. At no time did he bother to ponder that the nontechnical brain is not without its virtues, or that there are times and circumstances when it is worth dropping the short view of what is practicable for the sake of the long view of what is remotely possible. So as best he could he concentrated upon the elder seven, educating them through the dragging months, stimulating their minds, encouraging their curiosity, and continually impressing upon them the idea that fear of disease can become a folk-separating dogma unless they conquered it within their souls.

He taught them that death is death, a natural process to be accepted philosophically and met with dignity—and there were times when he suspected that he was teaching them nothing, he was merely reminding them, for deep within their growing minds was the ancestral strain of Terrestrialism which had mulled its way to the same conclusions ten or twenty thousands of years before. Still, he was helping to remove this disease-block from the path of the stream, and was driving child-logic more rapidly toward adult outlook. In that respect he was satisfied. He could do little more.

In time, they organized group concerts, humming or making singing noises to the accompaniment of the harp, now and again improvising lines to suit Fander's tunes, arguing out the respective merits of chosen words until by process of elimination they had a complete song. As songs grew to a repertoire and singing grew more adept, more polished, Old Graypate displayed interest, came to one performance, then another, until by custom he had established his own place as a one-man audience.

One day the eldest boy, who was named Redhead, came to Fander and grasped a tentacle-tip. "Devil, may I operate your food-machine?"

"You mean you would like me to show you how to work it?"

"No, Devil, I know how to work it." The boy gazed self-assuredly into the other's great bee-eyes.

"Then how is it operated?"

"You fill its container with the tenderest blades of grass, being careful not to include roots. You are equally careful not to turn a switch before the container is full and its door completely closed. You then turn the red switch for a count of two hundred eighty, reverse the container, turn the green switch for a count of forty-seven. You then close both switches, empty the container's warm pulp into the end molds and apply the press until the biscuits are firm and dry."

"How have you discovered all this?"

"I have watched you make biscuits for us many times. This morning, while you were busy, I tried it myself." He extended a hand. It held a biscuit. Taking it from him, Fander examined it. Firm, crisp, well-shaped. He tasted it. Perfect.

Redhead became the first mechanic to operate and service a Martian lifeboat's emergency premasticator. Seven years later, long after the machine had ceased to function, he managed to repower it, weakly but effectively, with dust that gave forth alpha sparks. In another five years he had improved it, speeded it up. In twenty years he had duplicated it and had all the know-how needed to turn out premasticators on a large scale. Fander could not have equalled this performance for, as a nontechnician, he'd no better notion than the average Terrestrial of the principles upon which the machine worked, neither did he know what was meant by radiant digestion or protein enrichment. He could do little more than urge Redhead along and leave the rest to whatever inherent genius the boy possessed—which was plenty.

In similar manner, Speedy and two youths named Blacky and Bigears took the load-sled out of his charge. On rare occasions, as a great privilege, Fander had permitted them to take up the sled for one-hour trips, alone. This time they were gone from dawn to dusk. Graypate mooched around, gun under arm, another smaller one stuck in his belt, going frequently to the top of a rise and scanning the skies in all directions.

The delinquents swooped in at sunset, bringing with them a strange boy.

Fander summoned them to him. They held hands so that his touch would give him simultaneous contact with all three.

"I am a little worried. The sled has only so much power. When it is all gone there will be no more."

They eyed each other aghast.

"Unfortunately, I have neither the knowledge nor the ability to energize the sled once its power is exhausted. I lack the wisdom of the friends who left me here—and that is my shame." He paused, watching them dolefully, then went on, "All I do know is that its power does not leak away. If not used much, the reserves will remain for many years." Another pause before he added, "And in a few years you will be men."

Blacky said, "But, Devil, when we are men we'll be much heavier, and the sled will use so much more power."

"How do you know that?" Fander put it sharply.

"More weight, more power to sustain it," opined Blacky with the air of one whose logic is incontrovertible. "It doesn't need thinking out. *It's obvious.*"

Very slowly and softly, Fander told him, "You'll do. May the twin moons shine upon you someday, for I know you'll do."

"Do what, Devil?"

"Build a thousand sleds like this one, or better—and explore the whole world."

From that time onward they confined their trips strictly to one hour, making them less frequently than of yore, spending more time poking and prying around the sled's innards.

Graypate changed character with the slow reluctance of the aged. Leastways, as two years then three rolled past, he came gradually out of his shell, was less taciturn, more willing to mix with those swiftly growing up to his own height. Without fully realizing what he was doing he joined forces with Fander, gave the children the remnants of Earthly wisdom passed down from his father's father. He taught the boys how to use the guns of which he had as many as eleven, some maintained mostly as a source of spares for others. He took them shell-hunting; digging deep beneath rotting foundations into stale, half-filled cellars in search of ammunition not too far corroded for use.

"Guns ain't no use without shells, and shells don't last forever."

Neither do buried shells. They found not one.

Of his own wisdom Graypate stubbornly withheld but a single item until the day when Speedy and Redhead and Blacky chivvied it out of him. Then, like a father facing the hangman, he gave them the truth about babies. He made no comparative mention of bees because there were no bees, nor of flowers because there were no flowers. One cannot analogize the non-existent. Nevertheless he managed to explain the matter more or less to their satisfaction, after which he mopped his forehead and went to Fander.

"These youngsters are getting too nosy for my comfort. They've been asking me how kids come along."

"Did you tell them?"

"I sure did." He sat down, staring at the Martian, his pale gray eyes bothered. "I don't mind giving in to the boys when I can't beat 'em off any longer, but I'm durned if I'm going to tell the girls."

Fander said, "I have been asked about this many a time before. I could not tell much because I was by no means certain whether you breed precisely as we breed. But I told them how *we* breed."

"The girls too?"

"Of course."

"Jeepers!" Graypate mopped his forehead again. "How did they take it?"

"Just as if I'd told them why the sky is blue or why water is wet."

"Must've been something in the way you put it to them," opined Graypate.

"I told them it was poetry between persons."

Throughout the course of history, Martian, Venusian, or Terrestrial, some years are more noteworthy than others. The twelfth one after Fander's marooning was outstanding for its series of events each of which was pitifully insignificant by cosmic standards but loomed enormously in this small community life.

To start with, on the basis of Redhead's improvements to the premasticator, the older seven—now bearded men—contrived to repower the exhausted sled and again took to the air for the first time in forty months. Experiments showed that the Martian load-carrier was now slower, could bear less weight, but had far longer range. They used it to visit the

ruins of distant cities in search of metallic junk suitable for
the building of more sleds, and by early summer they had
constructed another, larger than the original, clumsy to the
verge of dangerousness, but still a sled.

On several occasions they failed to find metal but did find
people, odd families surviving in under-surface shelters, cling-
ing grimly to life and passed-down scraps of knowledge. Since
all these new contacts were strictly human to human, with no
weirdly tentacled shape to scare off the parties of the second
part, and since many were finding fear of plague more to be
endured than their terrible loneliness, many families returned
with the explorers, settled in the shelters, accepted Fander,
added their surviving skills to the community's riches.

Thus local population grew to seventy adults and four
hundred children. They compounded with their plague-fear
by spreading through the shelters, digging through half-
wrecked and formerly unused expanses, and moving apart to
form twenty or thirty lesser communities each one of which
could be isolated should death reappear.

Growing morale born of added strength and confidence in
numbers soon resulted in four more sleds, still clumsy but
slightly less dangerous to manage. There also appeared the
first rock house above ground, standing four-square and solid-
ly under the gray skies, a defiant witness that mankind still
considered itself a cut above the rats and rabbits. The community presented the house to Blacky and Sweetvoice, who had
announced their desire to associate. An adult who claimed to
know the conventional routine spoke solemn words over the
happy couple before many witnesses, while Fander attended
the groom as best Martian.

Toward summer's end Speedy returned from a solo sled-
trip of many days, brought with him one old man, one boy
and four girls, all of strange, outlandish countenance. They
were yellow in complexion, had black hair, black, almond-
shaped eyes, and spoke a language that none could understand. Until these newcomers had picked up the local speech,
Fander had to act as interpreter, for his mind-pictures and
theirs were independent of vocal sounds. The four girls were
quiet, modest, and very beautiful. Within a month Speedy had
married one of them whose name was a gentle clucking sound
which meant Precious Jewel Ling.

After this wedding, Fander sought Graypate, placed a tentacle-tip in his right hand. "There were differences between

the man and the girl, distinctive features wider apart than any we know upon Mars. Are these some of the differences which caused your war?"

"I dunno. I've never seen one of these yellow folk before. They must live mighty far off." He rubbed his chin to help his thoughts along. "I only know what my old man told me and his old man told him. There were too many folk of too many different sorts."

"They can't be all that different if they can fall in love."

"Mebbe not," agreed Graypate.

"Supposing most of the people still in this world could assemble here, breed together, and have less different children; the children bred others still less different. Wouldn't they eventually become all much the same—just Earth-people?"

"Mebbe so."

"All speaking the same language, sharing the same culture? If they spread out slowly from a central source, always in contact by sled, continually sharing the same knowledge, same progress, would there be any room for new differences to arise?"

"I dunno," said Graypate evasively. "I'm not so young as I used to be, and I can't dream as far ahead as I used to do."

"It doesn't matter so long as the young ones can dream it." Fander mused a moment. "If you're beginning to think yourself a back number, you're in good company. Things are getting somewhat out of hand as far as I'm concerned. The onlooker sees the most of the game, and perhaps that's why I'm more sensitive than you to a certain peculiar feeling."

"To what feeling?" inquired Graypate, eyeing him.

"That Terra is on the move once more. There are now many people where there were few. A house is up and more are to follow. They talk of six more. After the six they will talk of sixty, then six hundred, then six thousand. Some are planning to haul up sunken conduits and use them to pipe water from the northward lake. Sleds are being built. Premasticators will soon be built, and force-screens likewise. Children are being taught. Less and less is being heard of your plague, and so far no more have died of it. I feel a dynamic surge of energy and ambition and genius which may grow with appalling rapidity until it becomes a mighty flood. I feel that I, too, am a back number."

"Bunk!" said Graypate. He spat on the ground. "If you dream often enough, you're bound to have a bad one once in a while."

"Perhaps it is because so many of my tasks have been taken over and done better than I was doing them. I have failed to seek new tasks. Were I a technician I'd have discovered a dozen by now. Reckon this is as good a time as any to turn to a job with which you can help me."

"What is that?"

"A long, long time ago I made a poem. It was for the beautiful thing that first impelled me to stay here. I do not know exactly what its maker had in mind, nor whether my eyes see it as he wished it to be seen, but I have made a poem to express what I feel when I look upon his work."

"Humph!" said Graypate, not very interested.

"There is an outcrop of solid rock beneath its base which I can shave smooth and use as a plinth on which to inscribe my words. I would like to put them down twice—in the script of Mars and the script of Earth." Fander hesitated a moment, then went on. "Perhaps this is presumptuous of me, but it is many years since I wrote for all to read—and my chance may never come again."

Graypate said, "I get the idea. You want me to put down your notions in our writing so you can copy it."

"Yes."

"Give me your stylus and pad." Taking them, Graypate squatted on a rock, lowering himself stiffly, for he was feeling the weight of his years. Resting the pad on his knees, he held the writing instrument in his right hand while his left continued to grasp a tentacle-tip. "Go ahead."

He started drawing thick, laborious marks as Fander's mind-pictures came through, enlarging the letters and keeping them well separated. When he had finished he handed the pad over.

"Asymmetrical," decided Fander, staring at the queer letters and wishing for the first time that he had taken up the study of Earth-writing. "Cannot you make this part balance with that, and this with this?"

"It's what you said."

"It is your own translation of what I said. I would like it better balanced. Do you mind if we try again?"

They tried again. They made fourteen attempts before Fander was satisfied with the perfunctory appearance of letters and words he could not understand.

Taking the paper, he found his ray-gun, went to the base-rock of the beautiful thing and sheared the whole front to a flat, even surface. Adjusting his beam to cut a V-shaped channel one inch deep, he inscribed his poem on the rock in long, unpunctuated lines of neat Martian curlicues. With less confidence and much greater care, he repeated the verse in Earth's 'awkward, angular hieroglyphics. The task took him quite a time, and there were fifty people watching him when he finished. They said nothing. In utter silence they looked at the poem and at the beautiful thing, and were still standing there brooding solemnly when he went away.

One by one the rest of the community visited the site next day, going and coming with the air of pilgrims attending an ancient shrine. All stood there a long time, returned without comment. Nobody praised Fander's work, nobody damned it, nobody reproached him for alienizing something wholly Earth's. The only effect—too subtle to be noteworthy—was a greater and still growing grimness and determination that boosted the already swelling Earth-dynamic.

In that respect, Fander wrought better than he knew.

A plague-scare came in the fourteenth year. Two sleds had brought back families from afar, and within a week of their arrival the children sickened, became spotted.

Metal gongs sounded the alarm, all work ceased, the affected section was cut off and guarded, the majority prepared to flee. It was a threatening reversal of all the things for which many had toiled so long; a destructive scattering of the tender roots of new civilization.

Fander found Graypate, Speedy, and Blacky, armed to the teeth, facing a drawn-faced and restless crowd.

"There's most of a hundred folk in that isolated part," Graypate was telling them. "They ain't all got it. Maybe they won't get it. If they don't it ain't so likely you'll go down either. We ought to wait and see. Stick around a bit."

"Listen who's talking," invited a voice in the crowd. "If you weren't immune you'd have been planted thirty-forty years ago."

"Same goes for near everybody," snapped Graypate. He glared around, his gun under one arm, his pale blue eyes bellicose. "I ain't much use at speechifying, so I'm just saying flatly that nobody goes before we know whether this really is the plague." He hefted his weapon in one hand, held it forward. "Anyone fancy himself at beating a bullet?"

The heckler in the audience muscled his way to the front. He was a swarthy man of muscular build, and his dark eyes looked belligerently into Graypate's. "While there's life there's hope. If we beat it, we live to come back, when it's safe to come back, if ever—and you know it. So I'm calling your bluff, see?" Squaring his shoulders, he began to walk off.

Graypate's gun already was halfway up when he felt the touch of Fander's tentacle on his arm. He lowered the weapon, called after the escapee.

"I'm going into that cut-off section and the Devil is going with me. We're running into things, not away from them. I never did like running away." Several of the audience fidgeted, murmuring approval. He went on, "We'll see for ourselves just what's wrong. We mightn't be able to put it right, but we'll find out what's the matter."

The walker paused, turned, eyed him, eyed Fander, and said, "You can't do that."

"Why not?"

"You'll get it yourself—and a heck of a lot of use you'll be dead and stinking."

"What, and me immune?" cracked Graypate grinning.

"The Devil will get it," hedged the other.

Graypate was about to retort, "What do *you* care?" but altered it slightly in response to Fander's contacting thoughts. He said, more softly, "Do you *care?*"

It caught the other off-balance. He fumbled embarrassedly within his own mind, avoided looking at the Martian, said lamely, "I don't see reason for any guy to take risks."

"He's taking them, because *he* cares," Graypate gave back. "And I'm taking them because I'm too old and useless to give a darn."

With that, he stepped down, marched stubbornly toward the isolated section, Fander slithering by his side, tentacle in hand. The one who wished to flee stayed put, staring after them. The crowd shuffled uneasily, seemed in two minds whether to accept the situation and stick around, or whether to rush Graypate and Fander and drag them away. Speedy and Blacky made to follow the pair but were ordered off.

No adult sickened; nobody died. Children in the affected sector went one after another through the same routine of liverishness, high temperature, and spots, until the epidemic of measles had died out. Not until a month after the last case had been cured by something within its own constitution did Graypate and Fander emerge.

The innocuous course and eventual disappearance of this suspected plague gave the pendulum of confidence a push, swinging it farther. Morale boosted itself almost to the verge of arrogance. More sleds appeared, more mechanics serviced them, more pilots rode them. More people flowed in; more oddments of past knowledge came with them.

Humanity was off to a flying start with the salvaged seeds of past wisdom and the urge to do. The tormented ones of Earth were not primitive savages, but surviving organisms of a greatness nine-tenths destroyed but still remembered, each contributing his mite of know-how to restore at least some of those things which had been boiled away in atomic fires.

When, in the twentieth year, Redhead duplicated the premasticator, there were eight thousand stone houses standing around the hill. A community hall seventy times the size of a house, with a great green dome of copper, reared itself upon the eastward fringe. A dam held the lake to the north. A hospital was going up in the west. The nuances and energies and talents of fifty races had built this town and were still building it. Among them were ten Polynesians and four Icelanders and one lean, dusky child who was the last of the Seminoles.

Farms spread wide. One thousand heads of Indian corn rescued from a sheltered valley in the Andes had grown to ten thousand acres. Water buffaloes and goats had been brought from afar to serve in lieu of the horses and sheep that would never be seen again—and no man knew why one species survived while another did not. The horses had died; the water buffalos lived. The canines hunted in ferocious packs; the felines had departed from existence. The small herbs, some tubers, and a few seedy things could be rescued and cultivated for hungry bellies; but there were no flowers for the hungry mind. Humanity carried on, making do with what was available. No more than that could be done.

Fander was a back-number. He had nothing left for which to live but his songs and the affection of the others. In everything but his harp and his songs the Terrans were way ahead of him. He could do no more than give of his own affection in return for theirs and wait with the patience of one whose work is done.

At the end of that year they buried Graypate. He died in his sleep, passing with the undramatic casualness of one who ain't much use at speechifying. They put him to rest on a knoll behind the community hall, and Fander played his mourning song, and Precious Jewel, who was Speedy's wife, planted the grave with sweet herbs.

In the spring of the following year Fander summoned Speedy and Blacky and Redhead. He was coiled on a couch, blue and shivering. They held hands so that his touch would speak to them simultaneously.

"I am about to undergo my *amafa*."

He had great difficulty in putting it over in understandable thought-forms, for this was something beyond their Earthly experience.

"It is an unavoidable change of age during which my kind must sleep undisturbed." They reacted as if the casual reference to his kind was a strange and startling revelation, a new aspect previously unthought-of. He continued, "I must be left alone until this hibernation has run its natural course."

"For how long, Devil?" asked Speedy, with anxiety.

"It may stretch from four of your months to a full year, or—"

"Or what?" Speedy did not wait for a reassuring reply. His agile mind was swift to sense the spice of danger lying far back in the Martian's thoughts. "Or it may never end?"

"It may never," admitted Fander, reluctantly. He shivered again, drew his tentacles around himself. The brilliance of his blueness was fading visibly. "The possibility is small, but it is there."

Speedy's eyes widened and his breath was taken in a short gasp. His mind was striving to readjust itself and accept the appalling idea that Fander might not be a fixture, permanent, established for all time. Blacky and Redhead were equally aghast.

"We Martians do not last forever," Fander pointed out, gently. "All are mortal, here and there. He who survives his *amafa* has many happy years to follow, but some do not survive. It is a trial that must be faced as everything from beginning to end must be faced."

"But—"

"Our numbers are not large," Fander went on. "We breed slowly and some of us die halfway through the normal span. By cosmic standards we are a weak and foolish people much in need of the support of the clever and the strong. You are clever and strong. Whenever my people visit you again, or any other still stranger people come, always remember that you are clever and strong."

"We are strong," echoed Speedy, dreamily. His gaze swung around to take in the thousands of roofs, the copper dome, the thing of beauty on the hill. "We are strong."

A prolonged shudder went through the ropy, bee-eyed creature on the couch.

"I do not wish to be left here, an idle sleeper in the midst of life, posing like a bad example to the young. I would rather rest within the little cave where first we made friends and grew to know and understand each other. Wall it up and fix a door for me. Forbid anyone to touch me or let the light of day fall upon me until such time as I emerge of my own accord." Fander stirred sluggishly, his limbs uncoiling with noticeable lack of sinuousness. "I regret I must ask you to carry me there. Please forgive me; I have left it a little late and cannot . . . cannot . . . make it by myself."

Their faces were pictures of alarm, their minds bells of sorrow. Running for poles, they made a stretcher, edged him onto it, bore him to the cave. A long procession was following by the time they reached it. As they settled him comfortably and began to wall up the entrance, the crowd watched in the same solemn silence with which they had looked upon his verse.

He was already a tightly rolled ball of dull blueness, with filmed eyes, when they fitted the door and closed it, leaving him to darkness and slumber. Next day a tiny, brown-skinned man with eight children, all hugging dolls, came to the door. While the youngsters stared huge-eyed at the door, he fixed upon it a two-word name in metal letters, taking great pains over his self-imposed task and making a neat job of it.

The Martian vessel came from the stratosphere with the slow, stately fall of a grounding balloon. Behind the transparent band its bluish, nightmarish crew were assembled and looking with great, multifaceted eyes at the upper surface of the clouds. The scene resembled a pink-tinged snowfield beneath which the planet still remained concealed.

Captain Rdina could feel this as a tense, exciting moment even though his vessel had not the honor to be the first with such an approach. One Captain Skhiva, now long retired, had done it many years before. Nevertheless, this second venture retained its own exploratory thrill.

Someone stationed a third of the way around the vessel's belly came writhing at top pace toward him as their drop brought them near to the pinkish clouds. The oncomer's signaling tentacle was jiggling at a seldom-used rate.

"Captain, we have just seen an object swoop across the horizon."

"What sort of an object?"

"It looked like a gigantic load-sled."

"It couldn't have been."

"No, Captain, of course not—but that is exactly what it appeared to be."

"Where is it now?" demanded Rdina, gazing toward the side from which the other had come.

"It dived into the mists below."

"You must have been mistaken. Long-standing anticipation can encourage the strangest delusions." He stopped a moment as the observation band became shrouded in the vapor of a cloud. Musingly, he watched the gray wall of fog slide upward as his vessel continued its descent. "That old report says definitely that there is nothing but desolation and wild animals. There is no intelligent life except some fool of a minor poet whom Skhiva left behind, and twelve to one he's dead by now. The animals may have eaten him."

"Eaten him? Eaten *meat?*" exclaimed the other, thoroughly revolted.

"Anything is possible," assured Rdina, pleased with the extreme to which his imagination could be stretched. "Except a load-sled. That was plain silly."

At which point he had no choice but to let the subject drop for the simple and compelling reason that the ship came out of the base of the cloud, and the sled in question was floating alongside. It could be seen in complete detail, and even their own instruments were responding to the powerful output of its numerous flotation-grids.

The twenty Martians aboard the sphere sat staring bee-eyed at this enormous thing which was half the size of their own vessel, and the forty humans on the sled stared back with equal intentness. Ship and sled continued to descend side by side, while both crews studied each other with dumb fascination which persisted until simultaneously they touched ground.

It was not until he felt the slight jolt of landing that Captain Rdina recovered sufficiently to look elsewhere. He saw the houses, the green-domed building, the thing of beauty poised upon its hill, the many hundreds of Earth-people streaming out of their town and toward his vessel.

None of these queer, two-legged life forms, he noted, betrayed slightest sign of revulsion or fear. They galloped to the tryst with a bumptious self-confidence which would still be evident any place the other side of the cosmos.

It shook him a little, and he kept saying to himself, again and again, "They're not scared—why should you be? They're not scared—why should you be?"

He went out personally to meet the first of them, suppressing his own apprehensions and ignoring the fact that many of them bore weapons. The leading Earthmen, a big-built, spade-bearded two-legger, grasped his tentacle as to the manner born.

There came a picture of swiftly moving limbs. "My name is Speedy."

The ship emptied itself within ten minutes. No Martian would stay inside who was free to smell new air. Their first visit, in a slithering bunch, was to the thing of beauty. Rdina stood quietly looking at it, his crew clustered in a half-circle around him, the Earth-folk a silent audience behind.

It was a great rock statue of a female of Earth. She was broad-shouldered, full-bosomed, wide-hipped, and wore voluminous skirts that came right down to her heavy-soled shoes. Her back was a little bent, her head a little bowed, and her face was hidden in her hands, deep in her toilworn hands. Rdina tried in vain to gain some glimpse of the tired features behind those hiding hands. He looked at her a long while before his eyes lowered to read the script beneath, ignoring the Earth-lettering, running easily over the flowing Martian curlicues:

> *Weep, my country, for your sons asleep,*
> *The ashes of your homes, your tottering towers.*
> *Weep, my country, O, my country, weep!*
> *For birds that cannot sing, for vanished flowers,*
> > *The end of everything,*
> > *The silenced hours.*
> > *Weep! my country.*

There was no signature. Rdina mulled it through many minutes while the others remained passive. Then he turned to Speedy, pointed to the Martian script.

"Who wrote this?"

"One of your people. He is dead."

"Ah!" said Rdina. "That songbird of Skhiva's. I have forgotten his name. I doubt whether many remember it. He was only a very small poet. How did he die?"

"He ordered us to enclose him for some long and urgent sleep he must have, and—"

"The *amafa*," put in Rdina, comprehendingly. "And then?"

"We did as he asked. He warned us that he might never come out." Speedy gazed at the sky, unconscious that Rdina was picking up his sorrowful thoughts. "He has been there nearly two years and has not emerged." The eyes came down to Rdina. "I don't know whether you can understand me, but he was one of us."

"I think I understand." Rdina was thoughtful. He asked, "How long is this period you call nearly two years?"

They managed to work it out between them, translating it from Terran to Martian time-terms.

"It is long," pronounced Rdina. "Much longer than the usual *amafa*, but not unique. Occasionally, for no known reason, someone takes even longer. Besides, Earth is Earth and Mars is Mars." He became swift, energetic as he called to one of his crew. "Physician Traith, we have a prolonged-*amafa* case. Get your oils and essences and come with me." When the other had returned, he said to Speedy, "Take us to where he sleeps."

Reaching the door to the walled-up cave, Rdina paused to look at the names fixed upon it in neat but incomprehensible letters. They read: DEAR DEVIL.

"What do those mean?" asked Physician Traith, pointing.

"Do not disturb," guessed Rdina carelessly. Pushing open the door, he let the other enter first, closed it behind him to keep all others outside.

They reappeared an hour later. The total population of the city had congregated outside the cave to see the Martians. Rdina wondered why they had not permitted his crew to satisfy their natural curiosity, since it was unlikely that they would be more interested in other things—such as the fate of one small poet. Ten thousand eyes were upon them as they came into the sunlight and fastened the cave's door. Rdina made contact with Speedy, gave him the news.

Stretching himself in the light as if reaching toward the sun, Speedy shouted in a voice of tremendous gladness which all could hear.

"He will be out again within twenty days."

At that, a mild form of madness seemed to overcome the two-leggers. They made pleasure-grimaces, piercing mouth-noises, and some went so far as to beat each other.

Twenty Martians felt like joining Fander that same night. The Martian constitution is peculiarly susceptible to emotion.

THE BEST POLICY

By Randall Garrett

When human beings begin to encounter strangers in the universe, conflict is likely to erupt. Earthmen, by and large, are an aggressive sort of people, and it would not be surprising to run into a race of equally aggressive, militaristic creatures Out There. This could produce a nasty crash as one culture meets the other in a head-on impact.

However, one feature of alien beings is their alienness: They are not likely to think the way we do. This story suggests, in a deliciously deadpan way, how a suitably clever human can befuddle and bamboozle his extraterrestrial captors simply by telling the truth. Randall Garrett, who wrote it, is a bearded, booming-voiced man who now makes his home in Texas and who has spent considerable time studying the art of creating confusion without exactly lying. His high-spirited stories have been appearing in science fiction's leading magazines since 1944, with some time out for service with the United States Marine Corps.

Thagobar Larnimisculus Verf, Borgax of Fenigwisnok, had a long name and an important title, and he was proud of both. The title was roughly translatable as "High-Sheriff-Admiral of Fenigwisnok," and Fenigwisnok was a rich and important planet in the Dal Empire. Title and name looked very impressive together on documents, of which there were a great many to be signed.

Thagobar himself was a prime example of his race, a race of power and pride. Like the terrestrial turtles, he had both an exo- and an endoskeleton, although that was his closest resemblance to the *chelonia*. He was humanoid in general shape, looking something like a cross between a medieval knight in full armor and a husky football player clad for the gridiron. His overall color was similar to that of a well-boiled lobster, fading to a darker purple at the joints of his exoskeleton. His clothing was sparse, consisting only of an abbreviated kilt embroidered with fanciful designs and emblazoned with a swirl of glittering gems. The emblem of his rank was engraved in gold on his plastron and again on his carapace, so that he would be recognizable both coming and going.

All in all, he made quite an impressive figure, in spite of his five feet two in height.

As commander of his own spaceship, the *Verf,* it was his duty to search out and explore planets which could be colonized by his race, the Dal. This he had done diligently for many years, following exactly his General Orders as a good commander should.

And it had paid off. He had found some nice planets in his time, and this one was the juiciest of the lot.

Gazing at the magniscreen, he rubbed his palms together in satisfaction. His ship was swinging smoothly in an orbit high above a newly-discovered planet, and the magniscreen was focused on the landscape below. No Dal ship had ever been in this part of the galaxy before, and it was comforting to have discovered a colonizable planet so quickly.

"A magnificent planet!" he said. "A wonderful planet! Look at that green! And the blue of those seas!" He turned to Lieutenant Pelquesh. "What do you think? Isn't it fine?"

"It certainly is, Your Splendor," said Pelquesh. "You should receive another citation for this one."

Thagobar started to say something, then suddenly cut it short. His hands flew out to the controls and slapped at switch plates; the ship's engines squealed with power as they brought the ship to a dead stop in relation to the planet below. In the magniscreen, the landscape became stationary.

He twisted the screen's magnification control up, and the scene beneath the ship ballooned outward, spilling off the edges as the surface came closer.

"There!" he said. "Pelquesh, what is that?"

It was a purely rhetorical question. The wavering currents of two hundred odd miles of atmosphere caused the image to shimmer uncertainly, but there was no doubt that it was a city of some kind. Lieutenant Pelquesh said as much.

"Plague take it!" Thagobar snarled. "An occupied planet! Only intelligent beings build cities."

"That's so," agreed Pelquesh.

Neither of them knew what to do. Only a few times in the long history of the Dal had other races been found—and un-

der the rule of the Empire, they had all slowly become ex-
tinct. Besides, none of them had been very intelligent, anyway.

"We'll have to ask General Orders," Thagobar said at last.
He went over to another screen, turned it on, and began dial-
ing code numbers into it.

Deep in the bowels of the huge ship, the General Orders
robot came sluggishly to life. In its vast memory lay ten thousand years of accumulated and ordered facts, ten thousand
years of the experiences of the Empire, ten thousand years of
the final decisions on every subject ever considered by Thagobar's race. It was more than an encyclopedia—it was a way of
life.

In a highly logical way, the robot sorted through its memory until it came to the information requested by Thagobar;
then it relayed the data to the screen.

"Hm-m-m," said Thagobar. "Yes. General Order 333,953,-
216-A-j, Chapter MMCMXLIX, Paragraph 402. 'First discovery of an intelligent or semi-intelligent species shall be
followed by the taking of a specimen selected at random. No
contact shall be made until the specimen has been examined
according to Psychology Directive 659-B, Section 888,077-q,
at the direction of the Chief Psychologist. The data will be
correlated by General Orders. If contact has already been
made inadvertently, refer to GO 472,678-R-s, Ch. MMMCCX,
Par. 553. Specimens shall be taken according to . . .'"

He finished reading off the General Order and then turned
to the lieutenant. "Pelquesh, you get a spaceboat ready to pick
up a specimen. I'll notify psychologist Zandoplith to be ready
for it."

Ed Magruder took a deep breath of spring air and closed
his eyes. It was beautiful; it was filled with spicy aromas and
tangy scents that, though alien, were somehow homelike—
more homelike than Earth.

He was a tall, lanky man, all elbows and knees, with non-
descript brown hair and bright hazel eyes that tended to crin-
kle with suppressed laughter.

He exhaled the breath and opened his eyes. The city was
still awake, but darkness was coming fast. He liked his
evening stroll, but it wasn't safe to be out after dark on New
Hawaii, even yet. There were little night things that fluttered
softly in the air, giving little warning of their poisonous bite,
and there were still some of the larger predators in the neighborhood. He started walking back toward New Hilo, the little

city that marked man's first foothold on the new planet.

Magruder was a biologist. In the past ten years, he had prowled over half a dozen planets, collecting specimens, dissecting them with precision, and entering the results in his notebooks. Slowly, bit by bit, he was putting together a pattern —a pattern of life itself. His predecessors stretched in a long line, clear back to Karl von Linné, but none of them had realized what was missing in their work. They had had only one type of life to deal with—terrestrial life. And all terrestrial life is, after all, homogenous.

But, of all the planets he'd seen, he liked New Hawaii best. It was the only planet besides Earth where a man could walk around without a protective suit of some kind—at least, it was the only one discovered so far.

He heard a faint swishing in the air over his head and glanced up quickly. The night things shouldn't be out this early!

And then he saw that it wasn't a night thing; it was a metallic-looking globe of some kind, and—

There was a faint greenish glow that suddenly flashed from a spot on the side of the globe, and all went blank for Ed Magruder.

Thagobar Verf watched dispassionately as Lieutenant Pelquesh brought the unconscious specimen into the biological testing section. It was a queer-looking specimen; a soft-skinned, sluglike parody of a being, with a pale, pinkish-tan complexion and a repulsive, fungoidal growth on its head and various other areas.

The biologists took the specimen and started to work on it. They took nips of skin and samples of blood and various electrical readings from the muscles and nerves.

Zandoplith, the Chief Psychologist, stood by the commander, watching the various operations.

It was Standard Procedure for the biologists; they went about it as if they would with any other specimen that had been picked up. But Zandoplith was going to have to do a job he had never done before. He was going to have to work with the mind of an intelligent being.

He wasn't worried, of course; it was all down in the Handbook, every bit of Proper Procedure. There was nothing at all to worry about.

As with all other specimens, it was Zandoplith's job to discover the Basic Reaction Pattern. Any given organism could react only in a certain very large, but finite number of ways, and these ways could be reduced to a Basic Pattern. All that was necessary to destroy a race of creatures was to get their Basic Pattern and then give them a problem that couldn't be solved by using that pattern. It was all very simple, and it was all down in the Handbook.

Thagobar turned his head from the operating table to look at Zandoplith. "Do you think it really will be possible to teach it our language?"

"The rudiments, Your Splendor," said the psychologist. "Ours is, after all, a very complex language. We'll give him all of it, of course, but it is doubtful whether he can assimilate more than a small portion of it. Our language is built upon logic, just as thought is built upon logic. Some of the lower animals are capable of the rudiments of logic, but most are unable to grasp it."

"Very well; we'll do the best we can. I, myself, will question it."

Zandoplith looked a little startled. "But, Your Splendor! The questions are all detailed in the Handbook!"

Thagobar Verf scowled. "I can read as well as you, Zandoplith. Since this is the first semi-intelligent life discovered in the past thousand years or so, I think the commander should be the one to do the questioning."

"As you say, Your Splendor," the psychologist agreed.

Ed Magruder was placed in the Language Tank when the biologists got through with him. Projectors of light were fastened over his eyes so that they focused directly on his retinas; sound units were inserted into his ears; various electrodes were fastened here and there; a tiny network of wires was attached to his skull. Then a special serum which the biologists had produced was injected into his bloodstream. It was all very efficient and very smoothly done. Then the Tank was closed, and a switch was thrown.

Magruder felt himself swim dizzily up out of the blackness. He saw odd-looking, lobster-colored things moving around while noises whispered and gurgled into his ears.

Gradually, he began to orient himself. He was being taught to associate sounds with actions and things.

Ed Magruder sat in a little four-by-six room, naked as a jay-bird, looking through a transparent wall at a sextette of the aliens he had seen so much of lately.

Of course, it wasn't these particular bogeys he'd been watching, but they looked so familar that it was hard to believe they were here in the flesh. He had no idea how long he'd been learning the language; with no exterior references, he was lost.

Well, he thought, I've picked up a good many specimens, and here I am, a specimen myself. He thought of the treatment he'd given his own specimens and shuddered a little.

Oh, well. Here he was; might as well put on a good show— stiff upper lip, chin up, and all that sort.

One of the creatures walked up to an array of buttons and pressed one. Immediately, Magruder could hear sounds from the room on the other side of the transparent wall.

Thagobar Verf looked at the specimen and then at the question sheet in his hand. "Our psychologists have taught you our language, have they not?" he asked coldly.

The specimen bobbled his head up and down. "Yup. And that's what I call real force-feeding, too."

"Very well; I have some questions to ask; you will answer them truthfully."

"Why, sure," Magruder said agreeably. "Fire away."

"We can tell if you are lying," Thagobar continued. "It will do you no good to tell us untruths. Now—what is your name?"

"Theophilus Q. Hassenpfeffer," Magruder said blandly.

Zandoplith looked at a quivering needle and then shook his head slowly as he looked up at Thagobar.

"That is a lie," said Thagobar.

The specimen nodded. "It sure is. That's quite a machine you've got there."

"It is good that you appreciate the superiority of our instruments," Thagobar said grimly. "Now—your name."

"Edwin Peter St. John Magruder."

Psychologist Zandoplith watched the needle and nodded.

"Excellent," said Thagobar. "Now, Edwin—"

"Ed is good enough," said Magruder.

Thagobar blinked. "Good enough for what?"

"For calling me."

Thagobar turned to the psychologist and mumbled something. Zandoplith mumbled back. Thagobar spoke to the specimen.

"Is your name Ed?"

"Strictly speaking, no," said Magruder.

"Then why should I call you that?"

"Why not? Everyone else does," Magruder informed him.

Thagobar consulted further with Zandoplith and finally said: "We will come back to that point later. Now . . . uh . . . Ed, what do you call your home planet?"

"Earth."

"Good. And what does your race call itself?"

"Homo sapiens."

"And the significance of that, if any?"

Magruder considered. "It's just a name," he said, after a moment.

The needle waggled.

"Another lie," said Thagobar.

Magruder grinned. "Just testing. That really *is* a whizzer of a machine."

Thagobar's throat and face darkened a little as his copper-bearing blue blood surged to the surface in suppressed anger. "You said that once," he reminded blackly.

"I know. Well, if you really want to know, *Homo sapiens* means 'wise man.' "

Actually, he hadn't said "wise man"; the language of the Dal didn't quite have that exact concept, so Magruder had to do the best he could. Translated back into English, it would have come out something like "beings with vast powers of mind."

When Thagobar heard this, his eyes opened a little wider, and he turned his head to look at Zandoplith. The psychologist spread his horny hands; the needle hadn't moved.

"You seem to have high opinions of yourselves," said Thagobar, looking back at Magruder.

"That's possible," agreed the Earthman.

Thagobar shrugged, looked back at his list, and the questioning went on. Some of the questions didn't make too much sense to Magruder; others were obviously psychological testing.

But one thing was quite clear; the lie detector was indeed quite a whizzer. If Magruder told the exact truth, it didn't indicate. But if he lied just the least tiny bit, the needle on the machine hit the ceiling—and, eventually, so did Thagobar.

Magruder had gotten away with his first few lies—they were unimportant, anyway—but finally, Thagobar said: "You have lied enough, Ed."

He pressed a button, and a nerve-shattering wave of pain swept over the Earthman. When it finally faded, Magruder found his belly muscles tied in knots, his fists and teeth clenched, and tears running down his cheeks. Then nausea overtook him, and he lost the contents of his stomach.

Thagobar Verf turned distastefully away. "Put him back in his cell and clean up the interrogation chamber. Is he badly hurt?"

Zandoplith had already checked his instruments. "I think not, Your Splendor; it is probably only slight shock and nothing more. However, we will have to retest him in the next session anyhow. We'll know then."

Magruder sat on the edge of a shelflike thing that doubled as a low table and a high bed. It wasn't the most comfortable seat in the world, but it was all he had in the room; the floor was even harder.

It had been several hours since he had been brought here, and he still didn't feel good. That stinking machine had *hurt!* He clenched his fists; he could still feel the knot in his stomach and—

And then he realized that the knot in his stomach hadn't been caused by the machine; he had thrown that off a long time back.

The knot was caused by a towering, thundering-great, ice-cold rage.

He thought about it for a minute and then broke out laughing. Here he was, like a stupid fool, so angry that he was making himself sick! And that wasn't going to do him *or* the colony any good.

It was obvious that the aliens were up to no good, to say the least. The colony at New Hilo numbered six thousand souls—the only humans on New Hawaii, except for a couple of bush expeditions. If this ship tried to take over the planet, there wouldn't be a devil of a lot the colonists could do about it. And what if the aliens found Earth itself? He had no idea what kind of armament this spaceship carried nor how big it was—but it seemed to have plenty of room inside it.

He knew it was up to him. He was going to have to do something, somehow. What? Could he get out of his cell and try to smash the ship?

Nope. A naked man inside a bare cell was about as helpless as a human being can get. What, then?

Magruder lay on his back and thought about it for a long time.

Presently, a panel opened in the door and a red-violet face appeared on the other side of a transparent square in the door.

"You are doubtless hungry," it said solemnly. "An analysis of your bodily processes has indicated what you need in the way of sustenance. Here."

The quart-size mug that slid out of a niche in the wall had an odd aroma drifting up from it. Magruder picked it up and looked inside. It was a grayish-tan, semitranslucent liquid about the consistency of thin gravy. He touched the surface with his finger and then touched the finger with his tongue. Its palate appeal was definitely on the negative side of zero.

He could guess what it contained: a score, more or less, of various amino acids, a dozen vitamins, a handful of carbohydrates, and a few percent of other necessities. A sort of pseudo-protoplasmic soup; an overbalanced meal.

He wondered whether it contained anything that would do him harm, decided it probably didn't. If the aliens wanted to dope him, they didn't need to resort to subterfuge, and besides, this was probably the gunk they had fed him while he was learning the language.

Pretending to himself that it was beef stew, he drank it down. Maybe he could think better on a full stomach. And, as it turned out, he was right.

Less than an hour later, he was back in the interrogation chamber. This time, he was resolved to keep Thagobar's finger off that little button.

After all, he reasoned to himself, I might want to lie to someone, when and if I get out of this. There's no point in getting a conditioned reflex against it.

And the way the machine had hurt him, there was a strong possibility that he just might get conditioned if he took very many jolts like that.

He had a plan. It was highly nebulous—little more than a principle, really, and it was highly flexible. He would simply have to take what came, depend on luck, and hope for the best.

He sat down in the chair and waited for the wall to become transparent again. He had thought there might be a way to get out as he was led from his cell to the interrogation chamber, but he didn't feel like tackling six heavily armored aliens all at once. He wasn't even sure he could do much with just one of them. Where do you slug a guy whose nervous system you know nothing about, and whose body is plated like a boiler?

The wall became transparent, and the alien was standing on the other side of it. Magruder wondered whether it was the same being who had questioned him before, and after looking at the design on the plastron, decided that it was.

He leaned back in his chair, folded his arms, and waited for the first question.

Thagobar Verf was a very troubled Dal. He had very carefully checked the psychological data with General Orders after the psychologists had correlated it according to the Handbook. He definitely did not like the looks of his results.

General Orders merely said: "No race of this type has ever been found in the galaxy before. In this case, the commander will act according to GO 234,511,006-R-g, Ch. MMCDX, Par. 666."

After looking up the reference, he had consulted with Zandoplith. "What do you think of it?" he asked. "And why doesn't your science have any answers?"

"Science, Your Splendor," said Zandoplith, "is a process of obtaining and correlating data. We haven't enough data yet, true, but we'll get it. We absolutely must not panic at this point; we must be objective, purely objective." He handed Thagobar another printed sheet. "These are the next questions to be asked, according to the Handbook of Psychology."

Thagobar felt a sense of relief. General Orders had said that in a case like this, the authority of action was all dependent on his own decision; it was nice to know that the scientist knew what he was doing, and had authority to back it.

He cut off the wall polarizer and faced the specimen on the other side.

"You will answer the next several questions in the negative," Thagobar said. "It doesn't matter what the real and truthful answer may be, you will say No; is that perfectly clear?"

"No," said Magruder.

Thagobar frowned. The instructions seemed perfectly lucid to him; what was the matter with the specimen? Was he possibly more stupid than they had at first believed?

"He's lying," said Zandoplith.

It took Thagobar the better part of half a minute to realize what had happened, and when he did, his face became unpleasantly dark. But there was nothing else he could do; the specimen had obeyed orders.

His Splendor took a deep breath, held it for a moment,

eased it out, and began reading the questions in a mild voice.

"Is your name Edwin?"

"No."

"Do you live on the planet beneath us?"

"No."

"Do you have six eyes?"

"No."

After five minutes of that sort of thing, Zandoplith said: "That's enough, Your Splendor; it checks out; his nervous system wasn't affected by the pain. You may proceed to the next list."

"From now on, you will answer truthfully," Thagobar said. "Otherwise, you will be punished again. Is *that* clear?"

"Perfectly clear," said Magruder.

Although his voice sounded perfectly calm, Magruder, on the other side of the transparent wall, felt just a trifle shaky. He would have to think quickly and carefully from now on. He didn't believe he'd care to take too much time in answering, either.

"How many *Homo sapiens* are there?"

"Several billions." There were actually about four billions, but the Dal equivalent of "several" was vaguely representative of numbers larger than five, although not necessarily so.

"Don't you know the actual number?"

"No," said Magruder. *Not right down to the man, I don't*. The needle didn't quiver. Naturally not—he was telling the truth, wasn't he?

"All of your people surely aren't on Earth, then?" Thagobar asked, deviating slightly from the script. "In only one city?"

With a sudden flash of pure joy, Magruder saw the beautifully monstrous mistake the alien had made. He had not suspected until now that Earthmen had developed space travel. Therefore, when he had asked the name of Magruder's home planet, the answer he'd gotten was "Earth." But the alien had been thinking of New Hawaii! *Wheeee!*

"Oh, no," said Magruder truthfully. "We have only a few thousand down there." Meaning, of course, New Hawaii, which was "down there."

"Then most of your people have deserted Earth?"

"Deserted Earth?" Magruder sounded scandalized. "Heavens to Betsy, no! We have merely colonized; we're all under one central government."

"How many are there in each colony?" Thagobar had completely abandoned the script now.

"I don't know exactly," Magruder told him, "but not one of our colonized planets has any more occupants on it than Earth."

Thagobar looked flabbergasted and flicked off the sound transmission to the prisoner with a swift movement of his finger.

Zandoplith looked pained. "You are not reading the questions from the Handbook," he complained.

"I know, I know. But did you hear what he said?"

"I heard it." Zandoplith's voice sounded morose.

"It wasn't true, was it?"

Zandoplith drew himself up to his full five feet one. "Your Splendor, you have taken it upon yourself to deviate from the Handbook, but I will not permit you to question the operation of the Reality Detector. Reality is truth, and therefore truth is reality; the Detector hasn't erred since—since *ever!*"

"I know," Thagobar said hastily. "But do you realize the implications of what he said? There are a few thousand people on the home planet; all the colonies have less. And yet, there are *several billion* of his race! That means they have occupied around ten million planets!"

"I realize it sounds queer," admitted Zandoplith, "but the Detector never lies!" Then he realized whom he was addressing and added, "Your Splendor."

But Thagobar hadn't noticed the breach of etiquette. "That's perfectly true. But, as you said, there's something queer here. We must investigate further."

Magruder had already realized that his mathematics was off kilter; he was thinking at high speed.

Thagobar's voice said: "According to our estimates, there are not that many habitable planets in the galaxy. How do you account, then, for your statement?"

With a quick shift of viewpoint, Magruder thought of Mars, so many light-years away. There had been a scientific outpost on Mars for a long time, but it was a devil of a long way from being a habitable planet.

"My people," he said judiciously, "are capable of living on planets with surface conditions which vary widely from those of Earth."

Before Thagobar could ask anything else, another thought occurred to the Earthman. The thousand-inch telescope on Luna had discovered, spectroscopically, the existence of large planets in the Andromeda Nebula. "In addition," he continued blandly, "we have found planets in other galaxies than this."

There! *That* ought to confuse them!

Again the sound was cut off, and Magruder could see the two aliens in hot discussion. When the sound came back again, Thagobar had shifted to another tack.

"How many spaceships do you have?"

Magruder thought that one over for a long second. There were about a dozen interstellar ships in the Earth fleet—not nearly enough to colonize ten million planets. He was in a jam!

No! Wait! A supply ship came to New Hawaii ever six months. But there were no ships on New Hawaii.

"Spaceships?" Magruder looked innocent. "Why, we have no spaceships."

Thagobar Verf shut off the sound again, and this time, he made the wall opaque, too. "No spaceships? *No spaceships?* He lied . . . I hope?"

Zandoplith shook his head dolefully. "Absolute truth."

"But—but—but—"

"Remember what he said his race called themselves?" the psychologist asked softly.

Thagobar blinked very slowly. When he spoke, his voice was a hoarse whisper. *"Beings with minds of vast power."*

"Exactly," said Zandoplith.

Magruder sat in the interrogation chamber for a long time without hearing or seeing a thing. Had they made sense out of his statements? Were they beginning to realize what he was doing? He wanted to chew his nails, bite his lips, and tear his hair; instead, he forced himself to outward calm. There was a long way to go yet.

When the wall suddenly became transparent once more, he managed to keep from jumping.

"Is it true," asked Thagobar, "that your race has the ability to move through space by means of mental power alone?"

For a moment, Magruder was stunned. It was beyond his wildest expectations. But he rallied quickly.

How does a man walk? he thought.

"It is true that by using mental forces to control physical energy," he said carefully, "we are able to move from place to place without the aid of spaceships or other such machines."

Immediately, the wall blanked again.

Thagobar turned around slowly and looked at Zandoplith. Zandoplith's face looked a dirty crimson; the healthy violet had faded.

"I guess you'd best call in the officers," he said slowly; "we've got a monster on our hands."

It took three minutes for the twenty officers of the huge *Verf* to assemble in the Psychology Room. When they arrived, Thagobar asked them to relax and then outlined the situation.

"Now," he said, "are there any suggestions?"

They were definitely *not* relaxed now. They looked as tense as bowstrings.

Lieutenant Pelquesh was the first to speak. "What are the General Orders, Your Splendor?"

"The General Orders," Thagobar said, "are that we are to protect our ship and our race, if necessary. The methods for doing so are left up to the commander's discretion."

There was a rather awkward silence. Then a light seemed to come over Lieutenant Pelquesh's face. "Your Splendor, we could simply drop an annihilation bomb on the planet."

Thagobar shook his head. "I've already thought of that. If they can move themselves through space by means of thought alone, they would escape, and their race would surely take vengeance for the vaporization of one of their planets."

Gloom descended.

"Wait a minute," said Pelquesh. "If he can do that, *why hasn't he escaped from us?*"

Magruder watched the wall become transparent. The room was filled with aliens now. The big cheese, Thagobar, was at the pickup.

"We are curious," he said, "to know why, if you can go anywhere at will, you have stayed here. Why don't you escape?"

More fast thinking. "It is not polite," Magruder said, "for a guest to leave his host until the business at hand is finished."

"Even after we . . . ah . . . disciplined you?"

"Small discomforts can be overlooked, especially when the host is acting in abysmal ignorance."

There was a whispered question from one of Thagobar's underlings and a smattering of discussion, and then:

"Are we to presume, then, that you bear us no ill will?"

"Some," admitted Magruder candidly. "It is only because of your presumptuous behavior toward me, however, that I personally am piqued. I can assure you that my race as a whole bears no ill will whatever toward your race as a whole or any member of it."

Play it up big, Magruder, he told himself. *You've got 'em rocking—I hope.*

More discussion on the other side of the wall.

"You say," said Thagobar, "that your race holds no ill will toward us; how do you know?"

"I can say this," Magruder told him; "I know—beyond any shadow of a doubt—exactly what every person of my race thinks of you at this very moment.

"In addition, let me point out that I have not been harmed as yet; they would have no reason to be angry. After all, you haven't been destroyed yet."

Off went the sound. More heated discussion. On went the sound.

"It has been suggested," said Thagobar, "that, in spite of appearances, it was intended that we pick you, and you alone, as a specimen. It is suggested that you were sent to meet us."

Oh, brother! This one would have to be handled with *very* plush gloves.

"I am but a very humble member of my race," Magruder said as a prelude—mostly to gain time. But wait! He was an extraterrestrial biologist, wasn't he? "However," he continued with dignity, "my profession is that of meeting alien beings. I was, I must admit, appointed to the job."

Thagobar seemed to grow tenser. "That, in turn, suggests that you knew we were coming."

Magruder thought for a second. It had been predicted for centuries that mankind would eventually meet an intelligent alien race.

"We have known you were coming for a long time," he said quite calmly.

Thagobar was visibly agitated now. "In that case, you must know where our race is located in the galaxy; you must know where our home base is."

Another tough one. Magruder looked through the wall at Thagobar and his men standing nervously on the other side of it. "I know where you are," he said, "and I know exactly where every one of your fellows is."

There was sudden consternation on the other side of the wall, but Thagobar held his ground.

"What is our location then?"

For a second, Magruder thought they'd pulled the rug out from under him at last. And then he saw that there was a perfect explanation. He'd been thinking of dodging so long that he almost hadn't seen the honest answer.

He looked at Thagobar pityingly. "Communication by voice is so inadequate. Our coordinate system would be completely unintelligible to you, and you did not teach me yours if you will recall." Which was perfectly true; the Dal would have been foolish to teach their coordinate system to a specimen—the clues might have led to their home base. Besides, General Orders forbade it.

More conversation on the other side.

Thagobar again: "If you are in telepathic communication with your fellows, can you read *our* minds?"

Magruder looked at him superciliously. "I have principles, as does my race; we do not enter any mind uninvited."

"Do the rest of your people know the location of our bases, then?" Thagobar asked plaintively.

Magruder's voice was placid. "I assure you, Thagobar Verf, that every one of my people, on every planet belonging to our race, knows as much about your home base and its location as I do."

Magruder was beginning to get tired of the on-and-off sound system, but he resigned himself to wait while the aliens argued among themselves.

"It has been pointed out," Thagobar said, after a few minutes, "that it is very odd that your race has never contacted us before. Ours is a very old and powerful race, and we have taken planets throughout a full half of the galaxy, and yet, your race has never been seen nor heard of before."

"We have a policy," said Magruder, "of not disclosing our presence to another race until it is to our advantage to do so. Besides, we have no quarrel with your race, and we have never had any desire to take your homes away from you. Only if a race becomes foolishly and insanely belligerent do we trouble ourselves to show them our power."

It was a long speech—maybe too long. Had he stuck strictly to the truth? A glance at Zandoplith told him; the chief psychologist had kept his beady black eyes on the needle all through the long proceedings, and kept looking more and more worried as the instrument indicated a steady flow of truth.

Thagobar looked positively apprehensive. As Magruder had become accustomed to the aliens, it had become more and more automatic to read their expressions. After all, he held one great advantage: they had made the mistake of teaching him their language. He knew them, and they didn't know him.

Thagobar said: "Other races, then, have been . . . uh . . . punished by yours?"

"Not in my lifetime," Magruder told him. He thought of *Homo neanderthalensis* and said: "There was a race, before my time, which defied us. It no longer exists."

"Not in your lifetime? How old are you?"

"Look into your magniscreen at the planet below," said the Earthman in a solemn tone. "When I was born, not a single one of the plants you see existed on Earth. The continents of Earth were nothing like that; the seas were entirely different.

"The Earth on which I was born had extensive ice caps; look below you, and you will see none. And yet, we have done nothing to change the planet you see; any changes that have taken place have come by the long process of geologic evolution."

"Gleek!" It was a queer sound that came from Thagobar's throat just before a switch cut off the wall and the sound again.

Just like watching a movie on an old film, Magruder thought. *No sound half the time, and it breaks every so often.*

The wall never became transparent again. Instead, after about half an hour, it slid up silently to disclose the entire officer's corp of the *Verf* standing at rigid attention.

Only Thagobar Larnimisculus Verf, Borgax of Fenigwisnok, stood at ease, and even so, his face seemed less purple than usual.

"Edwin Peter St. John Magruder," he intoned, "as commander of this vessel, Noble of the Grand Empire, and representative of the Emperor himself, we wish to extend to you our most cordial hospitality.

"Laboring under the delusion that you represented a lower form of life, we have treated you ignominiously, and for that we offer our deepest apologies."

"Think nothing of it," said Magruder coolly. "The only thing that remains is for you to land your ship on our planet so that your race and mine can arrange things to our mutual happiness." He looked at all of them. "You may relax," he added imperiously. "And bring me my clothes."

The human race wasn't out of the hole yet; Magruder was perfectly well aware of that. Just what should be done with the ship and the aliens when they landed, he wasn't quite sure;

it would have to be left up to the decision of the President of New Hawaii and the Government of Earth. But he didn't foresee any great difficulties.

As the *Verf* dropped toward the surface of New Hawaii, its commander sidled over to Magruder and said, in a troubled voice: "Do you think your people will like us?"

Magruder glanced at the lie detector. It was off.

"*Like* you? Why, they'll *love* you," he said.

He was sick and tired of being honest.

ALAREE

By Robert Silverberg

The German word "gestalt" means "shape" or "pattern," but it also has the sense of "group" or "formation." The science-fictional concept of the gestalt *mind has frequently been examined—the intelligence that includes more than one individual. On Earth, the rule of one-body-one-intelligence seems to hold true, but who knows what we may find on other worlds? We already know of some simple creatures, like the corals and sponges, that exist in colonies numbering many individuals. Such linkings are purely physical; the possibility exists, though, that on another planet some higher form of life may have developed a colony of linked minds. What it would be like to encounter such a form of life is considered in this story.*

When our ship left its carefully planned trajectory and started to wobble through space in dizzy circles, I knew we shouldn't have passed up that opportunity for an overhauling on Spica IV. My men and I were anxious to get back to Earth, and a hasty check had assured us that the *Aaron Burr* was in tip-top shape, so we had turned down the offer of an overhaul, which would have meant a month's delay, and set out straight for home.

As so often happens, what seemed like the most direct route home turned out to be the longest. We had spent far too much time on this survey trip already, and we were rejoicing in the prospect of an immediate return to Earth when the ship started turning cartwheels.

Willendorf, computerman first class, came to me looking sheepish, a few minutes after I'd noticed we were off course.

"What is it, Gus?" I asked.

"The feed network's oscillating, sir," he said, tugging at his unruly reddish-brown beard. "It won't stop, sir."

"Is Ketteridge working on it?"

"I've just called him," Willendorf said. His stolid face reflected acute embarrassment. Willendorf always took it personally whenever one of the cybers went haywire, as if it were his own fault. "You know what this means, don't you, sir?"

I grinned. "Take a look at this, Willendorf," I said, shoving the trajectory graphs toward him. I sketched out with my stylus the confused circles we had been traveling in all morning. "That's what your feed network's doing to us," I said. "And we'll keep on doing it until we get it fixed."

"What are you going to do, sir?"

I sensed his impatience with me. Willendorf was a good man, but his psych charts indicated a latent desire for officerhood. Deep down inside, he was sure he was at least as competent as I was to run this ship and probably a good deal more so.

"Send me Upper Navigating Technician Haley," I snapped. "We're going to have to find a planet in the neighborhood and put down for repairs."

It turned out there was an insignificant solar system in the vicinity, consisting of a small but hot white star and a single unexplored planet, Terra-size, a few hundred million miles out. After Haley and I had decided that that was the nearest port of refuge, I called a general meeting.

Quickly and positively I outlined our situation and explained what would have to be done. I sensed the immediate disappointment, but, gratifyingly, the reaction was followed by a general feeling of resigned pitching in. If we all worked, we'd get back to Earth, sooner or later. If we didn't, we'd spend the next century flip-flopping aimlessly through space.

After the meeting, we set about the business of recovering control of the ship and putting it down for repairs. The feed network, luckily, gave up the ghost about ninety minutes later; it meant we had to stoke the fuel by hand, but at least it stopped that accursed oscillating.

We got the ship going, and Haley, navigating by feel in a way I never would have dreamed possible, brought us into the nearby solar system in hardly any time at all. Finally we swung into our landing orbit and made our looping way down to the surface of the little planet.

I studied my crew's faces carefully. We had spent a great deal of time together in space—much too much, really, for comfort—and an incident like this might very well snap them all if we didn't get going again soon enough. I could foresee disagreements, bickering, declaration of opinion where no opinion was called for.

I was relieved to discover that the planet's air was breathable. A rather high nitrogen concentration, to be sure—82 percent—but that left 17 percent for oxygen, plus some miscellaneous inerts, and it wouldn't be too rough on the lungs. I decreed a one-hour free break before beginning repairs.

Remaining aboard ship, I gloomily surveyed the scrambled feed network and tried to formulate a preliminary plan of action for getting the complex cybernetic instrument to function again, while my crew went outside to relax.

Ten minutes after I had opened the lock and let them out, I heard someone clanking around in the aft supplies cabin.

"Who's there?" I yelled.

"Me," grunted a heavy voice that could only be Willendorf's. "I'm looking for the thought-converter, sir."

I ran hastily through the corridor, flipped up the latch on the supplies cabin, and confronted him. "What do you want the converter for?" I snapped.

"Found an alien, sir," he said laconically.

My eyes widened. The survey chart had said nothing about intelligent extraterrestrials in this limb of the galaxy, but then again this planet hadn't been explored yet.

I gestured toward the rear cabinet. "The converter helmets are in there," I said. "I'll be out in a little while. Make sure you follow technique in making contact."

"Of course, sir." Willendorf took the converter helmet and went out, leaving me standing there. I waited a few minutes, then climbed the catwalk to the air lock and peered out.

They were all clustered around a small alien being, who looked weak and inconsequential in the midst of the circle. I smiled at the sight. The alien was roughly humanoid in shape, with the usual complement of arms and legs, and a pale green complexion that blended well with the muted violet coloring of his world. He was wearing the thought-converter somewhat lopsidedly, and I saw a small, green, furry ear protruding from the left side. Willendorf was talking to him.

Then someone saw me standing at the open air lock, and I heard Haley yell to me, "Come on down, Chief!"

They were ringed around the alien in a tight circle. I shouldered my way into their midst. Willendorf turned to me.

"Meet Alaree, sir," he said. "Alaree, this is our commander."

"We are pleased to meet you," the alien said gravely. The converter automatically turned his thoughts into English, but maintained the trace of his oddly inflected accent. "You have been saying that you are from the skies."

"His grammar's pretty shaky," Willendorf interposed. "He keeps referring to any of us as 'you'—even you, who just got here."

"Odd," I said. "The converter's supposed to conform to the rules of grammar." I turned to the alien, who seemed perfectly at ease among us. "My name is Bryson," I said. "This is Willendorf, over here."

The alien wrinkled his soft-skinned forehead in momentary confusion. "We are Alaree," he said again.

"We? You and who else?"

"We and we else," Alaree said blandly. I stared at him for a moment, then gave up. The complexities of an alien mind are often too much for a mere Terran to fathom.

"You are welcome to our world," Alaree said after a few moments of silence.

"Thanks," I said. "Thanks."

I turned away, leaving the alien with my men. They had twenty-six minutes left of the break I'd given them, after which we would have to get back to the serious business of repairing the ship. Making friends with floppy-eared aliens was one thing; getting back to Earth was another.

The planet was a warm, friendly sort of place, with rolling fields and acres of pleasant-looking purple vegetation. We had landed in a clearing at the edge of a fair-sized copse. Great broad-beamed trees shot up all around us.

Alaree returned to visit us every day, until he became almost a mascot of the crew. I liked the little alien myself and spent some time with him, although I found his conversation generally incomprehensible. No doubt he had the same trouble with us. The converter had only limited efficiency, after all.

He was the only representative of his species who came. For all we knew, he was the only one of his kind on the whole planet. There was no sign of life elsewhere, and, although Willendorf led an unauthorized scouting party during some free time on the third day, he failed to find a village of any sort. Where Alaree went every night, and how he had found us in the first place, remained mysteries.

As for the feed network, progress was slow. Ketteridge, the technician in charge, had tracked down the foul-up and was trying to repair it without building a completely new network.

Shortcuts again. He tinkered away for four days, setting up a tentative circuit, trying it out, watching it sputter and blow out, building another.

There was nothing I could do. But I sensed tension heightening among the crewmen. They were annoyed at themselves, at each other, at me, at everything.

On the fifth day, Ketteridge and Willendorf finally let their accumulated tenseness explode. They had been working together on the network, but they quarreled, and Ketteridge came storming into my cabin immediately afterward.

"Sir, I demand to be allowed to work on the network by myself. It's my specialty, and Willendorf's only snarling things up."

"Get me Willendorf," I said.

When Willendorf showed up I heard the whole story, decided quickly to let Ketteridge have his way—it was, after all, his specialty—and calmed Willendorf down. Then, reaching casually for some papers on my desk, I dismissed both of them. I knew they'd come to their senses in a day or so.

I spent most of the next day sitting placidly in the sun, while Ketteridge tinkered with the feed network some more. I watched the faces of the men. They were starting to smoulder. They wanted to get home, and they weren't getting there. Besides, this was a fairly dull planet, and even the novelty of Alaree wore off after a while. The little alien had a way of hanging around men who were busy scraping fuel deposits out of the jet tubes, or something equally unpleasant, and bothering them with all sorts of questions.

The following morning I was lying blissfully on the grass near the ship, talking to Alaree. Ketteridge came to me, and by the tightness of his lips I knew he was in trouble.

I brushed some antlike blue insects off my trousers and rose to a sitting position, leaning against the tall, tough-barked tree behind me. "What's the matter, Ketteridge? How's the feed network?"

He glanced uneasily at Alaree for a moment before speaking. "I'm stuck, sir. I'll have to admit I was wrong. I can't fix it by myself."

I stood up and put my hand on his shoulder. "That's a noble thing to say, Ketteridge. It takes a big man to admit he's been a fool. Will you work with Willendorf now?"

"If he'll work with me, sir," Ketteridge said miserably.

"I think he will," I said. Ketteridge saluted and turned away, and I felt a burst of satisfaction. I'd met the crisis in the only way possible; if I had *ordered* them to cooperate, I would have gotten no place. The psychological situation no longer allowed for unbending military discipline.

After Ketteridge had gone, Alaree, who had been silent all this time, looked up at me in puzzlement. "We do not understand," he said.

"Not *we*," I corrected. "*I.* You're only one person. *We* means many people."

"We are only one person?" Alaree said tentatively.

"No. *I* am only one person. Get it?"

He worried the thought around for a few moments; I could see his browless forehead contract in deep concentration.

"Look," I said. "I'm one person. Ketteridge is another person. Willendorf is another. Each one of them is an independent individual—an *I.*"

"And together you make *We?*" Alaree asked brightly.

"Yes and no," I said. "*We* is composed of many *I*'s—but we still remain *I.*"

Again he sank deep in concentration, and then he smiled, scratched the ear that protruded from one side of the thought-helmet, and said, "*We* do not understand. But *I* do. Each of you is—is an *I.*"

"An individual," I said.

"An individual," he repeated. "A complete person. And together, to fly your ship, you must become a *We.*"

"But only temporarily," I said. "There still can be conflict between the parts. That's necessary, for progress. I can always think of the rest of them as *They.*"

"I . . . They," Alaree repeated slowly. "*They.*" He nodded. "It is difficult for me to grasp all this. I . . . think differently. But I am coming to understand, and I am worried."

That was a new idea. Alaree worried? Could be, I reflected. I had no way of knowing. I knew so little about Alaree— where on the planet he came from, what his tribal life was like, what sort of civilization he had, were all blanks.

"What kind of worries, Alaree?"

"You would not understand," he said solemnly and would say no more.

Toward afternoon, as golden shadows started to slant through the closely packed trees, I returned to the ship. Willendorf and Ketteridge were aft, working over the feed network, and the whole crew had gathered around to watch and offer suggestions. Even Alaree was there, looking absurdly comical in his copper-alloy thought-converter helmet, standing on tiptoe and trying to see what was happening.

About an hour later, I spotted the alien sitting by himself beneath the long-limbed tree that towered over the ship. He was lost in thought. Evidently whatever his problem was, it was really eating him.

Toward evening, he made a decision. I had been watching him with a great deal of concern, wondering what was going on in that small but unfathomable mind. I saw him brighten, leap up suddenly, and cross the field, heading in my direction.

"Captain!"

"What is it, Alaree?"

He waddled up and stared gravely at me. "Your ship will be ready to leave soon. What was wrong is nearly right again."

He paused, obviously uncertain of how to phrase his next statement, and I waited patiently. Finally he blurted out; "May I come back to your world with you?"

Automatically, the regulations flashed through my mind. I pride myself on my knowledge of the rules. And I knew this one.

ARTICLE 101A

No intelligent extraterrestrial life is to be transported from its own world to any civilized world under any reason whatsoever, without explicit beforehand clearance. The penalty for doing so is . . .

And it listed a fine of more money than was ever dreamt of in my philosophy.

I shook my head. "Can't take you, Alaree. This is your world, and you belong here."

A ripple of agony ran over his face. Suddenly he ceased to be the cheerful, roly-poly creature it was so impossible to take seriously, and became a very worried entity indeed. "You cannot understand," he said. "I no longer belong here."

No matter how hard he pleaded, I remained adamant. And when to no one's surprise Ketteridge and Willendorf announced, a day later, that their pooled labors had succeeded in repairing the feed network, I had to tell Alaree that we were going to leave—without him.

He nodded stiffly, accepting the fact, and without a word stalked tragically away, into the purple tangle of foliage that surrounded our clearing.

He returned a while later, or so I thought. He was not wearing the thought-converter. That surprised me. Alaree knew the helmet was a valuable item, and he had been cautioned to take good care of it.

I sent a man inside to get another helmet for him. I put it on him—this time tucking that wayward ear underneath properly—and looked at him sternly. "Where's the other helmet, Alaree?"

"We do not have it," he said.

"*We?* No more I?"

"We," Alaree said. And as he spoke, the leaves parted and another alien—Alaree's very double—stepped out into the clearing.

Then I saw the helmet on the newcomer's head, and realized that he was no double. He was Alaree, and the other alien was the stranger!

"I see you're here already," the alien I knew as Alaree said to the other. They were standing about ten feet apart, staring coldly at each other. I glanced at both of them quickly. They might have been identical twins.

"We are here," the stranger said. "We have come to get you."

I took a step backward, sensing that some incomprehensible drama was being played out here among these aliens.

"What's going on, Alaree?" I asked.

"We are having difficulties," both of them said, as one. *Both* of them.

I turned to the second alien. "What's your name?"

"Alaree," he said.

"Are you all named that?" I demanded.

"We are Alaree," Alaree Two said.

"They are Alaree," Alaree One said. "And *I* am Alaree. *I.*"

At that moment there was a disturbance in the shrubbery, and half a dozen more aliens stepped through and confronted Alarees One and Two.

"We are Alaree," Alaree Two repeated exasperatingly. He made a sweeping gesture that embraced all seven of the aliens to my left, but pointedly excluded Alaree One at my right.

"Are we—you coming with we—us?" Alaree Two demanded. I heard the six others say something in approximately the same tone of voice, but since they weren't wearing converters, their words were only scrambled nonsense to me.

Alaree One looked at me in pain, then back at his seven fel-

lows. I saw an expression of sheer terror in the small creature's eyes. He turned to me.

"I must go with them," he said softly. He was quivering
with fear.

Without a further word, the eight marched silently away. I
stood there, shaking my head in bewilderment.

We were scheduled to leave the next day. I said nothing to
my crew about the bizarre incident of the evening before, but
noted in my log that the native life of the planet would require careful study at some future time.

Blast-off was slated for 1100. As the crew moved efficiently
through the ship, securing things, packing, preparing for departure, I sensed a general feeling of jubilation. They were
happy to be on their way again, and I didn't blame them.

About half an hour before blast-off, Willendorf came to
me. "Sir, Alaree's down below," he said. "He wants to come
up and see you. He looks very troubled, sir."

I frowned. Probably the alien still wanted to go back with
us. Well, it was cruel to deny the request, but I wasn't going
to risk that fine. I intended to make that clear to him.

"Send him up," I said.

A moment later Alaree came stumbling into my cabin. Before he could speak I said, "I told you before—I can't take
you off this planet, Alaree. I'm sorry about it."

He looked up pitiably and said, "You mustn't leave me!"
He was trembling uncontrollably.

"What's wrong, Alaree?" I asked.

He stared intensely at me for a long moment, mastering
himself, trying to arrange what he wanted to tell me into a
coherent argument. Finally he said, "They would not take me
back. I am alone."

"Who wouldn't take you back, Alaree?"

"*They*. Last night, Alaree came for me, to take me back.
They are a *We*—an entity, a oneness. You cannot understand. When they saw what I had become, they cast me out."

I shook my head dizzily. "What do you mean?"

"You taught me . . . to become an *I*," he said, moistening
his lips. "Before, I was part of *We—They*. I learned your
ways from you, and now there is no room for me here. They
have cut me off. When the final break comes, I will not be
able to stay on this world."

Sweat was pouring down his pale face, and he was
breathing harder. "It will come any minute. They are gath-

ering strength for it. But I am *I*," he said triumphantly. He shook violently and gasped for breath.

I understood now. They were *all* Alaree. It was one planet-wide, self-aware corporate entity, composed of any number of individual cells. He had been one of them—but he had learned independence.

Then he had returned to the group—but he carried with him the seeds of individualism, the deadly, contagious germ we Terrans spread everywhere. Individualism would be fatal to such a group mind; it was cutting him loose to save itself. Just as diseased cells must be excised for the good of the entire body. Alaree was inexorably being cut off from his fellows lest he destroy the bond that made them one.

I watched him as he sobbed weakly on my acceleration cradle. "They . . . are . . . cutting . . . me . . . loose . . . *now!*"

He writhed horribly for a brief moment, and then relaxed and sat up on the edge of the cradle. "It is over," he said calmly. "I am fully independent."

I saw a stark *aloneness* reflected in his eyes, and behind that a gentle indictment of me for having done this to him. This world, I realized, was no place for Earthmen. What had happened was our fault—mine more than anyone else's.

"Will you take me with you?" he asked again. "If I stay here, Alaree will kill me."

I scowled wretchedly for a moment, fighting a brief battle within myself, and then I looked up. There was only one thing to do—and I was sure, once I explained on Earth, that I would not suffer for it.

I took his hand. It was cold and limp; whatever he had just been through, it must have been hell. "Yes," I said softly. "You can come with us."

And so Alareee joined the crew of the *Aaron Burr*. I told them about it just before blast-off, and they welcomed him aboard in traditional manner.

We gave the sad-eyed little alien a cabin near the cargo hold, and he established himself quite comfortably. He had no personal possessions—"It is not *Their* custom," he said—and promised that he'd keep the cabin clean.

He had brought with him a rough-edged, violet fruit that he said was his staple food. I turned it over to Kechnie for synthesizing, and we blasted off.

Alaree was right at home aboard the *Burr*. He spent much time with me—asking questions.

"Tell me about Earth," Alaree would ask. The alien wanted desperately to know what sort of a world he was going to.

He would listen gravely while I explained. I told him of cities and wars and spaceships, and he nodded sagely, trying to fit the concepts into a mind only newly liberated from the *gestalt.* I knew he could comprehend only a fraction of what I was saying, but I enjoyed telling him. It made me feel as if Earth were coming closer that much faster, simply to talk about it.

And he went around begging everyone, "Tell me about Earth." They enjoyed telling him, too—for a while.

Then it began to get a little tiresome. We had grown accustomed to Alaree's presence on the ship, flopping around the corridors doing whatever menial job he had been assigned to. But—although I had told the men why I had brought him with us, and though we all pitied the poor lonely creature and admired his struggle to survive as an individual entity—we were slowly coming to the realization that Alaree was something of a nuisance aboard ship.

Especially later, when he began to change.

Willendorf noticed it first, twelve days out from Alaree's planet. "Alaree's been acting pretty strange these days, sir," he told me.

"What's wrong?" I asked.

"Haven't you spotted it, sir? He's been moping around like a lost soul—very quiet and withdrawn, like."

"Is he eating well?"

Willendorf chuckled loudly. "I'll say he is! Kechnie made up some synthetics based on that piece of fruit he brought with him, and he's been stuffing himself wildly. He's gained ten pounds since he came on ship. No, it's not lack of food!"

"I guess not," I said. "Keep an eye on him, will you? I feel responsible for his being here, and I want him to come through the voyage in good health."

After that, I began to observe Alaree more closely myself, and I detected the change in his personality too. He was no longer the cheerful, childlike being who delighted in pouring out questions in endless profusion. Now he was moody, silent, always brooding, and hard to approach.

On the sixteenth day out—and by now I was worried seriously about him—a new manifestation appeared. I was in the hallway, heading from my cabin to the chartroom, when Alaree stepped out of an alcove. He reached up, grasped my uniform lapel, and, maintaining his silence, drew my head down and stared pleadingly into my eyes.

Too astonished to say anything, I returned his gaze for nearly thirty seconds. I peered into his transparent pupils, wondering what he was up to. After a good while had passed, he released me, and I saw something like a tear trickle down his cheek.

"What's the trouble, Alaree?"

He shook his head mournfully and shuffled away.

I got reports from the crewmen that day and next that he had been doing this regularly for the past eighteen hours— waylaying crewman, staring long and deep at them as if trying to express some unspeakable sadness, and walking away. He had approached almost everyone on the ship.

I wondered now how wise it had been to allow an extrater-restrial, no matter how friendly, to enter the ship. There was no telling what this latest action meant.

I started to form a theory. I suspected what he was aiming at, and the realization chilled me. But once I reached my con-clusion, there was nothing I could do but wait for con-firmation.

On the nineteenth day, Alaree again met me in the cor-ridor. This time our encounter was more brief. He plucked me by the sleeve, shook his head sadly and shrugged his shoul-ders, and walked away.

That night, he took to his cabin, and by morning he was dead. He had apparently died peacefully, in his sleep.

"I guess we'll never understand him, poor fellow," Wil-lendorf said, after we had committed the body to space. "You think he had too much to eat, sir?"

"No," I said. "It wasn't that. He was lonely, that's all. He didn't belong here, among us."

"But you said he had broken away from that group-mind," Willendorf objected.

I shook my head. "Not really. That group-mind arose out of some deep psychological and physiological needs of those people. You can't just declare your independence and be able to exist as an individual from then on if you're part of that group-entity. Alaree had grasped the concept intellectually, to some extent, but he wasn't suited for life away from the cor-porate mind, no matter how much he wanted to be."

"He couldn't stand alone?"

"Not after his people had evolved that *gestalt*-setup. He learned independence from us," I said. "But he couldn't live with us, really. He needed to be part of a whole. He found out his mistake after he came aboard and tried to remedy things."

I saw Willendorf pale. "What do you mean, sir?"

"You know what I mean. When he came up to us and stared soulfully into our eyes. *He was trying to form a new gestalt—out of us!* Somehow he was trying to link us together, the way his people had been linked."

"He couldn't do it, though," Willendorf said fervently.

"Of course not. Human beings don't have whatever need it is that forced those people to merge. He found that out, after a while, when he failed to get anywhere with us."

"He just couldn't do it," Willendorf repeated.

"No. And then he ran out of strength," I said somberly, feeling the heavy weight of my guilt. "He was like an organ removed from a living body. It can exist for a little while by itself, but not indefinitely. He failed to find a new source of life —and he died." I stared bitterly at my fingertips.

"What do we call it in my medical report?" asked Ship Surgeon Thomas, who had been silent up till then. "How can we explain what he died from?"

"Call it—*malnutrition*," I said.

LIFE CYCLE

By Poul Anderson

Earthly life has developed many methods of reproducing itself. The amoeba is content to split in half; the hydra produces a bud that develops into a new hydra; the small crustacean known as daphnia lays eggs that do not need to be fertilized in order to bring forth young daphnias. Most animals, though, rely on two sexes, female and male, one to produce eggs and the other to fertilize them.

The variations within this scheme are great—take, for example, the case of the oyster, which is male at one time of the year and female at another. Given such biological variations, it was inevitable that science-fiction writers would begin to speculate about the unearthly aspects reproduction might take among alien beings. Poul Anderson, a lanky chap of Viking descent who lives in California, is better qualified to make scientific speculations than most of his colleagues. He took a degree in physics at the University of Minnesota before turning to science fiction, and keeps abreast of the latest technical developments in a way that gives his stories the solid ring of authenticity.

In this example, he provides a convincing blend of science and imagination that yields insight into a wholly alien race. But because recent scientific research has given us a view of conditions on Mercury different from the one that was accepted in 1957, when this story was written, Anderson has added his own introduction to the story in the interest of maintaining accuracy.

AUTHOR'S NOTE

A science-fiction writer may, of course, speculate about things that science has not yet discovered. But whenever he deals with what is already known, he should get his facts straight.

That's what I tried to do in this story. The planet Mercury was depicted as accurately as possible by me, according to the best available data and theories, as of 1957.

The trouble is, scientific "facts" won't stay put. In the spring of 1965, radar and radio observations indicated that Mercury does *not* eternally turn the same face toward the sun and that the dark side—even in the course of a very long night—does not get especially cold.

So perhaps this story should not now be reprinted, or perhaps it should at least have been rewritten. But information is still coming in; we are not quite sure that the new data mean what we think they mean; surely all our ideas are due for another upset or two before we get to Mercury and see for ourselves. It is not yet impossible that the older picture may turn out to have been right after all. Be that as it may, theory at the moment is in such a state of flux that one can't say with any confidence what Mercury, or any other part of the universe, really is like.

Let this older story remain unchanged, then, as an intellectual exercise if nothing else.

—Poul Anderson

"Well, all right! I'll go to their temple myself!"

"You must be crazy even to think of such a *tonteria*," said Juan Navarro. He sucked hard on his pipe, decided it was finished, and knocked out the dottle. "They would tear you in pieces."

"Quicker than starving to death on this hellbound lump of rock."

"*Very* small pieces." Navarro sat down on a workbench and swung his legs. He was a Basque, medium-sized, long-headed, dark-haired, with the mountaineer's bony independence in his face. He was also a biologist of distinction, an amateur violinist, and a hungry man waiting to die. "You don't understand, Joe. Those Dayside beings are not just another race. They are *gods*."

Joe Kingsbury Thayendanegea, who was a stocky Mohawk from upper New York State, paced the caging space of the room, hands behind his back, and swore. If he had had a tail, he would have lashed it. He was the pilot and engineer, the only other Terrestrial on Mercury. When you dived this far down into the sun's monstrous gravitational well, you couldn't take a big crew along.

"So what else can you think of?" he challenged. "Shall we draw straws and barbecue the loser?"

Antella, the owl-faced Martian mineralogist, made a harsh cawing in his gray-feathered throat. "Best it be me," he advised. "Then no one is technically guilty of cannibalism."

"Not much meat on that skinny little frame of yours, *amigo*," said Navarro. "And a human body would have so many other uses after one was finished with the organic parts. Make the vertebrae into chessmen—the ribs into Venetian blinds for bay windows—yes, and the skulls would make distinctive mousetraps."

Kingsbury shook heavy shoulders and thrust his beaky face forward. "What are we yattering about?" he demanded. "We've got a week's slim rations left aboard this clunk. After that we start starving."

"So you are going to the temple and confront the gods and convince them of the error of their ways. Ka!" Antella clicked his short, curved bill. "Or did you think to threaten them with our one solitary pistol?"

"I'm going to try and find out what the Twonks—or their gods, if you insist—have against us," said Kingsbury. "Here's the idea: It's getting close to sunrise time, and there'll be a crowd of 'em at the temple. I'll go out on Dayside and find me an empty Twonk shell and get into it. With luck, I'll pass unnoticed long enough to—"

Antella's brass-colored eyes widened. "The scheme is a bold one," he admitted. "As far as I know, there is strict silence during the ceremonies, whatever they are. You just might accomplish it."

Navarro leered. "I know exactly what you would accomplish, Joe. Do you remember that story you tell me, oh, last year I think it was? About the tourist in the North forest, and the Canuck guide, and the moose call?"

"Yeah. 'Ze moose, she—' Hey! What do you mean?"

"Precisely. That temple is a breeding place. They go there to breed."

"How do *you* know? I've been tramping around arguing with the Twonks, and you've just sat here in the lab."

Navarro shrugged. "What else could I do but my research? I studied the biochemistry of Mercurian life. I worked out the life cycle of a few plants and one insectoidal form."

"They all look like insects. But go on."

"The first expedition established no more than that Mercurian life has a silicate base," recapitulated Navarro. "Otherwise they were too busy staying alive and teaching English to the natives and making maps. But they brought home specimens, which were analyzed. And one strange fact became evident: Those specimens could not reproduce under Twilight Zone conditions. Yet they live here! And we see the natives lay eggs, which hatch; and lower forms bring forth their own kind in various ways—"

"I know," grunted Kingsbury. "But why? I mean, what's so puzzling about their reproduction?"

"The cells are totally different, both physically and chemically, from protoplasmic life," said Navarro. "But there are analogues; there have to be. The basic process is the same, meiosis and mitosis, governed by a molecular 'blue-print' not unlike our chromosomes. However, though we know that such processes *must* take place, the silicate materials involved are too stable to undergo them. The ordinary exothermic reactions which fuel Mercurian life do not produce enough energy for the cell-duplication which is growth. In fact, adult Mercurians are even incapable of self-repair; wounds do not heal, they must depend on being so tough that in this low gravity they suffer few injuries."

"So what happens?"

Navarro shrugged. "I do not know, except this much: that somehow, at breeding time, they must pick up an extra charge of energy. Analyzing small animals, I have identified the compound which is formed to store this energy and release it, by gradually breaking down, as the organism grows. It is all used up at maturity. But where is the temperature necessary to build up this molecule? Only on Dayside.

"Now these gods are said to live on Dayside and meet the Twonks of Twilight at the temple. You know the breeding ceremonies take place when libration has brought the temple into the sunlight."

"Go on," said Antella thoughtfully.

"*Pues,* one of the plants, has this life cycle; it grows in the Twilight Zone, on the sunward side, and its vines are phototropic. Eventually their growth and the libration bring them into the light. The spore-pods burst and the spores are scattered into the air. A few are blown back into Twilight, and they are now fertile; radiation has formed the necessary compound. Or consider one of the small insectoids I studied. It breeds here in the usual manner, then the female crawls out into the light to lay her eggs. When they hatch, the little ones scurry back to the shade, and some of them reach shelter before they fry. Wasteful, of course, but even on this barren planet nature is a notorious spendthrift."

"Wait a minute!" interrupted Kingsbury. Navarro liked to hear himself talk, but there are limits. "Are you implying that the Dayside gods are merely the sun? That because the Twonks have to have light when they breed, they've built up a sort of Apollo-cum-fertility cult?"

"Why not? There are races on Earth and Mars with similar beliefs. To this day, here and there in my own Pyrenees, many women believe the wind can make them pregnant." Navarro laughed. "It is a good excuse anyhow, no?"

"But there's Dayside life too. Life that never comes into Twilight."

"Yes, yes, of course. Quite different from Twilight biology —after all, it has to live at a temperature of four hundred degrees Centigrade. Possibly the Twonks regard some Dayside animal as a sort of fertility totem. I am only saying this—that if the gods are actually the sun, you will have Satan's own time persuading the sun to take back its edict that we must die."

In the end, there was a decision. Navarro thought Kingsbury a suicidal idiot . . . but what choice was there? They would go to the temple together, disguised, and find out what they could; if there were no gods, but only some fanatically conservative priestess behind the death sentence, a .20-caliber Magnum automatic might make her see reason. Antella would stay behind to guard the ship; he couldn't take heat as well as an Earthling.

The humans donned their spacesuits and went through the air lock. Navarro had the gun, Kingsbury armed himself with a crowbar; at last and worst, he thought savagely, he'd crack a few Mercurian carapaces.

They stepped out into desolation. Behind them lay the *Explorer,* a crippled metal giant, no more to them than a shelter. In the end, perhaps, a coffin. There was no possibility of rescue from Earth—radio communication was out, with the sun so close, and Mercury Expedition Two wasn't due back for six months. Earth wouldn't even realize they were in trouble till they had already died.

To right and left, the dry valley lifted into gaunt ocherous peaks against a dusky sky where a few hard stars glittered. There were bushes scattered about, low things with blue metallic-looking leaves. A small animal bounded from them, its shell agleam in the wan light. The ground was slaty rubble, flaked off in departed ages when Mercury still had weather. Above the peaks to the left hung a white glare, the invisible sun. It would never be seen from here, but a few miles further west the planet's libration would lift it briefly and unendurably over the near horizon.

There was a wind blowing; the wind is never quiet on Mercury, where one side is hot enough to melt lead and the other close to absolute zero. It sent a ghostly whirl of dust devils across the valley. There wasn't much air—a man would have called it a soft vacuum and not fit to breathe at any density. Most of it had long ago escaped into space or frozen on Darkside, but now vapor pressure had struck a balance, and there was some carbon dioxide, nitrogen, ammonia, and inert gas free. Enough to blow fine dust up against the weak gravity and to form an ionosphere which made radio communication possible over the horizon.

Kingsbury shuddered, remembering green forests and clear streams under the lordly sky of Earth. What the devil had inspired him to come here? Money, he supposed. Earth needed fissionable ores, and Mercury had them, and Expedition Two was sent to negotiate an agreement with the natives. The pay was proportional to the risk—but what use is all the money in the cosmos to a dead man?

"When I get home," said Navarro wistfully, "after the parades and banquets—yes, surely there will be parades, with all the pretty girls throwing flowers and kisses at us—after that I shall retire to my own village and sit down before the tavern and order a bottle of the best Amontillado. Three days later I will ask them to sweep the cobwebs off me. A week later I shall go home and sleep."

"I'll settle for a tall cold beer in Gavagan's," said Kingsbury. "You ought to let me take you pub crawling in New York sometime—bah!" His gauntleted hand made a vicious gesture at the tumbled ruin of a landscape. "What makes you think we ever will get home?"

"Nothing," said Navarro gently, "except that I will not permit myself to think otherwise."

They rounded a tall red crag and saw how the valley broadened into cultivated fields, ironberry bushes and flintgrain stalks. On the dusky edge of vision was the Mercurian hive, a giant dome of crushed rock in which several thousand natives dwelt. There were hundreds of such barracks, scattered around the Twilight Zone, with a temple for every dozen or so. Apparently there was no variation in language or culture over the whole planet—understandable when the habitable area was so small. And it was an open question how much individual personality a Mercurian had, and how much of her belonged to the hive-mind.

Close at hand was the hut which held their lives. It was a crude, roofless structure, four stone walls and an open doorway. The first expedition had erected it with native help, to store supplies and tools—it made the ship roomier. The *Explorer*'s crew had used it similarly, putting in most of their food and the bulky ion-control rings from the reaction drive. Again the natives had lent a willing hand.

There were four guards outside the hut. They were armed only with spears and clubs. It would be easy enough to shoot them down. But before anything could be transferred back to the ship, the entire hive would come swarming, and there weren't that many bullets.

"Let's go talk to them," said Navarro.

"What's the use?" asked Kingsbury. "I've talked to those animated hulks till my larynx needs a retread."

"I have an idea—I want to check on it." Navarro's clumsy suit went skimming over the ashen ground. Kingsbury followed with a mumbled oath.

The nearest guard hefted her spear and swiveled antennae in their direction. Otherwise there was no movement in her. She stood six feet tall, broad as a space-suited man, her exoskeleton shimmering blue, her head featureless except for the glassy eyes. With four three-fingered arms, tightly curled ovipositor, and sliding joints of armor, she looked like a nightmare insect. But she wasn't; a dragonfly or a beetle was man's brother beside this creature of silicone cells and silicate blood and shell of beryllium alloy. Kingsbury thought of her as a kind of robot—well, yes, she was alive, but where did you draw the line between the robot and the animal?

Navarro stopped before her. She waited. None of her sisters moved. It was a disconcerting habit, never to open conversation.

The Basque cleared his throat. "I have come—oh, wait." With his teeth he switched his helmet radio to the band the natives could sense. "I wish to ask again why you deny us permission to use our own food."

The answer crackled in their earphones. "It is the command of the gods."

Kingsbury stood listening to that nonhuman accent and speculating just what sort of religion these entities did have. They had emotions—they must, being alive—but the degree of correspondence to human or Martian feeling was doubtful.

It wasn't strange that they communicated by organically generated FM radio pulses. The atmosphere didn't carry enough sound to make ears worthwhile. But constant submergence in the thoughts of every other Mercurian within ten miles . . . it must do something to the personality. Make the society as a whole more intelligent, perhaps—the natives had readily learned English from the first expedition, while men hadn't yet made sense out of the native language. But there was probably little individual awareness. A sort of ant mind—ants collectively did remarkable things but were hopeless when alone.

Navarro smiled, a meaningless automatic grimace behind his face plate. "Can you not tell my why the gods have so decreed? You were all friendly enough when my race last visited you. What made the gods change their minds?"

No answer. That probably meant the Twonk didn't know either.

"You could at least let us have back our control rings and enough food for the journey home. I assure you, we would leave at once."

"No." The voice was alike empty of rancor and mercy. "It is required that you die. The next strangers to come will, then, not be forewarned, and we can dispose of them too. This land will be shunned."

"If we get desperate enough, we will start fighting you. We will kill many."

"That I—we do not understand. We are letting you die this way because it is easiest. If you fight us, then we shall fight you and overwhelm you with numbers; so why do you not die without making useless trouble for yourselves?"

"That isn't in our nature."

"I—we do not know what you mean by 'nature.' Every She, when she has laid as many eggs as she can, goes out to the sun and returns to those which you name gods. Death is a correct termination when there is no further use for the organism."

"Men think differently," said Navarro. "Of course, as a more or less good Catholic, I consider my body only a husk—but I still want to keep it as long as possible."

No reply, except for some crackling gibberish. The Mercurians were talking to each other. Weaker overtones made Kingsbury suspect that several Twonks within the hive were joining the discussion—or the stream of consciousness, or whatever you wanted to call the rumination of a semicollective mind.

"Look here, my friend," said Navarro. "You know our purposes. We want to get certain minerals from you. You have no use for them, and we would pay you well, in tools and machinery you cannot make for yourselves."

"It would be mutually advantageous," agreed the Twonk. "When the first ship came, we considered it an excellent idea. But since then the gods have told us your sort must not be allowed to live."

"Por Dios! Why?"

"The gods did not say."

"You serve these gods," said Navarro harshly. "I believe you give them food—right? And tools and anything else they want. You obey their least whim. What do *you* gain from them?"

No answer.

"Can we talk to these gods? Maybe we can persuade them—"

"It is forbidden you to see the Living Light." Another conference. "Perhaps you will agree to die and stop bothering us if we tell you the gods are needful to our life. They give us pure metal—"

"Most of which you make into tools for them," snapped Navarro. "We could do the same for you."

"That is a small thing. But the gods are needful to our life. It is the gods who put life into our eggs. Without them no young would be hatched. It is thus necessary that we obey them."

"Cut it out, Juan," snarled Kingsbury. "I've been through this rigmarole a hundred times. It's no use."

Navarro nodded absentmindedly and trudged off. They switched to a different radio band, one the natives could not "hear," but said nothing for a while.

"Has it ever occurred to you," asked Navarro finally, "that nobody has ever seen a male Mercurian?"

"Sure. They're hermaphrodites."

"That was assumed by the first expedition. An assumption only, of course. They could not vivisect a live Twonk—"

"I sure could!"

"—and the old ones all go out on Dayside to die. The only

chance for anatomical studies would be to find one which had met a violent end here in Twilight, and there was always too much else to do."

"Well, why shouldn't they be hermaphrodites? Oysters are."

"At certain times of the year. But oysters are a low form of life. On Earth, Mars, and Venus, the higher one goes on the evolutionary scale, the more sharp the distinction between the sexes."

"All right, maybe their males are very small."

"As with some fish? Possibly. But most improbable. All their eggs are about the same size, you know."

"Who cares?" snorted Kingsbury. "I just want to go home."

"I care. I have a tidy mind. And, too, Earth needs that uranium and thorium. We will never get it unless we can circumvent this religion of theirs, either by persuading the gods or by . . . hm . . . destroying the cult. But to accomplish the latter, we will first have to understand the creed."

They came out on a road of sorts, a narrow track in the shale, stamped out by thousands of years of feet. There were natives woking in the fields, and before the hive they could see smiths hammering cold iron and copper into implements. A few young were in sight, unhumanly solemn at their play. None paid any attention to the outworlders.

Navarro pointed to a smith. "It is true what the Twonk said, that the gods supply their metal?"

"Yes," said Kingsbury. "At least, so I've been told, and I do think the Twonks are unable to tell a lie. Being radio-telepathic, y'know, they couldn't lie to each other, so the idea would never occur to them."

"Hm . . . they do not have fire here, not in this sleazy atmosphere. They must have been in a crude neolithic stage until the gods started smelting ores for them. I imagine that could be done with mirrors focusing the Dayside heat on— oh, a mixture of crushed hematite and some reducing material."

"Uh-huh. And the gods get the pick of whatever the Twonks make out of the metal." Kingsbury cleared his throat to spit, remembered he was in a space suit, and swallowed. "It's perfectly clear, Juan. There are two intelligent races on Mercury. The Daysiders have set up in business as gods. They don't want humans around because they're afraid we'll spoil their racket and make 'em work for a living."

"Obviously," said Navarro. "The problem is, how to convince the Twonks of this? To do that, we shall first have to study the nature of the Dayside beings."

They mounted a razorback ridge and clapped down glare filters. Before them was the sun.

It burned monstrous on the horizon, a white fury that drowned the stars and leaped back off the withered land. Even here, with shadows lapping his feet and the refrigeration unit at full blast, Kingsbury felt how the heat licked at him.

"God!" he whispered. "How far can we go into that blazing hell?"

"Not very far," said Navarro. "We shall have to hope some Twonks died close by. Come!" He broke into long low-gravity bounds, down the slope and out onto the plain.

Squinting through tormented eyes, Kingsbury made out a shimmering pool at the horizon. It spouted as he watched . . . molten lead? With the speed he had and the sharp curvature of the surface, the sun was rising visibly as he ran.

Even here there was life. A crystalline tree squatted near a raw pinnacle, stiff and improbable. A small thing with many legs scuttered away, shell too bright to look at. Basically, Dayside life had the silicate form of Twilight, many of the compounds identical—a common ancestry a billion years ago, when Mercury still had water—but this life was adapted to a heat that made lead run liquid.

"This . . . road . . . goes on," panted Kingsbury. "Must be . . . a graveyard . . . somewhere. . . ."

His skin was prickling now, as charged particles ate in through the armor. His underclothing was limp with sweat. His tongue felt like a swollen lump of wood.

This was farther into Dayside than men had ever gone before. Through the dizziness, he wondered how even a Twonk could survive the trip. Only, of course, they didn't. The natives had told the first expedition that their old ones went out into the sunlight to die. There'd be no one to bury them, and the shells weren't volatile—

He stumbled over the first one before he knew it. When his gauntlets touched the ground, he yelled. Navarro pulled him up again. There was a dazzle in their helmets, they squinted and gasped with dry lungs and thought they heard their brains sizzling.

Dead Twonks, thousands of them, scattered around like broken machines, empty-eyed, but the light demonic on their carapaces. Kingsbury picked one up. Even in Mercurian gravity, it seemed to have oddly little weight. Navarro took another. Its arms and legs flapped horribly as he ran back eastward.

They never remembered that running. After they had fallen on the dark side of the ridge, they must have fainted, for the next memory was of stirring and a slow awareness that they were embracing dead Mercurians.

Kingsbury put his lips to his canteen nozzle and sucked water up the hose. It was nearly scalding, but he had never drained so sweet a draught. Then he lay and shuddered for another long while.

"Bueno," croaked his companion. "We made it."

They sat up and regarded their loot. Both shells had split open down the front, along the line of weakness where the ventral scutes joined. They had expected to find the shriveled remnants of "organic" material, dried flesh and blackened tendons and collapsed veins. But there was nothing.

The shells were empty.

It was a long circuitous walk back to the ship. They didn't want any natives to see them. After that there was a wonderful time of sleeping while Antella worked.

They didn't stop to think about the implications until it was too late to think very much at all. Sunrise would occur at the temple in a few hours, and it was quite a ways from here.

Antella's claw-like hands gestured proudly at the shells. "See, I have hinged the front plates so you can get in and out. Your radios are connected to the antennae, though how you expect to talk Mercurian if anyone converses with you, I do not understand. This harness will support the shells around your suits. Naturally, you cannot use the lower arms, but I have wired them into a lifelike position."

Kingsbury drew hard on a cigarette. It might be the last one he ever smoked. "Nice work," he said. "Now as for the plan itself, we'll just have to play by ear. We'll get inside the temple with the others, see what we can see, and hope to get out again undamaged. If necessary, we'll shuck these disguises and fight our way back here. Even in space suits, we can outrun any Twonk."

Navarro shook his head. "A most forlorn hope," he muttered. "And if we should succeed, do you realize how many xenologists will pour the vials of wrath on our heads for disrupting native culture?"

"That bothers me a lot," snorted Kingsbury.

"I, of course, can claim to be carrying out the historic traditions of my own people," said Navarro blandly. "It was not the Saracens but the Basques who slew Roland at Roncesvalles."

"Why'd they do that?"

"They didn't like the way Charlemagne was throwing his weight around. Unfortunately, you, my friend, cannot say you are merely preserving your own culture. These Twonks have no scalps to lift."

"That's a laugh," said Kingsbury, "my culture for the past hundred years has been building skyscrapers and bridges. Come on, let's shove."

It was a clumsy business getting into the shells, but once the plates were latched shut and the harness adjusted, it was not too awkward a disguise. The heads could not be turned on their necks when you wore a space helmet inside, but Antella had filled the empty eye sockets with wide-angle lenses. Kingsbury hoped he wouldn't be required to wink or move all four arms, or waggle the ovipositor or speak Mercurian; but otherwise, if he was careful, he ought to pass muster.

The humans left the ship and went down the valley, moving with the stiff native stride. Not till they were past the hive did they speak. Kingsbury's belly muscles were taut, but none of the autochthones paid him any special heed. It was fortunate that the Mercurians were not given to idle gossip.

Presently he found himself on a broad, smoothly laid road. It ran straight northwest, through a forest of gleaming barrel-shaped plants where the small wildlife of Twilight scuttled off into the dusk. More and more natives joined them, tall solemn figures streaming in from side roads onto the highway. Many were laden with gifts, iron tools and flashing gems and exquisitely wrought stone vessels. Did the gods drink molten lead out of those? There was no speech on the communication band, only the quiet pulse of currents oscillating in nerves that were silver wires.

Ghostly journey, through a dark chaotic wilderness of rock and crystalline forest, among a swarm of creatures out of dreams. It shocked Kingsbury how small man and man's knowledge were in the illimitable universe.

He switched to the other band and said harshly, "Juan, maybe we are nuts. Even if we get away with it, what can we hope to do? Suppose one of these Twonks pulled a similar stunt in your church—wouldn't that just make you fighting mad?"

"Yes, of course," answered the other man. "Unless by such means the Twonk proved to me that my faith was based on a fraud. Naturally, she would not be able to do so; but assuming for the sake of discussion that she did, my philosophy would come crashing down about my ears. Then I should be quite ready to listen to her."

"But God! How can we imagine these critters think like us?"

"They don't. But that is in our favor, because they are actually more logical than we humans. They have freely admitted that the only reason they obey the gods is that those are essential to fertility."

"Well . . . maybe the gods are!"

"Yes, yes, I am quite sure of it. But I am equally sure that there is nothing supernatural about it. Suppose, for instance, that a dose of sunlight is necessary for reproduction. A class of priestesses may have capitalized on this fact—I am not sure how, given the Mercurian telepathy, but perhaps the priestesses can think on a different band. Now if we can show that the sunlight alone is required, and the priestesses are mere window dressing, then I am sure the Twonks will get rid of them."

Kingsbury grinned with scant mirth. "And we're supposed to find this out and prove it in one glimpse?"

"This was originally your idea, *amigo.*"

"Yeah. Please don't rub it in."

They walked on, silent, thinking of Earth's remote loveliness. An hour passed. It grew hotter, and the western blaze climbed into the sky until you could see the great lens of zodiacal light just above the hills, and more natives joined the procession until there were several thousand pouring along the road. Kingsbury and Navarro stayed close together, near the middle of the crowd.

Black against the blinding sky, they saw the temple. It stood on a high ridge, a columned building of red granite, curiously reminiscent of old Egyptian work. A flat roof covered the front half; the rear was open, but walled off from sight.

The pilgrimage moved between basalt statues onto a flagged plaza before the temple. There it halted, motionless as only a nonbreathing Mercurian can be. Kingsbury tuned back to the communication band and heard that they were chanting—at least, he supposed the eery whining rise-and-fall of radio pulses was music. He kept his own mouth shut; no one in that entranced collectivity would realize he wasn't joining in.

A line of Mercurians emerged from the colonnade. They

must be priestesses or servitors, for there were geometric patterns daubed on their shells. They halted before the worshipers. Gravely, those who bore gifts advanced, bowed down, and laid them at the feet of the clergy. The articles were picked up and carried back into the temple.

Kingsbury sweated and shivered in his spacesuit. What if the ritual included some fancy dance? He hoped Navarro, who had the gun, could break out of his shell fast enough to use it. None of the natives was armed, and a human was a match for any ten Mercurians, but there must be five thousand of them around him.

The glare became a sudden flame. Sunrise! The shadow of the temple fell over the plaza, but Kingsbury narrowed his eyes to slits, and still his head ached.

He was dimly aware of the priestesses returning. Their voices twittered, and the chant ended. A hundred Mercurians walked forth, up the stairs and into the doorway. Another hundred and another hundred . . . They were not quite so impassive now. Kingsbury could see that those near him were trembling with excitement.

Now his and Navarro's line was on the move. He saw that one of the priestesses was leading them. They entered between the pillars and went across a room of mosaics and down a hall. At its end were passages leading to a number of roofless courts into which the sunlight fell. His party took one.

The priestess stood aside, and the procession went on in.

Against the radiance, Kingsbury could just see that there was a doorway on the western side and that daises were built into the floor. The Twonks were settling themselves on those, waiting. He switched to the private band: "Juan, what happens now?"

"What do you think?" answered the Basque. His voice shook, but there was a wryness in it. "This is where they breed, isn't it?"

"If one of 'em makes a pass at me, shall I try to play along?"

"I think there is something against it in Leviticus—nor could you, ah, respond. . . . We shall probably have to run for our lives. But they are all lying down. Find yourself a couch!"

There was a stillness that stretched. The heat blasted and gnawed. Even the Twonks couldn't endure it for very long at a time. Something would have to take place soon, unless—

"Juan! Maybe they're what-you-call-it, virgin birth. Maybe the sun fertilizes them."

"No. Not parthenogenetic. It has not the evolutionary potentiality to produce intelligent life—it does not give variant zygotes. Sunlight is necessary but not sufficient, I think. And I still cannot believe they are true hermaphrodites. Somewhere there must be males."

Almost, Kingsbury jerked. It was a tremendous effort to hold himself rigid, to wait in the shimmering, dazzling devildance of light as all the natives were waiting. "I've got it! The gods—*they* are the males!"

"That is clear enough," said Navarro impatiently. "I deduced it hours ago. But if the case is so simple, I am not hopeful. The males can still claim to be a different, superior order of life, as they indeed already do. We shall need a more fundamental discovery to upset this male-worshiping cult."

Navarro's voice snapped off. Flame stood in the doorway.

No . . . the tall lizardlike forms, in burnished coppery scales, wreathed in silvery vapor—they glowed, walking dragons, but they did not burn. They advanced, through the doorway and into the courtyard. Their beaks gaped, and the small dark eyes held sun sparks, and the tails lashed their taloned feet. More and more of them, stalking in, one to a Twonk, and approaching with hands held out.

The males of Mercury . . . Dayside life, charged with the energy from the sun which made new life possible, sweating out pure quicksilver to cool them so they wouldn't fry their mates. Was it any wonder they were thought divine?

But it wasn't possible! Male and female had to come from the same race, evolving together—they *couldn't* have arisen separately, one in the hell of dayside and one in the endless purgatorial dusk of Twilight. The same mothers had to bear them; and yet, and yet, Twonk eggs only brought forth Twonks. . . .

Then—

The knowledge bit home as a dragon neared Kingsbury. The male was hesitating, the lean head wove back and forth. . . . An alien smell? A subtle wrongness of posture?

The Mohawk sat up and yelled. The dragon spouted mercury vapor and crouched. Teeth made to shear through rock flashed in the open mouth.

"Juan, I've got it! I know what they are! Let's get back!"

Navarro was on his feet, fumbling at the belly of his disguise. Latches clicked free, and he scrambled out of it. The nearest dragon leaped. Navarro's gun bucked. The male fell with a hole blown through him. So much for the immortal gods, the heavenly showmen. Kingsbury was out of his own shell now. A female lunged at him. He got her around the waist and pitched her into the mob. Whirling, he slugged his way toward the door, Navarro covering his back.

The dragons snapped at them but didn't dare attack. There was a moment of fury, then the humans were out on the plaza. They began running.

"Now we've got to beat them back to the ship," panted Kingsbury.

"More than that," said Navarro. "We must reach safety before they come near enough to call the hive and have us intercepted. I wonder if we can."

"A man might try," said Kingsbury.

The forward port showed some thousands of armed Mercurian females. They ringed in the ship, waiting, too rational to batter with useless clubs at the hull and too angry to depart. There were more of them arriving every minute.

"I wonder—" Antella peered out. He spoke coolly, but his feathers stood erect with tension. "I wonder if they can do worse to us than they have already done. We will starve no faster besieged in here than walking freely around."

"They can get to us if they want to work at it," said Kingsbury. "And I think they do. They could rig up some kind of battering ram—"

Navarro lighted his pipe and puffed hard. "It is our task to persuade them otherwise," he said. "Do you believe they will listen?"

Kingsbury went over to the ship's radio and sat down and operated the controls with nervous fingers. "Let's hope so. It's our only chance. Do you want to talk to 'em?"

"Go ahead. You are better with the English language than I. I will perhaps put in an oar."

Kingsbury switched on the speaker and brought his lips to the microphone. "Hello, out there," he said.

His voice cut through the seething of Mercurian tones. It was weird how they snapped off all at once. English, clear and grammatical and subtly distorted, answered him:

"What do you wish to say? You have violated the temple. The gods order that you must die."

"The gods would say that," replied Kingsbury. "But they are not gods at all. They want to get rid of us because we can tell you the truth. They've lied and cheated you for I don't know how many centuries."

"Truth, lie, cheat. Those are words we do not know."

"Well . . . uh . . . truth is a correct statement, a statement of what is real. A lie is a statement which is not truth, but made on purpose, knowing it to be false. Cheating is . . . well . . . curse it, I wish we had a dictionary along! The gods have lied to you so you would do what they wanted. That's cheating."

"We think we understand," said the toneless voice. "It is a new concept to us, but a possible one. The gods do not speak so we can hear them. They—" Conference, presumably recalling what the first expedition had told about radio—"they use a different band. They communicate with us by gestures only. So are you implying that they are not what they claim to be and have made life unnecessarily difficult for us?"

"That's it, pal." Kingsbury still didn't like the Twonks much, but he was grateful they were so quick on the uptake. "Having seen what goes on in the temple, we know what these self-appointed gods are. They're nothing but the males of your own species."

"What does the word 'male' denote?"

"Well—" Kingsbury ground to a halt. Precisely how did you explain it in nickel words when Junior asked where he came from? He gave Navarro a helpless look. The Basque grinned, leaned over the microphone, and gave a simple account.

The female collectivity thought about it for a while, standing in burnished motionlessness, then said with an unaccustomed slowness: "That is logical. We have long observed that certain of the animals go through the same motions of fertilization as we with the gods. But whether you wish to call them gods or males makes no difference. They are still the great ones who give life."

"They don't give any more life than you do," snapped Kingsbury. "They need you just as much as you need them. In fact . . . *they are yourselves!*"

"That is an irrational statement." Was there a defensive overtone in the voice? "Our eggs bring forth only females, so it is reasonable to suppose that the gods are born directly of the sun. A Mercurian hatches from an egg after the god-male has given life. She grows up and in her turn visits the god-males and brings forth eggs. At last, grown old, she goes to the sunlands and dies. There is no missing period in which she could become a god-male."

"Oh, yeah? What about after she's gone sunside?"

Mercurian language gabbled at them.

Kingsbury spoke fast: "We went out there ourselves and found the shells of those you thought had died. But the shells were empty! You know you have muscles, nerves, guts, organs. Those ought to remain in a dried-out condition. But I repeat, the shells were empty!"

"Then— But we have only your statement."

"You can check up on it. We can rebuild a space suit for one of you, furnish enough protection from the sun for you to go out there a while, long enough to see."

"But what happens? What is the significance of the empty shells?"

"Isn't it obvious, you dunderheads? You're a kind of larval stage. At the proper time, you go out into the sun. Its radiation changes you. You're changed so much that all memory of your past state disappears—your whole bodies have to be reconstructed, to live on Dayside. But when the process is finished, you break out of the shell—and now you're male.

"*You* don't know that. The male comes out as if newly born—hatched, I mean. Probably his kind meet him and help him and teach him. The males discovered the truth somehow . . . well, it was easy enough for them, since they can watch the whole life cycle. Instead of helping you females, as nature intended, they set themselves up as gods and lived off you, taking more than they gave. And when they learned about us, they forbade you to have dealings with us—because they were afraid we'd learn the truth and expose them.

"But they need you! All you have to do is refuse to visit the temples for a few sunrises. Then see how fast they come to terms!"

For a time, then, the radio hissed and crackled with the thinking of many minds linked into one. Antella sat unmoving, Navarro fumbled with his pipe, Kingsbury gnawed his lips and drummed on the radio panel.

Finally: "This is astonishing news. We must investigate. You will provide one of us with a suit in which to inspect Dayside."

"Easy enough," said Kingsbury. His tone jittered. "And if you find the shells really are empty, as you will—what then?"

"We shall follow your advice. You will be given admittance to your supplies, and we will discuss arrangements for the mining of those ores which you desire."

Navarro found himself uncontrollably shaking. "St. Nicholas, patron of wanderers," he whispered, "I will build you a shrine for this."

"The males may make trouble," warned Antella.

"If their nature is as you claim," said the Twonk horde, "they will not be difficult to control."

Kingsbury, the American, wondered if he had planted the seeds of another matriarchy. Underneath all the rejoicing, he felt a vague sense of guilt.

THE GENTLE VULTURES

By Isaac Asimov

Randall Garrett's story examined, from the viewpoint of the Earthmen, a possible encounter between our species and hostile aliens. In the story that follows, Isaac Asimov handles the same theme from the viewpoint of the aliens themselves. Suppose, he says, strangers from afar have been watching us for years. Suppose, too, that they are the overlords of a galactic empire, eager to add us to their dominion. How will they react, though, when they learn what sort of creatures we Earthmen really are? To them, we are the aliens—and we are terribly, frighteningly alien.

Isaac Asimov, one of the science fiction's ablest practitioners, rarely deals with galactic matters these days. The Boston-based Dr. Asimov, who taught biochemistry while writing such famed s-f novels as The Currents of Space *and* The Caves of Steel, *now devotes himself to science fact with equal success. Though jovial and even boisterous in the flesh, Asimov is scholarly behind the typewriter, and he's won acclaim for such standard reference items as* The Intelligent Man's Guide to Science *and* Asimov's Biographical Encyclopedia of Science and Technology.

For fifteen years now, the Hurrians had maintained their base on the other side of the Moon.

It was unprecedented, unheard of. No Hurrian had dreamed it possible to be delayed so long. The decontamination squads had been ready—ready and waiting for fifteen years, ready to swoop down through the radioactive clouds and save what might be saved for the remnant of survivors. In return, of course, for fair payment.

But fifteen times, the planet had revolved about its sun. During each revolution, the satellite had rotated thirteen times about the primary. And in all that time the nuclear war had not come.

Nuclear bombs were exploded by the large-primate intelligences at various points on the planet's surface. The planet's stratosphere had grown amazingly warm with radioactive refuse. But still no war.

Devi-en hoped ardently that he would be replaced. He was the fourth Captain-in-charge of this colonizing expedition (if it could still be called so after fifteen years of suspended animation), and he was quite content that there should be a fifth. Now that the home world was sending an Archadministrator to make a personal survey of the situation, his replacement might come soon. Good!

He stood on the surface of the Moon, encased in his space suit, and thought of home, of Hurria. His long, thin arms moved restlessly with the thought, as though aching (through millions of years of instinct) for the ancestral trees. He stood only three feet high. What could be seen of him through the glass-fronted head plate was a black and wrinkled face with the fleshy, mobile nose dead-centered. The little tuft of fine beard was a pure white in contrast. In the rear of the suit, just below center, was the bulge within which the short and stuffy Hurrian tail might rest comfortably.

Devi-en took his appearance for granted, of course, but was well aware of the difference between the Hurrians and all the other intelligences in the Galaxy. The Hurrians alone were so small; they alone were tailed; they alone were vegetarians; they alone had escaped the inevitable nuclear war that had ruined every other known intelligent species.

He stood on the walled plain that extended for so many miles that the raised and circular rim (which on Hurria would have been called a crater, if it were smaller) was invisible beyond the horizon. Against the southern edge of the rim, where there was always some protection against the direct rays of the sun, a city had grown. It had begun as a temporary camp, of course, but with the years, women had been brought in, and children had been born. Now there were schools and elaborate hydroponics establishments, large water reservoirs, all that went with a city on an airless world.

It was ridiculous! All because one planet had nuclear weapons and would not fight a nuclear war.

The Archadministrator, who would be arriving soon, would undoubtedly ask, almost at once, the same question that Devi-en had asked himself a wearisome number of times.

Why had there not been a nuclear war?

Devi-en watched the hulking Mauvs preparing the ground now for the landing, smoothing out the unevennesses and laying down the ceramic bed designed to absorb the hyper-atomic field-thrusts with minimum discomfort to the passengers within the ship.

Even in their space suits, the Mauvs seemed to exude power, but it was the power of muscle only. Beyond them was the little figure of a Hurrian giving orders, and the docile Mauvs obeyed. Naturally.

The Mauvian race, of all the large-primate intelligences, paid their fees in the most unusual coin, a quota of themselves, rather than of material goods. It was a surprisingly useful tribute, better than steel, aluminum, or fine drugs in many ways.

Devi-en's receiver stuttered to life. "The ship is sighted, sir," came the report. "It will be landing within the hour."

"Very good," said Devi-en. "Have my car made ready to take me to the ship as soon as landing is initiated."

He did not feel that it was very good at all.

The Archadministrator came flanked by a personal retinue of five Mauvs. They entered the city with him, two on each side, three following. They helped him off with his space suit, then removed their own.

Their thinly haired bodies, their large, coarse-featured faces, their broad noses and flat cheekbones were repulsive but not frightening. Though twice the height of the Hurrians and more than twice the breadth, there was a blankness about their eyes, something completely submissive about the way they stood, with their thick-sinewed necks slightly bent, their bulging arms hanging listlessly.

The Archadministrator dismissed them, and they trooped out. He did not really need their protection, of course, but his position required a retinue of five, and that was that.

No business was discussed during the meal or during the almost endless ritual of welcome. At a time that might have been more appropriate for sleeping, the Archadministrator passed small fingers through his tuft of beard and said, "How much longer must we wait for this planet, Captain?"

He was visibly advancing in age. The hair on his upper arms was grizzled, and the tufts at the elbows were almost as white as his beard.

"I cannot say, your Height," said Devi-en, humbly. "They have not followed the path."

"That is obvious. The point is, *why* have they not followed the path? It is clear to the Council that your reports promise more than they deliver. You talk of theories, but you give no details. Now we are tired of all this back on Hurria. If you know of anything you have not told us, now is the time to talk of it."

"The matter, your Height, is hard to prove. We have had no experience of spying on a people over such an extended period. Until recently, we weren't watching for the right things. Each year we kept expecting the nuclear war the year after, and it is only in my time as Captain that we have taken to studying the people more intensively. It is at least one benefit of the long waiting time that we have learned some of their principal languages."

"Indeed? Without even landing on their planet?"

Devi-en explained. "A number of radio messages were recorded by those of our ships that penetrated the planetary atmosphere on observation missions, particularly in the early years. I set our linguistics computers to work on them, and for the last year I have been attempting to make sense out of it all."

The Archadministrator stared. His bearing was such that any outright exclamation of surprise would have been superfluous. "And have you learned anything of interest?"

"I may have, your Height, but what I have worked out is so strange and the underpinning of actual evidence is so uncertain that I dared not speak of it officially in my reports."

The Archadministrator understood. He said, stiffly, "Would you object to explaining your views unofficially—to me."

"I would be glad to," said Devi-en, at once. "The inhabitants of this planet are, of course, large-primate in nature. And they are competitive."

The other blew out his breath in a kind of relief and passed his tongue quickly over his nose. "I had a queer notion," he muttered, "that they might *not* be competitive and that that might— But go on, go on."

"They *are* competitive," Devi-en assured him. "Much more so than one would expect on the average."

"Then why doesn't everything else follow?"

"Up to a point it does, your Height. After the usual long incubation period, they began to mechanize, and after that, the usual large-primate killings became truly destructive warfare. At the conclusion of the most recent large-scale war, nuclear weapons were developed and the war ended at once."

The Archadministrator nodded. "And then?"

Devi-en said. "What should have happened was that a nuclear war ought to have begun shortly afterward, and that in the course of the war, nuclear weapons would have developed quickly in destructiveness, have been used nevertheless in typical large-primate fashion, and have quickly reduced the population to starving remnants in a ruined world."

"Of course, but that didn't happen. Why not?"

Devi-en said, "There is one point. I believe these people, once mechanization started, developed at an unusually high rate."

"And if so?" said the other. "Does that matter? They reached nuclear weapons the more quickly."

"True. But after the most recent general war, they continued to develop nuclear weapons at an unusual rate. That's the trouble. The deadly potential had increased before the nuclear war had a chance to start, and now it has reached a point where even large-primate intelligences dare not risk a war."

The Archadministrator opened his small black eyes wide. "But that is impossible. I don't care how technically talented these creatures are. Military science advances rapidly only during a war."

"Perhaps that is not true in the case of these particular creatures. But even if it were, it seems they *are* having a war; not a real war, but a war."

"Not a real war, but a war," repeated the Archadministrator blankly. "What does that mean?"

"I'm not sure." Devi-en wiggled his nose in exasperation. "This is where my attempts to draw logic out of the scattered material we have picked up is least satisfactory. This planet has something called a Cold War. Whatever it is, it drives them furiously onward in research, and yet it does not involve complete nuclear destruction."

The Archadministrator said, "Impossible!"

Devi-en said, "There is the planet. Here we are. We have been waiting fifteen years."

The Archadministrator's long arms came up and crossed over his head and down again to the opposite shoulders. "Then there *is* only one thing to do. The Council has considered the possibility that the planet may have achieved a stale-

mate, a kind of uneasy peace that balances just short of a nuclear war. Something of the sort you describe though no one
suggested the actual reasons you advance. But it's something
we can't allow."

"No, your Height?"

"No." He seemed almost in pain. "The longer the stalemate
continues, the greater the possibility that large-primate individuals may discover the methods of interstellar travel. They
will leak out into the Galaxy in full competitive strength. You
see?"

"Then?"

The Archadministrator hunched his head deeper into his
arms, as though not wishing to hear what he himself must say.
His voice was a little muffled. "If they are balanced precar-
iously, we must push them a little, Captain. We must push
them."

Devi-en's stomach churned, and he suddenly tasted his dinner once more in the back of his throat. "Push them, your
Height?" He didn't want to understand.

But the Archadministrator put it bluntly: "We must help
them start their nuclear war." He looked as miserably sick as
Devi-en felt. He whispered, "We must!"

Devi-en could scarcely speak. He said, in a whisper, "But
how could such a thing be done, your Height?"

"I don't know how. And do not look at *me* so. It is not my
decision. It is the decision of the Council. Surely you understand what would happen to the Galaxy if a large-primate intelligence were to enter space in full strength without having
been tamed by nuclear war."

Devi-en shuddered at the thought. All that competitiveness
loosed on the Galaxy. He persisted, though. "But *how* does
one start a nuclear war? How is it done?"

"I don't know, I tell you. But there must be some way; perhaps a—a message we might send or a—a crucial rainstorm
we might start by cloud seeding. We could manage a great
deal with their weather conditions—"

"How would that start a nuclear war?" said Devi-en,
unimpressed.

"Maybe it wouldn't. I mention such a thing only as a possible example. But large primates would know. After all, they
are the ones who *do* start nuclear wars in actual fact. It is in
their brain pattern to know. That is the decision the Council
came to."

Devi-en felt the soft noise his tail made as it thumped slowly against the chair. He tried to stop it and failed. "What decision, your Height?"

"To trap a large-primate from the planet's surface. To kidnap one."

"A *wild* one?"

"It's the only kind that exists at the moment on the planet. Of course, a wild one."

"And what do you expect him to tell us?"

"That doesn't matter, Captain. As long as he says enough about anything, mentalic analysis will give us the answer."

Devi-en withdrew his head as far as he could into the space between his shoulder blades. The skin just under his armpits quivered with repulsion. A wild large-primate being! He tried to picture one, untouched by the stunning aftermath of nuclear war, unaltered by the civilizing influence of Hurrian eugenic breeding.

The Archadministrator made no attempt to hide the fact that he shared the repulsion, but he said, "You will have to lead the trapping expedition, Captain. It is for the good of the Galaxy."

Devi-en had seen the planet a number of times before, but each time a ship swung about the Moon and placed the world in his line of sight, a wave of unbearable homesickness swept him.

It was a beautiful planet, so like Hurria itself in dimensions and characteristics but wilder and grander. The sight of it, after the desolation of the Moon, was like a blow.

How many other planets like it were on Hurrian master listings at this moment? he wondered. How many other planets were there concerning which meticulous observers had reported seasonal changes in appearance that could be interpreted only as being caused by artificial cultivation of food plants? How many times in the future would a day come when the radioactivity in the stratosphere of one of these planets would begin to climb, when colonizing squadrons would have to be sent out at once.

As they were to this planet.

It was almost pathetic, the confidence with which the Hurrians had proceeded at first. Devi-en could have laughed, as he read through those initial reports, if he weren't trapped in this project himself now. The Hurrian scout ships had moved close to gather geographical information, to locate population centers. They were sighted, of course, but what did it matter? Any time, now, they thought, the final explosion.

Any time . . . But useless years had passed, and the scout ships wondered if they ought not to be cautious. They moved back.

Devi-en's ship was cautious now. All the crew was on edge because of the unpleasantness of the mission; not all Devi-en's assurances that there was no harm intended to the large-primate could quite calm them. Even so, they could not hurry matters. It had to be over a fairly deserted and uncultivated tract of uneven ground that they hovered. They stayed at a height of ten miles for days, while the crew became edgier and only the ever-stolid Mauvs maintained calm.

Then the scope showed them a creature, alone on the uneven ground, a long staff in one hand, a pack across the upper portion of his back.

They lowered silently, supersonically. Devi-en himself, skin crawling, was at the controls.

The creature was heard to say two definite things before he was taken, and they were the first comments recorded for use in mentalic computing.

The first, when the large-primate caught sight of the ship almost upon him, was picked up by the direction telemike. It was "My God! A flying saucer!"

Devi-en understood the first phrase. That was a term for the Hurrian ships that had grown common among the large-primates those first careless years.

The second remark was made when the wild creature was brought in to the ship, struggling with amazing strength, but helpless in the iron grip of the unperturbed Mauvs.

Devi-en, panting, with his fleshly nose quivering slightly, advanced to receive him and the creature (whose unpleasantly hairless face had become oily with some sort of fluid secretion) yelled, "Holy Toledo, a *monkey!*"

Again, Devi-en understood the second part. It was the word for little-primate in one of the chief languages of the planet.

The wild creature was almost impossible to handle. He required infinite patience before he could be spoken to reasonably. At first, there was nothing but a series of crises. The creature realized almost at once that he was being taken off Earth, and what Devi-en thought might prove an exciting experience for him proved nothing of the sort. He talked instead of his offspring and of a large-primate female.

They have wives and children, thought Devi-en compassionately, and, in their way, love them, for all they are large-primates.

Then he had to be made to understand that the Mauvs who kept him under guard and who restrained him when his violence made that necessary would not hurt him, that he was not to be damaged in any way.

Devi-en was sickened at the thought that one intelligent being might be damaged by another. It was very difficult to discuss the subject, even if only to admit the possibility long enough to deny it. The creature from the planet treated the very hesitation with great suspicion. It was the way the large-primates were.

On the fifth day, when, out of sheer exhaustion perhaps, the creature remained quiet over a fairly extended period, they talked in Devi-en's private quarters, and suddenly he grew angry again when the Hurrian first explained, matter-of-factly, that they were waiting for a nuclear war.

"Waiting!" cried the creature. "What makes you so sure there will be one?"

Devi-en wasn't sure, of course, but he said, "There is always a nuclear war. It is our purpose to help you afterward."

"Help us *afterward*." His words grew incoherent. He waved his arms violently, and the Mauvs who flanked him had to restrain him gently once again and lead him away.

Devi-en sighed. The creature's remarks were building in quantity and perhaps mentalics could do something with them. His own unaided mind could make nothing of it.

And meanwhile the creature was not thriving. His body was almost completely hairless, a fact that long-distance observation had not revealed owing to the artificial skins worn by them. This was either for warmth or because of an instinctive repulsion on the part even of these particular large-primates themselves for hairless skin. It might be an interesting subject to take up. Mentalics computation could make as much out of one set of remarks as another.

Strangely enough, the creature's face had begun to sprout hair; more in fact than the Hurrian face had and of a dark color.

But still, the central fact was that he was not thriving. He had grown thinner because he was eating poorly and if he was kept too long, his health might suffer. Devi-en had no wish to feel responsible for that.

On the next day, the large-primate seemed quite calm. He talked almost eagerly, bringing the subject around to nuclear warfare almost at once. It had a terrible attraction for the large-primate mind, Devi-en thought.

The creature said, "You said nuclear wars always happen. Does that mean there are other people than yours and mine—and theirs?" He indicated the nearby Mauvs.

"There are thousands of intelligent species, living on thousands of worlds. Many thousands," said Devi-en.

"And they all have nuclear wars?"

"All who have reached a certain stage of technology. All but us. We were different. We lacked competitiveness. We had the cooperative instinct."

"You mean you know that nuclear wars will happen and you do nothing about it?"

"We *do,*" said Devi-en, pained. "Of course, we do. We try to help. In the early history of my people, when we first developed space travel, we did not understand large-primates. They repelled our attempts at friendship, and we stopped trying. Then we found worlds in radioactive ruins. Finally, we found one world actually in the process of a nuclear war. We were horrified but could do nothing. Slowly, we learned. We are ready, now, at every world we discover to be at the nuclear stage. We are ready with decontamination equipment and eugenic analyzers."

"What are eugenic analyzers?"

Devi-en had manufactured the phrase by analogy with what he knew of the wild one's language. Now he said, carefully, "We direct matings and sterilizations to remove, as far as possible, the competitive element in the remnant of the survivors."

For a moment, he thought the creature would grow violent again.

Instead, the other said in a monotone. "You make them docile, you mean, like these things?" Once again he indicated the Mauvs.

"No. No. These are different. We simply make it possible for the remnants to be content with a peaceful, nonexpanding, nonaggressive society under our guidance. Without this, they destroyed themselves, you see, and without it, they would destroy themselves again."

"What do you get out of it?"

Devi-en stared at the creature dubiously. Was it really necessary to explain the basic pleasure of life? He said, "Don't you enjoy helping someone?"

"Come on. Besides that. What's in it for you?"

"Of course, there are contributions to Hurria."

"Ha."

"Payment for saving a species is only fair," protested Devi-en, "and there are expenses to be covered. The contribution is not much and is adjusted to the nature of the world. It may be an annual supply of wood from a forested world; manganese salts from another. The world of these Mauvs is poor in physical resources, and they themselves offered to supply us with a number of individuals to use as personal assistants. They are extremely powerful even for large-primates, and we treat them painlessly with anticerebral drugs. . . ."

"To make zombies out of them!"

Devi-en guessed at the meaning of the noun and said, indignantly, "Not at all. Merely to make them content with their role as personal servants and forgetful of their homes. We would not want them to be unhappy. They are intelligent beings!"

"And what would you do with Earth if we had a war?"

"We have had fifteen years to decide that," said Devi-en. "Your world is very rich in iron and has developed a fine steel technology. Steel, I think, would be your contribution." He sighed. "But the contribution would not make up for our expense in this case, I think. We have overwaited now by ten years at least."

The large-primate said, "How many races do you tax in this way?"

"I do not know the exact number. Certainly, more than a thousand."

"Then you're the little landlords of the Galaxy, are you? A thousand worlds destroy themselves in order to contribute to your welfare. You're something else, too, you know." The wild one's voice was rising, growing shrill. "You're vultures."

"Vultures?" said Devi-en, trying to place the word.

"Carrion-eaters. Birds that wait for some poor creature to die of thirst in the desert and then come down to eat the body."

Devi-en felt himself turn faint and sick at the picture conjured up for him. He said, weakly, "No, no, we *help* the species."

"You wait for the war to happen like vultures. If you want to help, *prevent* the war. Don't save the remnants. Save them all."

Devi-en's tail twitched with sudden excitement. "How do we prevent a war? Will you tell me that?" What was prevention of war but the reverse of bringing about a war? Learn one process and surely the other would be obvious.

But the wild one faltered. He said, finally, "Get down there. Explain the situation."

Devi-en felt keen disappointment. That didn't help. Besides — He said, "Land among you? Quite impossible." His skin quivered in half a dozen places at the thought of mingling with the wild ones in their untamed billions.

Perhaps the sick look on Devi-en's face was so pronounced and unmistakable that the wild one could recognize it for what it was even across the barrier of species. He tried to fling himself at the Hurrian and had to be caught virtually in mid-air by one of the Mauvs, who held him immobile with an effortless constriction of biceps.

The wild one screamed. "No. Just sit here and wait! Vulture! Vulture! *Vulture!*"

It was days before Devi-en could bring himself to see the wild one again. He was almost brought to disrespect of the Archadministrator when the analysis of the mental makeup of these wild ones was made.

Devi-en said, boldly, "Surely there is enough to give some solution to our question."

The Archadministrator's nose quivered, and his pink tongue passed over it meditatively. "A solution of a kind, perhaps. I can't trust this solution. We are facing a very unusual species. We know that already. We can't afford to make mistakes. One thing, at least—we have happened upon a highly intelligent one. Unless—unless he is at his race's norm." The Archadministrator seemed upset at that thought.

Devi-en said, "The creature brought up the horrible picture of that—that bird—that—"

"Vulture," said the Archadministrator.

"It put our entire mission into such a distorted light. I have not been able to eat properly since or sleep. In fact, I am afraid I will have to ask to be relieved—"

"Not before we have completed what we have set out to do," said the Archadministrator firmly. "Do you think I enjoy the picture of—of carrion-eat— You *must* collect more data."

Devi-en nodded, finally. He understood, of course. The Archadministrator was no more anxious to cause a nuclear war than any Hurrian would be. He was putting off the moment of decision as long as possible.

Devi-en steeled himself for one more interview with the wild one. It turned out to be a completely unbearable one, and the last.

The wild one had a bruise across his cheek as though he

had been resisting the Mauvs again. In fact, it was certain he had. He had done so numerous times before, and the Mauvs, despite their most earnest attempts to do no harm, could not help but bruise him on occasion. One would expect the wild one to see how intensely they tried not to hurt him and to quiet his behavior as a result. Instead, it was as though the conviction of safety spurred him on to additional resistance.

These large-primate species were vicious, vicious, thought Devi-en sadly.

For over an hour, the interview hovered over useless small talk, and then the wild one said with sudden belligerence, "How long did you say you things have been here?"

"Fifteen of your years," said Devi-en.

"That figures. The first flying saucers were sighted just after World War II. How much longer before the nuclear war?"

With automatic truth, Devi-en said, "We wish we knew," and stopped suddenly.

The wild one said, "I thought nuclear war was inevitable. Last time you said you overstayed ten years. You expected the war ten years ago, didn't you?"

Devi-en said, "I can't discuss this subject."

"No?" The wild one was screaming. "What are you going to do about it? How long will you wait? Why not nudge it a little? Don't just wait, vulture. Start one."

Devi-en jumped to his feet. "What are you saying?"

"Why else are you waiting, you dirty—" He choked on a completely incomprehensible expletive, then continued, breathlessly, "Isn't that what vultures do when some poor miserable animal, or man, maybe, is taking too long to die? They can't wait. They come swirling down and peck out his eyes. They wait till he's helpless and just hurry him along the last step."

Devi-en ordered him away quickly and retired to his sleeping room, where he was sick for hours. Nor did he sleep then or that night. The word "vulture" screamed in his ears, and that final picture danced before his eyes.

Devi-en said firmly, "Your Height, I can speak with the wild one no more. If you need still more data, I cannot help you."

The Archadministrator looked haggard. "I know. This vulture business—very difficult to take. Yet you notice the thought didn't affect him. Large-primates are immune to such things, hardened, calloused. It is part of their way of thinking. Horrible."

"I can get you no more data."

"It's all right. I understand. Besides, each additional item only strengthens the preliminary answer; the answer I thought was only provisional; that I hoped earnestly was only provisional." He buried his head in his grizzled arms. "We have a way to start their nuclear war for them."

"Oh? What need be done?"

"It is something very direct, very simple. It is something I could never have thought of. Nor you."

"What is it, your Height?" He felt an anticipatory dread.

"What keeps them at peace now is that neither of two nearly equal sides dares take the responsibility of starting a war. If one side did, however, the other—well, let's be blunt about it —would retaliate in full."

Devi-en nodded.

The Archadministrator went on. "If a single nuclear bomb fell on the territory of either of the two sides, the victims would at once assume the other side had launched it. They would feel they could not wait for further attacks. Retaliation in full would follow within hours; the other side would retaliate in its turn. Within weeks it would be over."

"But how do we make one of them drop that first bomb."

"We don't, Captain. That is the point. We drop the first bomb ourselves."

"What?" Devi-en swayed.

"That is it. Compute a large-primate's mind, and that answer thrusts itself at you."

"But how can we?"

"We assemble a bomb. That is easy enough. We send it down by ship and drop it over some inhabited locality—"

"*Inhabited?*"

The Archadministrator looked away and said uneasily, "The effect is lost otherwise."

"I see," said Devi-en. He was picturing vultures; he couldn't help it. He visualized them as large, scaled birds (like the small harmless flying creatures on Hurria, but immensely large), with rubber-skinned wings and long razor-bills, circling down, pecking at dying eyes.

His hands covered his eyes. He said shakily, "Who will pilot the ship? Who will launch the bomb?"

The Archadministrator's voice was no stronger than Devi-en's. "I don't know."

"I won't," said Devi-en. "I can't. There is no Hurrian who can, at any price."

The Archadministrator rocked back and forth miserably. "Perhaps the Mauvs could be given orders—"

"Who could give them such orders?"

The Archadministrator sighed heavily. "I will call the Council. They have all the data. Perhaps they will suggest something."

So after a little over fifteen years, the Hurrians were dismantling their base on the other side of the Moon.

Nothing had been accomplished. The large-primates of the planet had not had their nuclear war; they might never have.

And despite all the future horror that might bring, Devi-en was in an agony of happiness. There was no point in thinking of the future. For the present, he was getting away from this most horrible of horrible worlds.

He watched the Moon fall away and shrink to a spot of light, along with the planet, and the sun of the system itself till the whole thing was lost among the constellations.

It was only then that he could feel anything but relief. It was only then that he felt a first tiny twinge of it-might-have-been.

He said to the Archadministrator, "It might all have been well if we had been more patient. They might yet have blundered into nuclear war."

The Archadministrator said, "Somehow I doubt it. The mentalic analysis of—"

He stopped, and Devi-en understood the wild one had been replaced on his planet with minimal harm. The events of the past weeks had been blanked out of his mind. He had been placed near a small, inhabited locality not far from the spot where he had been first found. His fellows would assume he had been lost. They would blame his loss of weight, his bruises, his amnesia upon the hardships he had undergone.

But the harm done *by* him . . .

If only they had not brought him up to the Moon in the first place. They might have reconciled themselves to the thought of starting a war. They might somehow have thought of dropping a bomb and worked out some indirect, long-distance system for doing so.

It had been the wild one's word picture of the vulture that had stopped it all. It had ruined Devi-en and the Archadministrator. When all data was sent back to Hurria, the effect on the Council itself had been notable. The order to dismantle the base had come quickly.

Devi-en said, "I will never take part in colonization again."

The Archadministrator said, mournfully, "None of us may ever have to. The wild ones of that planet will emerge and with large-primates and large-primate thinking loose in the Galaxy, it will mean the end of—of—"

Devi-en's nose twitched. The end of everything; of all the good Hurria had done in the Galaxy; all the good it might have continued to do in the future.

He said, "We ought to have dropped—" and did not finish.

What was the use of saying that? They couldn't have dropped the bomb for all the Galaxy. If they could have, they would have been large-primate themselves in their manner of thinking, and there are worse things than merely the end of everything.

Devi-en thought of the vultures.

STRANGER STATION

By Damon Knight

Damon Knight is a slender, soft-spoken man with a deceptively mild smile. He seems gentle and relaxed, but behind the tranquil exterior there seethes a fiercely active mind. Knight has served science fiction as an editor of magazines and anthologies, as a feared and respected critic, as a translator from the French, and as a leader of writers' conferences and organizations. When not engaged in any of these activities, he writes a little of the stuff himself. His short stories are marked by graceful style, stunning execution, and a profound understanding of character.

All these virtues are on display in the present work—plus a chilling portrayal of a weird relationship between man and nonman. Few stories have captured the sense of differentness *in an alien being as awesomely well as this one.*

The clang of metal echoed hollowly down through the Station's many vaulted corridors and rooms. Paul Wesson stood listening for a moment as the rolling echoes died away. The maintenance rocket was gone, heading back to Home; they had left him alone in Stranger Station.

Stranger Station! The name itself quickened his imagination. Wesson knew that both orbital stations had been named a century ago by the then-British administration of the satellite service; "Home" because the larger, inner station handled the traffic of Earth and its colonies; "Stranger" because the outer station was designed specifically for dealings with foreigners—beings from outside the solar system. But even that could not diminish the wonder of Stranger Station, whirling out here alone in the dark—waiting for its once-in-two-decades visitor. . . .

One man, out of all Sol's billions, had the task and privilege of enduring the alien's presence when it came. The two races, according to Wesson's understanding of the subject, were so fundamentally different that it was painful for them to meet. Well, he had volunteered for the job, and he thought he could handle it—the rewards were big enough.

He had gone through all the tests, and against his own expectations he had been chosen. The maintenance crew had brought him up as dead weight, drugged in a survival hamper; they had kept him the same way while they did their work and then had brought him back to consciousness. Now they were gone. He was alone.

But not quite.

"Welcome to Stranger Station, Sergeant Wesson," said a pleasant voice. "This is your alpha network speaking. I'm here to protect and serve you in every way. If there's anything you want, just ask me." It was a neutral voice, with a kind of professional friendliness in it, like that of a good schoolteacher or rec supervisor.

Wesson had been warned, but he was still shocked at the human quality of it. The alpha networks were the last word in robot brains—computers, safety devices, personal servants, libraries, all wrapped up in one, with something so close to "personality" and "free will" that experts were still arguing the question. They were rare and fantastically expensive; Wesson had never met one before.

"Thanks," he said now, to the empty air. "Uh—what do I call you, by the way? I can't keep saying, 'Hey, alpha network.' "

"One of your recent predecessors called me Aunt Nettie," was the response.

Wesson grimaced. Alpha network—Aunt Nettie. He hated puns; that wouldn't do. "The aunt part is all right," he said. "Suppose I call you Aunt Jane. That was my mother's sister; you sound like her, a little bit."

"I am honored," said the invisible mechanism politely. "Can I serve you any refreshments now? Sandwiches? A drink?"

"Not just yet," said Wesson. "I think I'll look the place over first."

He turned away. That seemed to end the conversation as far as the network was concerned. A good thing; it was all right to have it for company, speaking when spoken to, but if it got talkative . . .

The human part of the Station was in four segments: bedroom, living room, dining room, bath. The living room was comfortably large and pleasantly furnished in greens and tans; the only mechanical note in it was the big instrument console in one corner. The other rooms, arranged in a ring around the living room, were tiny; just space enough for Wesson, a narrow encircling corridor, and the mechanisms that would serve him. The whole place was spotlessly clean, gleaming and efficient in spite of its twenty-year layoff.

This is the gravy part of the run, Wesson told himself. The month before the alien came—good food, no work, and an alpha network for conversation. "Aunt Jane, I'll have a small steak now," he said to the network. "Medium rare, with hashed brown potatoes, onions and mushrooms, and a glass of lager. Call me when it's ready."

"Right," said the voice pleasantly. Out in the dining room, the autochef began to hum and cluck self-importantly. Wesson wandered over and inspected the instrument console. Air locks were sealed and tight, said the dials; the air was cycling. The station was in orbit and rotating on its axis with a force at the perimeter, where Wesson was, of one g. The internal temperature of this part of the Station was an even 73°.

The other side of the board told a different story; all the dials were dark and dead. Sector Two, occupying a volume some eighty-eight thousand times as great as this one, was not yet functioning.

Wesson had a vivid mental image of the Station, from photographs and diagrams—a five-hundred-foot Duralumin sphere, onto which the shallow thirty-foot disk of the human section had been stuck apparently as an afterthought. The whole cavity of the sphere, very nearly—except for a honeycomb of supply and maintenance rooms and the all-important, recently enlarged vats—was one cramped chamber for the alien . . .

"Steak's ready!" said Aunt Jane.

The steak was good, bubbling crisp outside the way he liked it, tender and pink inside. "Aunt Jane," he said with his mouth full, "this is pretty soft, isn't it?"

"The steak?" asked the voice, with a faintly anxious note.

Wesson grinned. "Never mind," he said. "Listen, Aunt Jane, you've been through this routine—how many times? Were you installed with the Station, or what?"

"I was not installed with the Station," said Aunt Jane primly. "I have assisted at three contacts."

"Um. Cigarette," said Wesson, slapping his pockets. The autochef hummed for a moment, and popped a pack of G. I.'s out of a vent. Wesson lighted up. "All right," he said, "you've been through this three times. There are a lot of things you can tell me, right?"

"Oh, yes, certainly. What would you like to know?"

Wesson smoked, leaning back reflectively, green eyes narrowed. "First," he said, "read me the Pigeon report—you know, from the *Brief History*. I want to see if I remember it right."

"Chapter Two," said the voice promptly. "First contact with a non-Solar intelligence was made by Commander Ralph C. Pigeon on July 1, 1987, during an emergency landing on Titan. The following is an excerpt from his official report:

" 'While searching for a possible cause for our mental disturbance, we discovered what appeared to be a gigantic construction of metal on the far side of the ridge. Our distress grew stronger with the approach to this construction, which was polyhedral and approximately five times the length of the *Cologne*.

" 'Some of those present expressed a wish to retire, but Lt. Acuff and myself had a strong sense of being called or summoned in some indefinable way. Although our uneasiness was not lessened, we therefore agreed to go forward and keep radio contact with the rest of the party while they returned to the ship.

" 'We gained access to the alien construction by way of a large, irregular opening. . . . The internal temperature was minus seventy-five degrees Fahrenheit; the atmosphere appeared to consist of methane and ammonia. . . . Inside the second chamber, an alien creature was waiting for us. We felt the distress, which I have tried to describe, to a much greater degree than before, and also the sense of summoning or pleading. . . . We observed that the creature was exuding a thick yellowish fluid from certain joints or pores in its surface. Though disgusted, I managed to collect a sample of this exudate, and it was later forwarded for analysis. . . .'

"The second contact was made ten years later by Commodore Crawford's famous Titan Expedition—"

"No, that's enough," said Wesson. "I just wanted the Pigeon quote." He smoked, brooding. "It seems kind of chopped off, doesn't it? Have you got a longer version in your memory banks anywhere?"

There was a pause. "No," said Aunt Jane.

"There was more to it when I was a kid," Wesson complained nervously. "I read that book when I was twelve, and I remember a long description of the alien—that is, I remember its being there." He swung around. "Listen, Aunt Jane—you're a sort of universal watchdog, that right? You've got cameras and mikes all over the Station?"

"Yes," said the network, sounding—was it Wesson's imagination?—faintly injured.

"Well, what about Sector Two? You must have cameras up there, too, isn't that so?"

"Yes."

"All right, then you can tell me. What do the aliens look like?"

There was a definite pause. "I'm sorry, I can't tell you that," said Aunt Jane.

"No," said Wesson, "I didn't think you could. You've got orders not to, I guess, for the same reason those history books have been cut since I was a kid. Now, what would the reason be? Have you got any idea, Aunt Jane?"

There was another pause. "Yes," the voice admitted.

"Well?"

"I'm sorry, I can't—"

"—tell you that," Wesson repeated along with it. "All right. At least we know where we stand."

"Yes, Sergeant. Would you like some dessert?"

"No dessert. One other thing. *What happens to Station watchmen, like me, after their tour of duty?*"

"They are upgraded to Class Seven, students with unlimited leisure, and receive outright gifts of seven thousand stellors, plus free Class One housing. . . ."

"Yeah, I know all that," said Wesson, licking his dry lips. "But here's what I'm asking you. The ones you know—what kind of shape were they in when they left here?"

"The usual human shape," said the voice brightly. "Why do you ask, Sergeant?"

Wesson made a discontented gesture. "Something I remember from a bull session at the Academy. I can't get it out of my head; I know it had something to do with the Station. Just a part of a sentence: '. . . blind as a bat and white bristles all over . . .' Now, would that be a description of the alien—or the watchman when they came to take him away?"

Aunt Jane went into one of her heavy pauses. "All right, I'll save you the trouble," said Wesson. "You're sorry, you can't tell me that."

"I *am* sorry," said the robot sincerely.

As the slow days passed into weeks, Wesson grew aware of the Station almost as a living thing. He could feel its resilient metal ribs enclosing him, lightly bearing his weight with its own as it swung. He could feel the waiting emptiness "up there," and he sensed the alert electronic network that spread around him everywhere, watching and probing, trying to anticipate his needs.

Aune Jane was a model companion. She had a record library of thousands of hours of music; she had films to show him, and microprinted books that he could read on the scanner in the living room; or if he preferred, she would read to him. She controlled the Station's three telescopes, and on request would give him a view of Earth or the Moon or Home. . . .

But there was no news. Aunt Jane would obligingly turn on the radio receiver if he asked her, but nothing except static came out. That was the thing that weighed most heavily on Wesson, as time passed—the knowledge that radio silence was being imposed on all ships in transit, on the orbital stations, and on the planet-to-space transmitters. It was an enormous, almost a crippling handicap. Some information could be transmitted over relatively short distances by photophone, but ordinarily the whole complex traffic of the space lanes depended on radio.

But this coming alien contact was so delicate a thing that even a radio voice, out here where the Earth was only a tiny disk twice the size of the Moon, might upset it. It was so precarious a thing, Wesson thought, that only one man could be allowed in the Station while the alien was there, and to give that man the company that would keep him sane, they had to install an alpha network. . . .

"Aunt Jane?"

The voice answered promptly, "Yes, Paul."

"This distress that the books talk about—you wouldn't know what it is, would you?"

"No, Paul."

"Because robot brains don't feel it, right?"

"Right, Paul."

"So tell me this—why do they need a man here at all? Why can't they get along with just you?"

A pause. "I don't know, Paul." The voice sounded faintly wistful. Were those gradations of tone really in it, Wesson wondered, or was his imagination supplying them?

He got up from the living room couch and paced restlessly back and forth. "Let's have a look at Earth," he said. Obediently, the viewing screen on the console glowed into life: there was the blue Earth, swimming deep below him, in its first quarter, jewel bright. "Switch it off," Wesson said.

"A little music?" suggested the voice, and immediately began to play something soothing, full of woodwinds.

"*No*," said Wesson. The music stopped.

Wesson's hands were trembling; he had a caged and frustrated feeling.

The fitted suit was in its locker beside the air lock. Wesson had been topside in it once or twice; there was nothing to see up there, just darkness and cold. But he had to get out of this squirrel cage. He took the suit down and began to get into it.

"Paul," said Aunt Jane anxiously, "are you feeling nervous?"

"Yes," he snarled.

"Then don't go into Sector Two," said Aunt Jane.

"Don't tell me what to do, you hunk of tin!" said Wesson with sudden anger. He zipped up the front of his suit with a vicious motion.

Aunt Jane was silent.

Seething, Wesson finished his check-off and opened the lock door.

The air lock, an upright tube barely large enough for one man, was the only passage between Sector One and Sector Two. It was also the only exit from Sector One; to get here in the first place, Wesson had had to enter the big lock at the "south" pole of the sphere, and travel all the way down inside, by drop hole and catwalk. He had been drugged unconscious at the time, of course. When the time came, he would go out the same way; neither the maintenance rocket nor the tanker had any space, or time, to spare.

At the "north" pole, opposite, there was a third air lock, this one so huge it could easily have held an interplanet freighter. But that was nobody's business—no human being's.

In the beam of Wesson's helmet lamp, the enormous central cavity of the Station was an inky gulf that sent back only remote, mocking glimmers of light. The near walls sparkled with hoarfrost. Sector Two was not yet pressurized; there was only a diffuse vapor that had leaked through the airseal and had long since frozen into the powdery deposit that lined the walls. The metal rang cold under his shod feet; the vast emptiness of the chamber was the more depressing because it was airless, unwarmed and unlit. *Alone*, said his footsteps; *alone* . . .

He was thirty yards up the catwalk when his anxiety suddenly grew stronger. Wesson stopped in spite of himself and turned clumsily, putting his back to the wall. The support of the solid wall was not enough. The catwalk seemed threatening to tilt underfoot, dropping him into the lightless gulf.

Wesson recognized this drained feeling, this metallic taste at the back of his tongue. It was fear.

The thought ticked through his head: *They want me to be afraid.* But why? Why now? Of what?

Equally suddenly, he knew. The nameless pressure tightened, like a great fist closing, and Wesson had the appalling sense of something so huge that it had no limits at all, descending, with a terrible endless swift slowness. . . .

It was time.

His first month was up.

The alien was coming.

As Wesson turned, gasping, the whole huge structure of the Station around him seemed to dwindle to the size of an ordinary room—and Wesson with it, so that he seemed to himself like a tiny insect, frantically scuttling down the walls toward safety.

Behind him as he ran, the Station *boomed*.

In the silent rooms, all the lights were burning dimly. Wesson lay still, looking at the ceiling. Up there his imagination formed a shifting, changing image of the alien—huge, shadowy, formlessly menacing.

Sweat had gathered in globules on his brow. He stared, unable to look away.

"That was why you didn't want me to go topside, huh, Aunt Jane?" he said hoarsely.

"Yes. The nervousness is the first sign. But you gave me a direct order, Paul."

"I know it," he said vaguely, still staring fixedly at the ceiling. "A funny thing . . . Aunt Jane?"

"Yes, Paul?"

"You won't tell me what it looks like, right?"

"*No*, Paul."

"I don't want to know. Lord, I don't *want* to know. . . . Funny thing, Aunt Jane, part of me is just pure funk—I'm so scared I'm nothing but a jelly."

"I know," said the voice gently.

"—And part is real cool and calm, as if it didn't matter. Crazy, the things you think about. You know?"

"What things, Paul?"

He tried to laugh. "I'm remembering a kids' party I went to

twenty, twenty-five years ago. I was—let's see—I was nine. I remember, because that was the same year my father died.

"We were living in Dallas then, in a rented mobile house, and there was a family in the next tract with a bunch of red-headed kids. They were always throwing parties; nobody liked them much, but everybody always went."

"Tell me about the party, Paul."

He shifted on the couch. "This one—this one was a Hal-loween party. I remember the girls had on black and orange dresses, and the boys mostly wore spirit costumes. I was about the youngest kid there, and I felt kind of out of place. Then all of a sudden one of the redheads jumps up in a skull mask, hollering, 'C'mon, everybody get ready for hide-and-seek.' And he grabs *me,* and says, '*You* be it,' and before I can even move, he shoves me into a dark closet. And I hear that door lock behind me."

He moistened his lips. "And then—you know, in the darkness—I feel something hit my *face.* You know, cold and clammy, like—I don't know—something dead. . . .

"I just hunched up on the floor of that closet, waiting for that thing to touch me again. You know? That thing, cold and kind of gritty, hanging up there. You know what it was? A cloth glove, full of ice and bran cereal. A joke. Boy, that was one joke I never forgot. . . . Aunt Jane?"

"Yes, Paul."

"Hey, I'll bet you alpha networks made great psychs, huh? I could lie here and tell you anything, because you're just a machine—right?"

"Right, Paul," said the network sorrowfully.

"Aunt Jane, Aunt Jane . . . It's no use kidding myself along. I can *feel* that thing up there, just a couple of yards away."

"I know you can, Paul."

"I can't stand it, Aunt Jane."

"You can if you think you can, Paul."

He writhed on the couch. "It's—it's dirty, it's clammy. My God, is it going to be like that for *five* months? I can't, it'll kill me, Aunt Jane."

There was another thunderous boom, echoing down through the structural members of the Station. "What's that?" Wesson gasped. "The other ship—casting off?"

"Yes. Now he's alone, just as you are."

"Not like me. He can't be feeling what I'm feeling. Aunt Jane, you don't know. . . ."

Up there, separated from him only by a few yards of metal, the alien's enormous, monstrous body hung. It was that poised weight, as real as if he could touch it, that weighed down his chest.

Wesson had been a space dweller for most of his adult life and knew even in his bones that, if an orbital station ever collapsed, the "under" part would not be crushed but would be hurled away by its own angular momentum. This was not the oppressiveness of planetside buildings, where the looming mass above you seemed always threatening to fall. This was something else, completely distinct, and impossible to argue away.

It was the scent of danger, hanging unseen up there in the dark, waiting, cold and heavy. It was the recurrent nightmare of Wesson's childhood—the bloated unreal shape, no-color, no-size, that kept on hideously falling toward his face. . . . It was the dead puppy he had pulled out of the creek, that summer in Dakota—wet fur, limp head, cold, cold, *cold*. . . .

With an effort, Wesson rolled over on the couch and lifted himself to one elbow. The pressure was an insistent chill weight on his skull; the room seemed to dip and swing around him in slow, dizzy circles.

Wesson felt his jaw muscles contorting with the strain as he knelt, then stood erect. His back and legs tightened; his mouth hung painfully open. He took one step, then another, timing them to hit the floor as it came upright.

The right side of the console, the one that had been dark, was lighted. Pressure in Sector Two, according to the indicator, was about one and a third atmospheres. The air-lock indicator showed a slightly higher pressure of oxygen and argon; that was to keep any of the alien atmosphere from contaminating Sector One, but it also meant that the lock would no longer open from either side. Wesson found that irrationally comforting.

"Lemme see Earth," he gasped.

The screen lighted up as he stared into it. "It's a long way down," he said. A long, long way down to the bottom of that well. . . . He had spent ten featureless years as a servo tech in Home Station. Before that, he'd wanted to be a pilot, but had washed out the first year—couldn't take the math. But he had never once thought of going back to Earth.

Now, suddenly, after all these years, that tiny blue disk seemed infinitely desirable.

"Aunt Jane, Aunt Jane, it's beautiful," he mumbled.

Down there, he knew, it was spring; and in certain places, where the edge of darkness retreated, it was morning—a watery blue morning like the sea light caught in an agate, a morning with smoke and mist in it, a morning of stillness and promise. Down there, lost years and miles away, some tiny dot of a woman was opening her microscopic door to listen to an atom's song. Lost, lost, and packed away in cotton wool, like a specimen slide—one spring morning on Earth.

Black miles above, so far that sixty Earths could have been piled one on another to make a pole for his perch, Wesson swung in his endless circle within a circle. Yet, vast as the gulf beneath him was, all this—Earth, Moon, orbital stations, ships; yes, the Sun and all the rest of his planets, too—was the merest sniff of space, to be pinched up between thumb and finger.

Beyond—there was the true gulf. In that deep night, galaxies lay sprawled aglitter, piercing a distance that could only be named in a meaningless number, a cry of dismay: O . . . O . . . O . . .

Crawling and fighting, blasting with energies too big for them, men had come as far as Jupiter. But if a man had been tall enough to lie with his boots toasting in the Sun and his head freezing at Pluto, still he would have been too small for that overwhelming emptiness. Here, not at Pluto, was the outermost limit of man's empire; here the Outside funneled down to meet it, like the pinched waist of an hourglass; here, and only here, the two worlds came near enough to touch. Ours—and Theirs.

Down at the bottom of the board, now, the golden dials were faintly alight, the needles trembling ever so little on their pins.

Deep in the vats, the vats, the golden liquid was trickling down: *"Though disgusted, I took a sample of the exudate, and it was forwarded for analysis. . . ."*

Space-cold fluid, trickling down the bitter walls of the tubes, forming little pools in the cups of darkness; goldenly agleam there, half alive. The golden elixir. One drop of the concentrate would arrest aging for twenty years—keep your arteries soft, tonus good, eyes clear, hair pigmented, brain alert.

That was what the tests of Pigeon's sample had showed. That was the reason for the whole crazy history of the "alien trading post"—first a hut on Titan, then later, when people understood more about the problem, Stranger Station.

Once every twenty years, an alien would come down out of Somewhere, and sit in the tiny cage we had made for him, and make us rich beyond our dreams—rich with life—and still we did not know why.

Above him, Wesson imagined he could see that sensed body awallow in the glacial blackness, its bulk passively turning with the Station's spin, bleeding a chill gold into the lips of the tubes—drip . . . drop . . .

Wesson held his head. The pressure inside made it hard to think; it felt as if his skull were about to fly apart. "Aunt Jane," he said.

"Yes, Paul." The kindly, comforting voice, like a nurse. The nurse who stands beside your cot while you have painful, necessary things done to you. Efficient, trained friendliness.

"Aunt Jane," said Wesson, "do you know why they keep coming back?"

"No," said the voice precisely. "It is a mystery."

Wesson nodded. "I had," he said, "an interview with Gower before I left Home. You know Gower? Chief of the Outerworld Bureau. Came up especially to see me."

"Yes?" said Aunt Jane encouragingly.

"Said to me, 'Wesson, you got to find out. Find out if we can count on them to keep up the supply. You know? There's fifty million more of us,' he says, 'than when you were born. We need more of the stuff, and we got to know if we can count on it. Because,' he says, 'you know what would happen if it stopped?' Do you know, Aunt Jane?"

"It would be," said the voice, "a catastrophe."

"That's right," Wesson said respectfully. "It would. Like, he says to me, 'What if the people in the Nefud area were cut off from the Jordan Valley Authority? Why, there'd be millions dying of thirst in a week.

" 'Or what if the freighters stopped coming to Moon Base? Why,' he says, 'there'd be thousands starving and smothering to death.'

"He says, 'Where the water is, where you can get food and air, people are going to settle and get married, you know? And have kids.'

"He says, 'If the so-called longevity serum stopped coming. . . .' Says, 'Every twentieth adult in the Sol family is due for his shot this year.' Says, 'Of those, almost twenty percent are one hundred fifteen or older.' Says, 'The deaths in that group in the first year would be at least three times what the actuarial tables call for.' " Wesson raised a strained face.

"I'm thirty-four, you know?" he said. "That Gower, he made me feel like a baby."

Aunt Jane made a sympathetic noise.

"Drip, drip," said Wesson hysterically. The needles of the tall golden indicators were infinitesimally higher. "Every twenty years we need more of the stuff, so somebody like me has to come out and take it for five lousy months. And one of *them* has to come out and sit there, and *drip. Why,* Aunt Jane? What for? Why should it matter to them whether we live a long time or not? Why do they keep on coming back? What do they take *away* from here?"

But to these questions, Aunt Jane had no reply.

All day and every day, the lights burned cold and steady in the circular gray corridor around the rim of Sector One. The hard gray flooring had been deeply scuffed in that circular path before Wesson ever walked there—the corridor existed for that only, like a treadmill in a squirrel cage. It said "Walk," and Wesson walked. A man would go crazy if he sat still, with that squirming, indescribable pressure on his head; and so Wesson paced off the miles, all day and every day, until he dropped like a dead man in the bed at night.

He talked, too, sometimes to himself, sometimes to the listening alpha network; sometimes it was difficult to tell which. "Moss on a rock," he muttered, pacing. "Told him, wouldn't give twenty mills for any shell. . . . Little pebbles down there, all colors." He shuffled on in silence for a while. Abruptly: "I don't see *why* they couldn't have given me a cat."

Aunt Jane said nothing. After a moment Wesson went on, "Nearly everybody at Home has a cat, for God's sake, or a goldfish or something. You're all right, Aunt Jane, but I can't *see* you. My God, I mean if they couldn't send a man a woman for company—what I mean, my God, I never liked *cats.*" He swung around the doorway into the bedroom, and absentmindedly slammed his fist into the bloody place on the wall.

"But a cat would have been *something,*" he said.

Aunt Jane was still silent.

"Don't pretend your feelings are hurt. I know you, you're only a machine," said Wesson. "Listen, Aunt Jane, I remember a cereal package one time that had a horse and a cowboy on the side. There wasn't much room, so about all you saw was their faces. It used to strike me funny how much they looked alike. Two ears on the top with hair in the middle. Two eyes. Nose. Mouth with teeth in it. I was thinking, we're kind of distant cousins, aren't we, us and the horses. But compared to that thing up there—we're *brothers*. You know?"

"Yes," said Aunt Jane quietly.

"So I keep asking myself, why couldn't they have sent a horse or a cat *instead* of a man? But I guess the answer is because only a man could take what I'm taking. God, only a man. Right?"

"Right," said Aunt Jane with deep sorrow.

Wesson stopped at the bedroom doorway again and shuddered, holding onto the frame. "Aunt Jane," he said in a low, clear voice, "you take pictures of *him* up there, don't you?"

"Yes, Paul."

"And you take pictures of me. And then what happens? After it's all over, who looks at the pictures?"

"I don't know," said Aunt Jane humbly.

"You don't know. But whoever looks at 'em, it doesn't do any good. Right? We got to find out why, why, why. . . . And we never do find out, do we?"

"No," said Aunt Jane.

"But don't they figure that if the man who's going through it could see him, he might be able to tell something? That other people couldn't? Doesn't that make sense?"

"That's out of my hands, Paul."

He sniggered. "That's funny. Oh, that's funny." He chortled in his throat, reeling around the circuit.

"Yes, that's funny," said Aunt Jane.

"Aunt Jane, tell me what happens to the watchmen."

"I can't tell you that, Paul."

He lurched into the living room, sat down before the console, beat on its smooth, cold metal with his fists. "What are you, some kind of monster? Isn't there any blood in your veins, or oil or *anything*?"

"Please, Paul—"

"Don't you see, all I want to know, can they talk? Can they tell anything after their tour is over?"

"No, Paul."

He stood upright, clutching the console for balance. "They can't? No, I figured. And you know why?"

"No."

"Up there," said Wesson obscurely. "Moss on the rock."

"Paul, what?"

"We get changed," said Wesson, stumbling out of the room

again. "We get changed. Like a piece of iron next to a magnet. Can't help it. You—nonmagnetic, I guess. Goes right through you, huh, Aunt Jane? You don't get changed. You stay here, wait for the next one."

"Yes," said Aunt Jane.

"You know," said Wesson, pacing, "I can tell how he's lying up there. Head *that* way, tail the other. Am I right?"

"Yes," said Aunt Jane.

Wesson stopped. "Yes," he said intently. "So you *can* tell me what you see up there, can't you, Aunt Jane?"

"No. Yes. It isn't allowed."

"Listen, Aunt Jane, *we'll die* unless we can find out what makes those aliens tick! Remember that." Wesson leaned against the corridor wall, gazing up. "He's turning now—around this way. Right?"

"Yes."

"Well, what else is he doing? Come on, Aunt Jane, tell me!"

A pause. "He is twitching his—"

"What?"

"I don't know the words."

"My God, my God," said Wesson, clutching his head, "of course there aren't any words." He ran into the living room, clutched the console, and stared at the blank screen. He pounded the metal with his fist. "You've got to show me, Aunt Jane, come on and show me—show me!"

"It isn't allowed," Aunt Jane protested.

"You've got to do it just the same, or we'll *die,* Aunt Jane—millions of us, billions, and it'll be your fault, get it? *Your fault,* Aunt Jane!"

"Please," said the voice. There was a pause. The screen flickered to life, for an instant only. Wesson had a glimpse of something massive and dark, but half transparent, like a magnified insect—a tangle of nameless limbs, whiplike filaments, claws, wings. . . .

He clutched the edge of the console.

"Was that all right?" Aunt Jane asked.

"Of course! What do you think, it'll kill me to look at it? Put it back, Aunt Jane, put it back!"

Reluctantly, the screen lighted again. Wesson stared and went on staring. He mumbled something.

"What?" said Aunt Jane.

"Life of my love, I loathe thee," said Wesson, staring. He roused himself after a moment and turned away. The image of the alien stayed with him as he went reeling into the cor-

ridor again; he was not surprised to find that it reminded him of all the loathsome, crawling, creeping things the Earth was full of. That explained why he was not supposed to see the alien, or even know what it looked like—because that fed his hate. And it was all right for him to be afraid of the alien, but he was not supposed to hate it. . . . Why not? Why not?

His fingers were shaking. He felt drained, steamed, dried up and withered. The one daily shower Aunt Jane allowed him was no longer enough. Twenty minutes after bathing the acid sweat dripped again from his armpits, the cold sweat was beaded on his forehead, the hot sweat was in his palms. Wesson felt as if there were a furnace inside him, out of control, all the dampers drawn. He knew that, under stress, something of the kind did happen to a man; the body's chemistry was altered—more adrenalin, more glycogen in the muscles, eyes brighter, digestion retarded. That was the trouble—he was burning himself up, unable to fight the thing that tormented him, nor run from it.

After another circuit, Wesson's steps faltered. He hesitated, and went into the living room. He leaned over the console, staring. From the screen, the alien stared blindly up into space. Down in the dark side, the golden indicators had climbed: the vats were more than two thirds filled.

To *fight* or *run* . . .

Slowly Wesson sank down in front of the console. He sat hunched, head bent, hands squeezed tight between his knees, trying to hold onto the thought that had come to him.

If the alien felt a pain as great as Wesson's—or greater—

Stress might alter the alien's body chemistry, too.

Life of my love, I loathe thee.

Wesson pushed the irrelevant thought aside. He stared at the screen, trying to envisage the alien up there, wincing in pain and distress—sweating a golden sweat of horror. . . .

After a long time, he stood up and walked into the kitchen. He caught the table edge to keep his legs from carrying him on around the circuit. He sat down.

Humming fondly, the autochef slid out a tray of small glasses—water, orange juice, milk. Wesson put the water glass to his stiff lips; the water was cool and hurt his throat. Then the juice, but he could drink only a little of it; then he sipped the milk. Aunt Jane hummed approvingly.

Dehydrated. How long had it been since he had eaten or drunk? He looked at his hands. They were thin bundles of sticks, ropy-veined, with hard yellow claws. He could see the bones of his forearms under the skin, and his heart's beating stirred the cloth at his chest. The pale hairs on his arms and thighs—were they blond or white?

The blurred reflections in the metal trim of the dining room gave him no answers—only pale faceless smears of gray. Wesson felt light-headed and very weak, as if he had just ended a bout of fever. He fumbled over his ribs and shoulder bones. He was thin.

He sat in front of the autochef for a few minutes more, but no food came out. Evidently Aunt Jane did not think he was ready for it, and perhaps she was right. *Worse for them than for us*, he thought dizzily. *That's why the Station's so far out, why radio silence, and only one man aboard. They couldn't stand it at all, otherwise.* . . . Suddenly he could think of nothing but sleep—the bottomless pit, layer after layer of smothering velvet, numbing and soft. . . . His leg muscles quivered and twitched when he tried to walk, but he managed to get to the bedroom and fall on the mattress. The resilient block seemed to dissolve under him. His bones were melting.

He woke with a clear head, very weak, thinking cold and clear: *When two alien cultures meet, the stronger must transform the weaker with love or hate.* "Wesson's Law," he said aloud. He looked automatically for pencil and paper, but there was none, and he realized he would have to tell Aunt Jane, and let her remember it.

"I don't understand," she said.

"Never mind, remember it anyway. You're good at that, aren't you?"

"Yes, Paul."

"All right—I want some breakfast."

He thought about Aunt Jane, so nearly human, sitting up here in her metal prison, leading one man after another through the torments of hell—nursemaid, protector, torturer. They must have known that something would have to give. . . . But the alphas were comparatively new; nobody understood them very well. Perhaps they really thought that an absolute prohibition could never be broken.

. . . the stronger must transform the weaker. . . .

I'm the stronger, he thought. *And that's the way it's going to be.* He stopped at the console, and the screen was blank. He said angrily, "Aunt Jane!" And with a guilty start, the screen flickered into life.

Up there, the alien had rolled again in his pain. Now the

great clustered eyes were staring directly into the camera; the coiled limbs threshed in pain; the eyes were staring, asking, pleading. . . .

"No," said Wesson, feeling his own pain like an iron cap, and he slammed his hand down on the manual control. The screen went dark. He looked up, sweating, and saw the floral picture over the console.

The thick stems were like antennae, the leaves thoraxes, the buds like blind insect eyes. The whole picture moved slightly, endlessly, in a slow waiting rhythm.

Wesson clutched the hard metal of the console and stared at the picture, with sweat cold on his brow, until it turned into a calm, meaningless arrangement of lines again. Then he went into the dining room, shaking, and sat down.

After a moment he said, "Aunt Jane, does it get worse?"

"No. From now on, it gets better."

"How long?" he asked vaguely.

"One month."

A month, getting "better"—that was the way it had always been, with the watchman swamped and drowned, his personality submerged. Wesson thought about the men who had gone before him—Class Seven citizenship, with unlimited leisure, and Class One housing. Yes, sure—in a sanatorium.

His lips peeled back from his teeth, and his fists clenched hard. *Not me!* he thought.

He spread his hands on the cool metal to steady them. He said, "How much longer do they usually stay able to talk?"

"You are already talking longer than any of them. . . ."

Then there was a blank. Wesson was vaguely aware, in snatches, of the corridor walls moving past and the console glimpsed and of a thunderous cloud of ideas that swirled around his head in a beating of wings. The aliens—what did they want? And what happened to the watchmen in Stranger Station?

The haze receded a little, and he was in the dining room again, staring vacantly at the table. Something was wrong.

He ate a few spoonfuls of the gruel the autochef served him, then pushed it away; the stuff tasted faintly unpleasant. The machine hummed anxiously and thrust a poached egg at him, but Wesson got up from the table.

The Station was all but silent. The resting rhythm of the household machines throbbed in the walls, unheard. The blue-lighted living room was spread out before him like an empty stage setting, and Wesson stared as if he had never seen it before.

He lurched to the console and stared down at the pictured alien on the screen—heavy, heavy, asprawl with pain in the darkness. The needles of the golden indicators were high, the enlarged vats almost full. *It's too much for him,* Wesson thought with grim satisfaction. The peace that followed the pain had not descended as it was supposed to; no, not this time!

He glanced up at the painting over the console—heavy crustacean limbs that swayed gracefully in the sea. . . .

He shook his head violently. *I won't let it; I won't give in!* He held the back of one hand close to his eyes. He saw the dozens of tiny cuneiform wrinkles stamped into the skin over the knuckles, the pale hairs sprouting, the pink shiny flesh of recent scars. *I'm human,* he thought. But when he let his hand fall onto the console, the bony fingers seemed to crouch like crustaceans' legs, ready to scuttle.

Sweating, Wesson stared into the screen. Pictured there, the alien met his eyes, and it was as if they spoke to each other, mind to mind, an instantaneous communication that needed no words. There was a piercing sweetness to it, a melting, dissolving luxury of change into something that would no longer have any pain. . . . A pull, a calling.

Wesson straightened up slowly, carefully, as if he held some fragile thing in his mind that must not be handled roughly, or it would disintegrate. He said hoarsely, "Aunt Jane!"

She made some responsive noise.

He said, "Aunt Jane, I've got the answer! The whole thing! Listen, now wait—listen!" He paused a moment to collect his thoughts. *"When two alien cultures meet, the stronger must transform the weaker with love or hate.* Remember? You said you didn't understand what that meant. I'll *tell* you what it means. When these—monsters—met Pigeon a hundred years ago on Titan, *they knew* we'd have to meet again. They're spreading out, colonizing, and so are we. We haven't got interstellar flight yet, but give us another hundred years, we'll *get* it. *We'll wind up out there, where they are.* And they can't stop us. Because they're not killers, Aunt Jane, it isn't in them. They're *nicer* than us. See, they're like the missionaries, and we're the South Sea Islanders. *They* don't kill their enemies, oh, no—perish the thought!"

She was trying to say something, to interrupt him, but he rushed on. "Listen! The longevity serum—that was a lucky accident. But they played it for all it's worth. Slick and smooth. They come and give us the stuff free—they don't ask for a thing in return. Why not? Listen.

"They come here, and the shock of that first contact makes them sweat out that golden gook we need. Then, the last month or so, the pain always eases off. Why? Because the two minds, the human and alien, they stop fighting each other. Something gives way, it goes soft, and there's a mixing together. And that's where you get the human casualties of this operation—the bleary men that come out of here not even able to talk human language anymore. Oh, I suppose they're happy—happier than I am!—because they've got something big and wonderful inside 'em. Something that you and I can't even understand. But if you took them and put them together again with the aliens who spent time here, *they could all live together—they're adapted.*

"That's what they're aiming for!" He struck the console with his fist. "Not now—but a hundred, two hundred years from now! When we start expanding out to the stars—when we go a-conquering—we'll have already been conquered! Not by weapons, Aunt Jane, not by hate—by love! Yes, love! *Dirty, stinking, low-down, sneaking love!*"

Aunt Jane said something, a long sentence, in a high, anxious voice.

"What?" said Wesson irritably. He couldn't understand a word.

Aunt Jane was silent. "What, what?" Wesson demanded, pounding the console. "Have you got it through your tin head or not? *What?*"

Aunt Jane said something else, tonelessly. Once more, Wesson could not make out a single word.

He stood frozen. Warm tears started suddenly out of his eyes. "Aunt Jane—" he said. He remembered, *You are already talking longer than any of them.* Too late? Too late? He tensed, then whirled and sprang to the closet where the paper books were kept. He opened the first one his hand struck.

The black letters were alien squiggles on the page, little humped shapes, without meaning.

The tears were coming faster, he couldn't stop them—tears of weariness, tears of frustration, tears of hate. *"Aunt Jane!"* he roared.

But it was no good. The curtain of silence had come down

over his head. He was one of the vanguard—the conquered men, the ones who would get along with their strange brothers, out among the alien stars.

The console was not working anymore; nothing worked when he wanted it. Wesson squatted in the shower stall, naked, with a soup bowl in his hands. Water droplets glistened on his hands and forearms; the pale short hairs were just springing up, drying.

The silvery skin of reflection in the bowl gave him back nothing but a silhouette, a shadow man's outline. He could not see his face.

He dropped the bowl and went across the living room, shuffling the pale drifts of paper underfoot. The black lines on the paper, when his eye happened to light on them, were worm shapes, crawling things, conveying nothing. He rolled slightly in his walk; his eyes were glazed. His head twitched, every now and then, sketching a useless motion to avoid pain.

Once the bureau chief, Gower, came to stand in his way. "You fool," he said, his face contorted in anger, "you were supposed to go on to the end, like the rest. Now look what you've done!"

"I found out, didn't I?" Wesson mumbled, and as he brushed the man aside like a cobweb, the pain suddenly grew more intense. Wesson clasped his head in his hands with a grunt, and rocked to and fro a moment, uselessly, before he straightened and went on. The pain was coming in waves now, so tall that at their peak his vision dimmed out, violet, then gray.

It couldn't go on much longer. Something had to burst.

He paused at the bloody place and slapped the metal with his palm, making the sound ring dully up into the frame of the Station: *rroom . . . rroom . . .*

Faintly an echo came back: *boo-oom . . .*

Wesson kept going, smiling a faint and meaningless smile. He was only marking time now, waiting. Something was about to happen.

The kitchen doorway sprouted a sudden sill and tripped him. He fell heavily, sliding on the floor, and lay without moving beneath the slick gleam of the autochef.

The pressure was too great—the autochef's clucking was swallowed up in the ringing pressure, and the tall gray walls buckled slowly in. . . .

The Station lurched.

Wesson felt it through his chest, palms, knees, and elbows: the floor was plucked away for an instant and then swung back.

The pain in his skull relaxed its grip a little. Wesson tried to get to his feet.

There was an electric silence in the Station. On the second try, he got up and leaned his back against a wall. *Cluck,* said the autochef suddenly, hysterically, and the vent popped open, but nothing came out.

He listened, straining to hear. What?

The Station bounced beneath him, making his feet jump like a puppet's; the wall slapped his back hard, shuddered, and was still; but far off through the metal cage came a long angry groan of metal, echoing, diminishing, dying. Then silence again.

The Station held its breath. All the myriad clickings and pulses in the walls were suspended; in the empty rooms the lights burned with a yellow glare, and the air hung stagnant and still. The console lights in the living room glowed like witch fires. Water in the dropped bowl, at the bottom of the shower stall, shone like quicksilver, waiting.

The third shock came. Wesson found himself on his hands and knees, the jolt still tingling in the bones of his body, staring at the floor. The sound that filled the room ebbed away slowly and ran down into the silences—a resonant metallic sound, shuddering away now along the girders and hull plates, rattling tinnily into bolts and fittings, diminishing, noiseless, gone. The silence pressed down again.

The floor leaped painfully under his body, one great resonant blow that shook him from head to foot.

A muted echo of that blow came a few seconds later, as if the shock had traveled across the Station and back.

The bed, Wesson thought, and scrambled on hands and knees through the doorway, along a floor curiously tilted, until he reached the rubbery block.

The room burst visibly upward around him, squeezing the block flat. It dropped back as violently, leaving Wesson bouncing helplessly on the mattress, his limbs flying. It came to rest, in a long reluctant groan of metal.

Wesson rolled up on one elbow, thinking incoherently, *Air, the air lock.* Another blow slammed him down into the mattress, pinched his lungs shut, while the room danced grotesquely over his head. Gasping for breath in the ringing silence, Wesson felt a slow icy chill rolling toward him across the room—and there was a pungent smell in the air. *Ammonia!* he thought, and the odorless, smothering methane with it.

His cell was breached. The burst membrane was fatal—the alien's atmosphere would kill him.

Wesson surged to his feet. The next shock caught him off balance, dashed him to the floor. He arose again, dazed and limping; he was still thinking confusedly, *The air lock—get out.*

When he was halfway to the door, all the ceiling lights went out at once. The darkness was like a blanket around his head. It was bitter cold now in the room, and the pungent smell was sharper. Coughing, Wesson hurried forward. The floor lurched under his feet.

Only the golden indicators burned now—full to the top, the deep vats brimming, golden-lipped, gravid, a month before the time. Wesson shuddered.

Water spurted in the bathroom, hissing steadily on the tiles, rattling in the plastic bowl at the bottom of the shower stall. The light winked on and off again. In the dining room, he heard the autochef clucking and sighing. The freezing wind blew harder; he was numb with cold to the hips. It seemed to Wesson abruptly that he was not at the top of the sky at all, but down, *down* at the bottom of the sea—trapped in this steel bubble, while the dark poured in.

The pain in his head was gone, as if it had never been there, and he understood what that meant: Up there, the great body was hanging like butcher's carrion in the darkness. Its death struggles were over, the damage done.

Wesson gathered a desperate breath, shouted, "Help me! The alien's dead! He kicked the Station apart—the methane's coming in! Get help, do you hear me? *Do you hear me?*"

Silence. In the smothering blackness, he remembered: *She can't understand me anymore. Even if she's alive.*

He turned, making an animal noise in his throat. He groped his way on around the room, past the second doorway. Behind the walls, something was dripping with a slow cold tinkle and splash, a forlorn night sound. Small, hard, floating things rapped against his legs. Then he touched a smooth curve of metal—the air lock.

Eagerly he pushed his feeble weight against the door. It didn't move. Cold air was rushing out around the door frame, a thin knife-cold stream, but the door itself was jammed tight.

The suit! He should have thought of that before. If he just had some pure air to breathe and a little warmth in his fingers . . . But the door of the suit locker would not move, either. The ceiling must have buckled.

And that was the end, he thought, bewildered. There were no more ways out. But there *had* to be. . . . He pounded on the door until his arms would not lift anymore; it did not move. Leaning against the chill metal, he saw a single light blink on overhead.

The room was a wild place of black shadows and swimming shapes—the book leaves, fluttering and darting in the air stream. Schools of them beat wildly at the walls, curling over, baffled, trying again; others were swooping around the outer corridor, around and around; he could see them whirling past the doorways, dreamlike, a white drift of silent paper in the darkness.

The acrid smell was harsher in his nostrils. Wesson choked, groping his way to the console again. He pounded it with his open hand, crying weakly—he wanted to see Earth.

But when the little square of brightness leaped up, it was the dead body of the alien that Wesson saw.

It hung motionless in the cavity of the Station, limbs dangling stiff and still, eyes dull. The last turn of the screw had been too much for it. But Wesson had survived. . . .

For a few minutes.

The dead alien face mocked him; a whisper of memory floated into his mind: *We might have been brothers.* . . . All at once Wesson passionately wanted to believe it—wanted to give in, turn back. That passed. Wearily he let himself sag into the bitter *now*, thinking with thin defiance, *It's done— hate wins. You'll have to stop this big giveaway—can't risk this happening again. And we'll hate you for that—and when we get out to the stars—*

The world was swimming numbly away out of reach. He felt the last fit of coughing take his body, as if it were happening to someone else besides him.

The last fluttering leaves of paper came to rest. There was a long silence in the drowned room.

Then:

"Paul," said the voice of the mechanical woman brokenly; "Paul," it said again, with the hopelessness of lost, unknown, impossible love.

LOWER THAN ANGELS

By Algis Budrys

When we meet the aliens, how will we communicate with them? A standard piece of s-f equipment is generally offered as the answer: the "thought-converter." Most writers are content to haul the thought-converter from the closet, put it on their characters' heads, and let the conversation commence. One of the special features of this story is the care with which its author has depicted the communication problems that will be cropping up even when the handy thought-converter is available. He examines a deeper problem, too: how, when we drop down from the heavens to visit the inhabitants of other worlds, can we keep them from thinking of us as gods?

Algis Budrys, who has the general dimensions of an outstanding fullback and the story-telling ability of a master, was born in Lithuania in the decade before the outbreak of the Second World War and has spent most of his life in the United States. Since 1952 s-f readers have relished scores of his short stories and such thoughtful, searching novels as Rogue Moon *and* Who?

This was almost the end: Fred Imbry, standing tiredly at the jungle's edge, released the anchoring field. Streaming rain immediately began coming down on the parked sub-ship on the beach. The circle of sand formerly included in the field now began to splotch, and the sea dashed a wave against the landing jacks. The frothing water ran up the beach and curled around Imbry's ankles. In a moment, the sand was as wet as though nothing had ever held that bit of seashore free.

The wind was still at storm force. Under the boiling gray sky, the craft shivered from half-buried landing jacks to needle-nosed prow. Soggy fronds plastered themselves against the hull with sharp, liquid slaps.

Imbry trudged across the sand, slopping through the water,

wiping rain out of his face. He opened the sub-ship's airlock hatch and stopped, turning for one look back into the jungle.

His exhausted eyes were sunk deep into his face. He peered woodenly into the jungle's surging undergrowth. But there was no sign of anyone's having followed him; they'd let him go. Turning back, he hoisted himself aboard the ship and shut the hatch behind him. He opened the inside hatch and went through, leaving wet, sandy footprints across the deck.

He lay down in his piloting couch and began methodically checking off the board. When it showed green all around, he energized his starting engines, waited a bit, and moved his power switch to *Atmospheric*.

The earsplitting shriek of the jet throats beat back the crash of the sea and the keening of the wind. The jungle trees jerked away from the explosion of billowing air, and even the sea recoiled. The ship danced off the ground, and the landing jacks thumped up into their recesses. The sand poured out a shroud of towering steam.

The throttles advanced, and Imbry ascended into Heaven on a pillar of fire.

Almost at the beginning, a week earlier, Fred Imbry had been sitting in the *Sainte Marie*'s briefing room for the first time in his life, having been aboard the mother ship a little less than two weeks. He sat there staring up at Lindenhoff, whose reputation had long ago made him one of Imbry's heroes, and hated the carefully schooled way the Assignment Officer could create the impression of a judgment and capacity he didn't have.

Around Imbry, the other contact crewmen were listening carefully, taking notes on their thigh pads as Lindenhoff's pointer rapped the schematic diagram of the solar system they'd just moved into. Part of Imbry's hatred was directed at them, too. Incompetents and cowards though most of them were, they still knew Lindenhoff for what he was. They'd all served under him for a long time. They'd all been exposed to his dramatics. They joked about them. But now they were sitting and listening for all the world as if Lindenhoff was what he pretended to be—the fearless, resourceful leader in command of the vast, idealistic enterprise that was embodied in the *Sainte Marie*. But then, the mother ship, too, and the corporation that owned her, were just as rotten at the core.

Lindenhoff was a bear of a man. He was dressed in iron-gray coveralls; squat, thick, powerful-looking, he moved back and forth on the raised platform under the schematic. With the harsh overhead lighting, his close-cropped skull looked almost bald; naked and strong, a turret set on the short, seamed pillar of his neck. A thick white scar began over his right eye, crushed down through the thick jut of his brow ridge, the mashed arch of his blunt nose, and ended on the staved-in cheekbone under his left eye. Except for the scar, his face was burned brown and leathery, and even his lips were only a different shade of brown. The bright gold color of his eyebrows and the yellow straw of his lashes came close to glowing in contrast.

His voice was pitched deep. He talked in short, rumbled sentences. His thick arm jerked sharply each time he moved the pointer.

"Coogan, you're going into IV. You've studied the aerial surveys. No animal life. No vegetation. All naked rock where it isn't water. Take Petrick with you and do a mineralogical survey. You've got a week. If you hit anything promising, I'll extend your schedule. Don't go drawing any weapons. No more'n it takes to keep you happy, anyhow. Jusek's going to need 'em on VII."

Imbry's mouth twitched in disgust. The lighting. The platform on which Lindenhoff was shambling back and forth, never stumbling even when he stepped back without looking behind him. The dimensions of that platform must be clearly imprinted in his mind. Every step was planned, every gesture practiced. The sunburn, laid down by a battery of lamps. The careful tailoring of the coveralls to make that ursine body look taller.

Coogan and Petrick. The coward and the secret drunkard. Petrick had left a partner to die on a plague world. Coogan had shot his way out of a screaming herd of reptiles on his third contact mission—and had never gone completely unarmed, anywhere, in the ten years since.

The rest of them were no better. Ogin had certified a planet worthless. A year later, a small scavenger company had found a fortune in wolfram not six miles away from his old campsite. Lindenhoff hadn't seen fit to fire him. Kenton, the foulminded pathological liar. Maguire, who hated everything that walked or flew or crept, who ripped without pity at every world he contacted, and whose round face, with its boyish smile, was always broadcast along with a blushingly modest interview whenever the *Sainte Marie*'s latest job of opening up a new solar system was covered by the news programs.

Most of those programs, Imbry'd found out in the short time he'd been aboard, were bought and paid for by the Sainte Marie Development Corporation's public relations branch.

His thin hands curled up into tight knots.

The mother ships and the men who worked out of them were the legends of this generation—with the *Sainte Marie* foremost among them. Constantly working outward, putting system after system inside the known universe, they were the bright hungry wave of mankind reaching out to gather in the stars. The men were the towering figures marching into the wilderness—the men who died unprotestingly in the thousand traps laid by the unknown darkness beyond the Edge; the men who beat their way through the jungles of the night, leaving broad roads behind them for civilization to follow.

He had come aboard this ship like a man fulfilling a dream —and found Coogan sitting in the crew lounge.

"Imbry, huh? Pull up a chair. My name's Coogan." He was whipcord lean; a wiry, broad-mouthed man with a tough, easy grin and live brown eyes. "TSN man?"

Imbry'd shaken his hand before he sat down. It felt a little unreal, actually meeting a man he'd heard so much about, and having him act as friendly as this.

"That's right," Imbry said, trying to sound as casual as he could under the circumstances. Except for Lindenhoff and possibly Maguire, Coogan was the man he most admired. "My enlistment finally ran out last week. I was a rescue specialist."

Coogan nodded. "We get some good boys that way." He grinned and chuckled. "So Old Smiley slipped you a trial contract and here you are, huh?"

"Old Smiley?"

"Personnel manager. Glad hand, looks sincere, got distinguished white hair."

"Oh. Mr. Redstone."

Coogan grinned. "Sure. Mr. Redstone. Well—think you'll like it here?"

Imbry nodded. "It looks like it," he said carefully. He realized he had to keep his enthusiasm ruthlessly under control, or else appear to be completely callow and juvenile. Even before he'd known what he'd do after he got out, he'd been counting the days until his TSN enlistment expired. Having the Corporation offer him a contract on the day of his discharge had been a tremendous unexpected bonus. If he'd been sixteen instead of twenty-six, he would have said it was the greatest thing that could have happened to him. Being twenty-six, he said, "I figure it's a good deal."

Coogan winked at him. "You're not just kiddin', friend. We're on our way out to a system that looks pretty promising. Old Sainte Marie's in a position to declare another dividend if it pays off." He rubbed his thumb and forefinger together. "And how I do enjoy those dividends! Do a good job, lad. Do a bang-up job. Baby needs new shoes."

"I don't follow you."

"Buddy, I got half of my pay sunk into company stock. So do the rest of these guys. Couple years more, and I can get off this barge, settle down, and just cash checks every quarter for the rest of my life. And laugh like a fool every time I hear about you birds goin' out to earn me some more."

Imbry hadn't known what to make of it, at first. He'd mumbled an answer of some kind. But, listening to the other men talking—Petrick, with the alcohol puffing out on his breath; Kenton, making grandiose plans; Maguire, sneering coldly; Jusek, singlemindedly sharpening his bush knife—he'd gradually realized Coogan wasn't an exception in this crew of depraved, vicious fakes. Listening to them talk about the Corporation itself, he'd realized, too, that the "pioneers of civilization" line was something reserved for the bought-and-paid-for write-ups only. He wasn't dewy-eyed. He didn't expect the Corporation to be in business for its health. But neither had he expected it to be totally cynical and grasping, completely indifferent to whether anyone ever settled the areas it skimmed of their first fruits.

He learned, in a shatteringly short time, just what the contact crew men thought of each other, of the Corporation, and of humanity. They carped at, gossiped about, and despised each other. They took the Corporation's stock as part of their pay, and exploited all the more ruthlessly for it. They jockeyed for favored assignments, brought back as "souvenirs" anything valuable and sufficiently portable on the worlds they visited, and cordially hated the crews of all the rival mother ships. They weren't pioneers—they were looters, squabbling among themselves for the biggest share, and they made Imbry's stomach turn.

They were even worse than most of the TSN officers and men he'd known.

"Imbry."

He looked up. Lindenhoff was standing, arms akimbo, under the schematic at the head of the briefing room.

"Yes?" Imbry answered tightly.

"You take II. It's a rain-forest world. Humanoid inhabited."

"I've studied the surveys."

Lindenhoff's heavy mouth twitched. "I hope so. You're going alone. There's nothing the natives can do to you that you won't be able to handle. Conversely, there's nothing much of any value on the planet. You'll contact the natives and try to get them started on some kind of civilization. You'll explain what the Terran Union is, and the advantages of trade. They ought to be able to grow some luxury agricultural products. See how they'd respond toward developing a technology. If Coogan turns up some industrial ores on IV, they'd make a good market, in time. That's about the general idea. Nobody expects you to accomplish much—just push 'em in the right direction. Take two weeks. All straight?"

"Yes." Imbry felt his jaws tightening. Something for nothing, again. First the Corporation developed a market, then it sold it the ores it found on a neighboring world.

No, he wasn't angry about having been given an assignment that couldn't go wrong and that wouldn't matter much if it did. He was quite happy about it, because he intended to do as little for the Corporation as he could.

"All right, that's about it, boys," Lindenhoff finished up. He stepped off the platform and the lights above the schematic went out. "You might as well draw your equipment and get started. The quicker it all gets done, the quicker we'll get paid."

Coogan slapped him on the back as they walked out on the flight deck. "Remember what I said," he chuckled. "If there's any ambition in the gooks at all, shove it hard. Me, I'm going to be looking mighty hard for something to sell 'em."

"Yeah, sure!" Imbry snapped.

Coogan looked at him wide-eyed. "What's eating you, boy?"

Imbry took a deep breath. "You're eating me, Coogan. You and the rest of the setup." He stopped and glared tensely at Coogan. "I signed a contract. I'll do what I'm obligated to. But I'm getting off this ship when I come back, and if I ever hear about you birds again, I'll spit on the sidewalk when I do."

Coogan reddened. He took a step forward, then caught

himself and dropped his hands. He shook his head. "Imbry, I've been watching you go sour for the last week. All right, that's the breaks. Old Smiley made a mistake. It's not the first time—and you could have fooled me, too, at first. What's your gripe?"

"What d'you think it is? How about Lindenhoff's giving you Petrick for a partner?"

Coogan shook his head again, perplexed. "I don't follow you. He's a geologist, isn't he?"

Imbry stared at him in astonishment. "You don't follow me?" Coogan was the one who'd told him about Petrick's drinking. He remembered the patronizing lift to Coogan's lip as he looked across the lounge at the white-faced, muddy-eyed man walking unsteadily through the room.

"Let's move along," Lindenhoff said from behind them.

Imbry half turned. He looked down at the Assignment Officer in surprise. He hadn't heard the man coming. Neither had Coogan. Coogan nodded quickly.

"Just going, Lindy." Throwing another baffled glance at Imbry, he trotted across the deck toward his sub-ship, where Petrick was standing and waiting.

"Go on, son," Lindenhoff said. "You're holding up the show."

Imbry felt the knotted tension straining at his throat. He snatched up his pack.

"All right," he said harshly. He strode over to his ship, skirting out of the way of the little trucks that were humming back and forth around the ships, carrying supplies and maintenance crewmen. The flight deck echoed back to the clangs of slammed access hatches, the crash of a dropped wrench, and the soft whir of truck motors. Maintenance men were running back and forth, completing final checks, and armorers struggled with the heavy belts of ammunition being loaded into the guns on Jusek's ship. In the harsh glare of work lights, Imbry climbed up through his hatch, slammed it shut, and got up into his control compartment.

The ship was a slightly converted model of the standard TSN carrier scout.

He fingered the controls distastefully. Grimacing, he jacked in his communication leads and contacted the tower for a check. Then he set up his flight plan in the ballistic computer, interlocked his AutoNav, and sat back, waiting.

Lindenhoff and his fearsome scar. Souvenir of danger on a frontier world? Badge of courage? Symbol of intrepidness?

Actually, he'd gotten it when a piece of scaffolding fell on him during a production of *A Midsummer Night's Dream*, well before he ever came aboard the *Saint Marie*.

The flight deck cleared. Imbry set his ship's circulators. The flight-deck alarm blasted into life.

The deck canopy slid aside, and the flight deck's air billowed out into space. Imbry energized his main drive.

"Imbry clear for launch."

"Check, Imbry. Launch in ten."

He counted down, braced back against his couch. The catapult rammed him up off the deck, and he fired his engines. He rose high above the *Sainte Marie*, hovering, and then the ship nosed down and he trailed a wake of fire across the spangled night, in toward the foreign sun.

Almost from pole to pole, World II was the deep, lush color of rain-forest vegetation. Only at the higher latitudes was it interspersed with the surging brown-green of prairie grass and bush country, tapering into something like a temperate ecology at the very "top" and "bottom" of the planet. Where there was no land, there was the deeper, bluer, green of the sea. And on the sea, again, the green of islands.

Imbry balanced his ship on end, drifting slowly down. He wanted a good look and a long look.

His training in the TSN had fitted him admirably for this job. Admirably enough so that he depended more on his own observation than he did on the aerial survey results, which had been fed raw into a computer and emerged as a digested judgment on the planet's ecology and population, and the probable state and nature of its culture. The TSN applied this judgment from a military standpoint. The Corporation applied it to contact work. Imbry's experience had never known it to go far wrong. But he distrusted things mechanical, and so he hung in the sky for an hour or more, checking off promising-looking sites as they passed under him—and giving his bitterness and disillusion time to evaporate.

Down there was a race that had never heard of any people but itself; a race to which large portions of even its own planet must be unknown and enigmatic. A fairly happy race, probably. And if the Corporation found no significance in that, Imbry did. He was going to be their first touch with the incredible vastness in which they floated, and whatever he could do to smooth the shock and make their future easier, he meant to do, to the best of his ability. And if the Corporation had no feelings, he did. If there was no idealism aboard the *Sainte Marie,* there was some in him.

Finally, he picked an area on the eastern shore of the principal continent and drifted down toward it, slipping in over the swelling expanse of an island-speckled ocean. Following the curve of a chain of atolls extending almost completely across the sea, he lost altitude steadily, finding it possible now, with some of the tension draining out of him, to enjoy the almost effortless drift through the quiet sky and the quick responsiveness of his ship. It wasn't quite as he'd dreamed it, but it was good. The mother ship was far away, and here on this world he was alone, coming down just above the tops of the breakers, now, settling gently on a broad and gleaming beach.

The anchoring field switched on, and bored down until it found bedrock. The sand around the ship pressed down in a shallow depression. Imbry turned away from the beach and began to walk into the jungle, his detectors and pressor fields tingling out to all sides of him. He walked slowly in the direction of a village, wearing his suit with its built-in equipment, with his helmet slung back between his shoulder blades.

The jungle was typical rain forest. There were trees which met the climatic conditions, and therefore much resembled ordinary palms. The same was true of the thick undergrowth, and, from the sound of them, of the avian fauna. The chatter in the trees was not quite as harsh as the Terrestrial version, nor as shrill. From the little he'd seen, that seemed typical—a slightly more leisurely, slightly gentler world than the Pacific belt of Earth. He walked slowly, as much from quiet enjoyment as from caution. Overhead, the sky was a warm blue, with soft clouds hanging over the atolls at the horizon. The jungle ran with bright color and deep, cool green. Imbry's face lost its drawn-up tension, and his walk became relaxed.

He found a trail in a very short time, and began following it, trusting to his detectors and not looking around except in simple curiosity. And quite soon after that, his detector field pinged, and the pressor pushed back against the right side of his chest. He turned it down, stopped, and looked in that direction. The field was set for sentient life only, and he knew he was about to meet his first native. He switched on his linguistic computer and waited.

The native, when he stepped out on the trail, was almost humanoid enough to pass for a Terrestrial. His ears were set a bit differently, and his musculature was not quite the same. It was also impossible to estimate his age, for none of the usual Terrestrial clues were applicable. But those were the only differences Imbry could see. His skin was dark enough so there was no mistaking him for a Caucasian—if you applied human standards—but a great deal of that might be simple suntan. His hair was light brown, grew out of his scalp in an ordinary fashion, and had been cut. He was wearing a short, skirtlike garment, with a perfectly ordinary navel showing above it in a flat stomach. The pattern of his wrap-around was of the blocky type to which woven patterns are limited, and it was bright, in imitation of the forms and colors available in the jungle.

He looked at Imbry silently out of intelligent black eyes, with a tentative smile on his mouth. He was carrying nothing in his open hands, and he seemed neither upset nor timid.

Imbry had to wait until he spoke first. The computer had to have something to work with. Meanwhile, he smiled back. His TSN training had prepared him for situations exactly like this. In exercises, he'd duplicated this situation a dozen times, usually with ET's much more fearsome and much less human. So he merely smiled back, and there was no tension or misgiving in the atmosphere at all. There was only an odd, childlike shyness which, once broken, could only lead to an invitation to come over to the other fellow's house.

The native's smile broadened, and he raised one hand in greeting, breaking into soft, liquid speech that seemed to run on and on without stopping, for many syllables at a time.

The native finished, and Imbry had to wait for his translator to make up its mind. Finally, it whispered in his ear.

"This is necessarily a rough computation. The communication is probably: *Hello. Are you a god?* (That's an approximation. He means something between *ancestor* and *deity*.) *I'm very glad to meet you.*"

Imbry shook his head at the native, hoping this culture didn't take that to mean "yes." "No," he said to the computer, "I'm an explorer. And I'm glad to meet you." He continued to smile.

The computer hummed softly. "*Explorer* is inapplicable as yet," it told Imbry. It didn't have the vocabulary built up.

The native was looking curiously at the little box of the computer sitting on Imbry's shoulder. His jungle-trained ears were sharp, and he could obviously hear at least the sibilants as it whispered. His curiosity was friendly and intelligent; he seemed intrigued.

"All right, try: *I'm like you. Hello,*" Imbry told the computer.

The translator spoke to the native. He looked at Imbry in gentle unbelief and answered.

This time, it was easier. The translator sank its teeth into this new material, and after a much shorter lag, without qualification, gave Imbry the native's communication, in its colloquial English, somewhat flavored:

"Obviously, you're not like me very much. But we'll straighten that out later. Will you stay in my village for a while?"

Imbry nodded, to register the significance of the gesture. "I'd be glad to. My name's Imbry. What's yours?"

"Good. I'm Tylus. Will you walk with me? And who's the little ancestor on your shoulder?"

Imbry walked forward, and the native waited until they were a few feet apart and then began leading the way down the trail.

"That's not an ancestor," Imbry tried to explain. "It's a machine that changes your speech into mine and mine into yours." But the translator broke down completely at that. The best it could offer to do was to tell Tylus that it was a lever that talked. And *your speech* and *my speech* were concepts Tylus simply did not have.

In all conscience, Imbry had to cancel that, so he contented himself with saying it was not an ancestor. Tylus immediately asked which of Imbry's respected ancestors it would be if it *were* an ancestor, and it was obvious that the native regarded Imbry as being, in many respects, a charming liar. But it was also plain that charming liars were accorded due respect in Tylus's culture, so the two were fairly well acquainted by the time they reached the outskirts of the village, and there was no longer any lag in translation at all.

The village was built to suit the environment. The roofs and walls of the light, one-room houses were made of woven frond mats tied down to a boxy frame. Every house had a porch for socializing with passersby and a cookfire out front. Most of the houses faced in on a circular village square, with a big, communal cooking pit for special events, and the entire village was set in under the trees just a little away from the shoreline. There were several canoes on the sand above high water, and at some time this culture had developed the outrigger.

There was a large amount of shouting back and forth going on among the villagers, and a good-sized crowd had collected at the point where the trail opened out into the village clearing. But Tylus urged Imbry forward, passing proudly through the crowd, and Imbry went with him, feeling somewhat awkward about it, but not wanting to leave Tylus marching on alone. The villagers moved aside to let him through, smiling, some of them grinning at Tylus's straight back and proudly carried head, none of them, obviously, wanting to deprive their compatriot of his moment.

Tylus stopped when he and Imbry reached the big central cooking pit, turned around, and struck a pose with one arm around Imbry's shoulders.

"Hey! Look! I've brought a big visitor!" Tylus shouted, grinning with pleasure.

The villagers let out a whoop of feigned surprise, laughing and shouting congratulations to Tylus, and cordial welcomes to Imbry.

"He *says* he's not a god!" Tylus climaxed, giving Imbry a broad, sidelong look of grinning appreciation for his ability to be ridiculous. "He came out of a big *lhoni* egg on the beach, and he's got a father-ghost who sits on his shoulder in a little black pot and gives him advice!"

"Oh, that's ingenious!" someone in the crowd commented in admiration.

"Look how fair he is!" one of the women exclaimed.

"Look how much handsomer than us he is!"

"Look how richly he's dressed! Look at the jewels shining in his silver belt!"

Imbry's translator raced to give him representative crowd comments, and he grinned back at the crowd. His rescue training had always presupposed grim, hostile or at best noncommittal ET's that would have to be persuaded into helping him locate the crashed personnel of the stricken ship. Now, the first time he'd put it to actual use, he found reality giving theory a bland smile, and he sighed and relaxed completely. Once he'd disabused this village of its god-notions in connection with him, he'd be able to not only work but be friendly with these people. Not that they weren't already cordial.

He looked around at the crowd, both to observe it and to give everybody a look at his smile.

The crowd was composed, in nearly equal parts, of men

and women very much like Tylus, with no significant variation except for age and sex characteristics that ranged from
the appreciable to the only anthropologically interesting. In
lesser part, there were children, most of them a little timid,
some of them awestruck, all of them naked.

An older man, wearing a necklace of carved wood in addition to his wraparound, came forward through the crowd. Imbry had to guess at his age, but he thought he had it fairly accurately. The native had white hair, for one thing, and a slight
thickness to his waist. For another, he was rather obviously
the village head man, and that indicated age and the experience it brought with it.

The head man raised his arm in greeting, and Imbry
replied.

"I am Iano. Will you stay with us in our village?"

Imbry nodded. "My name's Imbry. I'd like to stay here for
a while."

Iano broke into a smile. "Fine! We're all very glad to meet
you. I hope your journey can be interrupted for a long time."
He smiled. "Well, if you say you're not a god, who do you say
you are?" There was a ripple of chuckling through the
crowd.

"I'm a man," Imbry answered. The translator had meanwhile worked out the proper wording for what he wanted to
say next. "I'm an explorer from another country." The local
word, of course, was not quite "explorer"—it was *traveler-from-
other-places-for-the-enjoyment-of-it-and-to-see-what-I-can-find*.

Iano chuckled. Then, gravely, he asked: "Do you always
travel in an *lhoni* egg, Imbry-who-says-he-is-Imbry?"

Imbry chuckled back in appreciation of Iano's shrewdness.
He was enjoying this, even if it was becoming more and more
difficult to approach the truth.

"That's no *lhoni* egg," he deprecated with a broad gesture
to match. "That's only my . . ." And here the translator had
to give up and render the word as *canoe*.

Iano nodded with a gravity so grave it was obviously no
gravity at all. Tylus, standing to one side, gave Imbry a look
of total admiration at this effort which overmatched all his
others.

"Ah. Your canoe. And how does one balance a canoe
shaped like an *lhoni* egg?"

Imbry realized what the translator had had to do. He'd
been afraid of as much. He searched for the best answer, and

the best answer seemed to be to tell the truth and stick to it. These people were intelligent. If he presented them with a consistent story and backed it up with as much proof as he could muster, they'd eventually see that nothing so scrupulously self-consistent could possibly be anything but the truth.

"Well," he said slowly, wondering what the effect would be at first, "it's a canoe that doesn't sail on water. It sails in the sky."

There was a chorus of admiration through the crowd. As much of it seemed to be meant for Iano as for Imbry. They appeared to think Imbry had made a damaging admission in this contest.

Iano smiled. "Is your country in the sky?"

Imbry struggled for some way of making it understandable. "Yes and no," he said carefully. "It's necessary to travel through the sky to get to my country, but when you get there you're in a place that's very much like here, in some ways."

Iano smiled again. "Well, of course. How else would you be happy if there weren't places like this to live, in the sky?"

He turned toward the other villagers. "He *said* he wasn't a god," he declared quietly, his eyes twinkling.

There was a burst of chuckling, and now all the admiring glances were for Iano.

The head man turned back to Imbry. "Will you stay in my house for a while? We will produce a feast later in the day."

Imbry nodded gravely. "I'd be honored." The villagers were smiling at him gently as they drifted away, and Imbry got the feeling that they were being polite and telling him that his discomfiture didn't really matter.

"Don't be sad," Tylus whispered. "Iano's a remarkably shrewd man. He could make anybody admit the truth. I'm quite sure that when he dies, he'll be some kind of god himself."

Then he waved a hand in temporary farewell and moved away, leaving Imbry alone with the gravely smiling Iano.

Imbry sat on the porch with Iano. Both of them looked out over the village square, sitting side by side. It seemed to be the expected posture for conversation between a god and someone who was himself a likely candidate for a similar position, and it certainly made for ease of quiet contemplation before each new sentence was brought out into words.

Imbry was still wearing his suit. Iano had politely suggested that he might be warm in it, but Imbry had explained.

"It cools me. That's only one of the things it does. For one thing, if I took it off I wouldn't be able to talk to you. In my country we have different words."

Iano had thought about it for a moment. Then he said: "Your wraparound must have powerful ancestors living in it." He thought a moment more. "Am I right in supposing that this is a new attribute you're trying out, and it hasn't grown up enough to go about without advice?"

Imbry'd been glad of several minutes in which to think. Then he'd tried to explain.

"No," he said, "the suit" (perforce, the word was *wraparound-for-the-whole-body*) "was made—was built—by other men in my country. It was built to protect me and to make me able to travel anywhere without being in any danger." But that was only just as much as repeating Iano's theory back to him in different form, and he realized it after Iano's polite silence had extended too long to be anything but an answer in itself.

He tried to explain the concept "machine."

"I'll teach you a new word for a new thing," he said. Iano nodded attentively.

Imbry switched off the translator, making sure Iano saw the motion and understood the result. Then he repeated "machine" several times, and, once Iano had accustomed himself to Imbry's new voice, which up to now he'd only heard as an indistinct background murmur to the translator's speaker, the head man picked it up quickly.

"Mahschin," he said at last, and Imbry switched his translator back on. "Go on, Imbry."

"A machine is a number of levers, working together. It is built by perfectly ordinary artisans—not gods, Iano, but men like yourself and myself—who have a good deal of knowledge and skill. With one lever, you can raise a tree trunk. With many levers, shaped into paddles, men can push the tree trunk through the water, after they have shaped it into a canoe.

"So a machine is like the many levers that move the canoe. But usually it doesn't need men to push it. It goes on by itself, because it—"

Here he had to stop for a minute. These people had no concept of storing energy and then releasing it to provide motive power. Iano waited, patient and polite.

"It has a little bit of fire in it," Imbry was forced to say lamely. "Fire can be put in a box—in something like two pots fastened tightly on top of each other—so that it can't get out.

But it wants to get out—it pushes against the inside of the two pots—so if you make a hole in the pots and put a lever in the way, the fire rushing out pushes the lever."

He looked at Iano, but couldn't make out whether he was being believed or not. Half the time, he had no idea what kind of almost-but-sadly-not-quite concepts the translator might be substituting for the things he was saying.

"A machine can be built to do almost anything that would otherwise require a lot of men. For instance, I could have brought another man with me who was skilled at learning words that weren't his. Then I wouldn't need the little black pot, which is a machine that learns words that aren't the same as mine. But the machine does it faster and in some ways better."

He stopped, hoping Iano had understood at least part of it.

After a time, Iano nodded gravely. "That's very ingenious. It saves your ancestors the inconvenience of coming with you and fatiguing themselves. I had no idea such a thing could be done. But of course, in your country there are different kinds of fires than we have here."

Which was a perfectly sound description, Imbry had to admit, granting Iano's viewpoint.

So now they'd been sitting quietly for a number of minutes, and Imbry had begun to realize that he might have to work for a long time before he extricated himself from this embarrassment. Finally he said, "Well, if you think I'm a god, what kind of a god do you think I am?"

Iano answered slowly. "Well, to tell you the truth, I don't know. You might be an ancestor. Or you might be only a man who has made friends with a lot of his ancestors." Imbry felt a flash of hope, but Iano went on: "Which, of course, would make you a god. Or—" He paused, and Imbry, taking a sideward look, caught Iano looking at him cautiously. "Or you might be no ancestor and no man-god. You might be one of the very-real-gods. You might be the cloud god, or the jungle god, taking the attribute of a man. Or . . . you might be *the* god. You might be the-father-of-all-*lhoni*."

Imbry took a deep breath. "Would you describe the *lhoni* to me, please," he said.

"Certainly." Iano's voice and manner were still cautious. "The *lhoni* are animals which live in the sea or on the beaches, as they choose. They leave their eggs on the beaches, but they rear their young in the sea. They are fishers, and they are

very wise. Many of them are ancestors. He said it with unusual respect and reverence.

Imbry sat quietly again. The god who was the-father-of-all-
the-*lhoni* would not only be the father of many ancestors,
who were themselves minor gods, he would also control the
sea, everything pertaining to the sea, the beaches, probably all
the islands, and the fates of those whose lives were tied to the
sea, who were themselves fishers, like the villagers. Imbry
wondered how much geography the villagers knew. They
might consider that the land was always surrounded by ocean
—that, as a matter of fact, the universe consisted of ocean
encircling a relatively small bit of land.

If Iano thought that was who Imbry might be, then he
might very well be thinking that he was in the presence of the
greatest god there was. A typical god, of course—there wasn't
a god in the world who didn't enjoy a joke, a feast, and a
good untruth-for-the-fun-of-everybody at least as much as
anybody else—but still, though you might not expect too
much of the household lares and penates, when it came to
Jupiter himself . . .

Imbry couldn't let that go on. Almost anything might happen. He might leave a religion behind him that, in a few gen-
erations of distortion, might twist itself—and the entire
culture—into something monstrous. He might leave the way
open for the next Corporation man to practice a brand of ex-
ploitation that would be near to unimaginable.

Imbry remembered what the *conquistadores* had done in
Central and South America, and his hackles rose.

"No!" he exploded violently, and Iano recoiled a little, startled. "No, I'm not a god. Not any kind. I'm a man—a different kind of man, maybe, but just a man. The fact that I have
a few machines doesn't prove anything. The fact that I know
more about some things than you do doesn't prove anything. I
come from a country where the people can keep records, so
nothing's lost when a man who has some wisdom dies. I've
been taught out of those records, and I'm helped by machines
built by other men who study other records. But you think my
people are any better than yours? You think the men I have
to work with are good or brave or kind? No more than you.
Less. We kill each other, we take away from other people
what isn't ours, we lie—we tell *untruths-for-unfair-advantage*
—we leave bad where we found good—we're just men, we're
not anything like gods, and we never will be!"

Iano had recovered his composure quickly. He nodded.

"No doubt," he said. "No doubt, to one god other gods are much like other men are to a man. Possibly even gods have gods. But that is not for us to say. We are men *here,* not in the country of the gods. There is the jungle, the sky, and the sea. And those who know more places than that must be our gods." He looked at Imbry with quick sympathy. "It's sad to know that even a god must be troubled."

The odds were low that any of the food served at the feast could hurt him. Aside from the fact that the ecology was closely parallel to Earth's, Imbry's system was flooded with Antinfect from the precautionary shot he'd gotten aboard the mother ship. But he couldn't afford to take the chance of getting sick. It might help destroy the legend gathered around him, but it would also leave him helpless. He had too much to do in too short a time to risk that. So he politely faked touching his tongue to each of the dishes as it was passed to him, and settled for a supper of rations out of his suit, grimacing as he heard someone whisper behind him that the god had brought his own god-food with him, because the food of men could not nourish him in this attribute.

No matter what he did, he couldn't shake the faith of the villagers. It was obvious at a glance that he was a god; therefore, *ipso facto,* everything he did was godlike.

He sat beside Iano and his wives, watching the fire roar in the communal pit and listening to the pounding beat of the musicians, but, even though the villagers were laughing happily and enjoying themselves immensely, he could not recapture the mood of easy relaxation he had borrowed from them and their world this afternoon. The *Sainte Marie* pressed too close to him. When he left here, he'd never be able to come back— and a ravaged world would haunt him for the rest of his life.

"Hey! Imbry! Look what I've got to show you!"

He looked up, and there was Tylus, coming toward him hand in hand with a quietly beautiful girl, and holding a baby just into the toddling stage. The child was being half led, half dragged, and seemed to be enjoying it.

Imbry smiled broadly. There was no getting away from it. Tylus enjoyed life so hugely that nobody near him could quite escape the infection.

"This is my woman, Pia," Tylus said with a proud grin, and the girl smiled shyly. "And this one hasn't got his name yet."

He reached down and slapped the baby playfully, and the boy grinned from ear to ear.

Everyone around the fire chuckled. Imbry grinned despite himself and nodded gravely to Tylus. "I'm glad to meet them." He smiled at Pia. "She must have been blind to pick you when she could have had so much better." The girl blushed, and everyone burst into laughter, while Tylus postured in proud glee. Imbry nodded toward the boy. "If he didn't look so much like his father, I'd say he was a fine one."

There was fresh laughter, and Imbry joined in it because he almost desperately needed to; but after it trailed away and Tylus and his family were gone back into their hut, after the fire died and the feast was over, when Imbry lay on the mat in Iano's house and the wind clashed the tree fronds while the surf washed against the beach—then Imbry lay tightly awake.

Given time—given a year or two—he might be able to break down the villagers' idea about him. But he doubted it. Iano was right. Even if he threw away his suit and left himself with no more equipment than any of the villagers possessed, he knew too much. Earth and the Terran Union were his heritage, and that was enough to make a god of any man among these people. If he so much as introduced the wheel into this culture, he was doing something none of these people had conceived of in all their history.

And he had nothing like a year. In two weeks' time, even using eidetic techniques, he could barely build up enough of a vocabulary in their language to do without his translator for simpler conversations. And, again, it wouldn't make a particle of difference whether he spoke their language or not. Words would never convince them.

But he had to get through to them somehow.

The cold fact was that during a half day's talk, he hadn't gotten anyone in the village to take literally even the slightest thing he said. He was a god. Gods speak in allegories, or gods proclaim laws. Gods do not speak man to man. And if they do, rest assured it is part of some divine plan, designed to meet inscrutable ends by subtle means.

What was it Lindenhoff had told him?

"You'll contact the natives and try to get them started on some kind of civilization. You'll explain what the Terran Union is and the advantages of trade. See how they'd respond toward developing a technology."

It couldn't be done. Not by a god who might, at worst, be only a demigod, who might at best even be *the* god, and who could not, under any circumstances, possibly be considered on a par with the other travelers-for-pleasure who occasionally turned up from over the sea but who were manifestly only other men.

He wasn't supposed to be a stern god or an omnipotent god or a being above the flesh. That kind of deity took a monotheist to appreciate him. He was simply supposed to be a god of these people—vain and happily boastful at times, a liar at times, a glutton at times, a drunkard at times, timid at times, adventurous at times, a hero at times, and heir to other sins of the flesh at other times, but always powerful, always above the people in wisdom of his own kind, always a god. Always a mute with a whispering ancestor on his shoulder.

But if he left them now, they'd be lost. Someone else would come down, and be a god. Kenton, or Ogin or Maguire the killer. And when the new god realized the situation, he'd stop trying to make these people into at least some kind of rudimentary market. They wouldn't even have that value to turn them into an interest to be protected. Lindenhoff would think of something else to do with them, for the Corporation's good. Turn them into a labor force for the mines Coogan would be opening up on IV, perhaps. Or else enslave them here. Have the god nudge them into becoming farmers for the luxury market or introduce a technology whether they understood it or not.

That might work. If the god and his fellow gods found stones for them to dig and smelt into metal, and showed them how to make machines, they might do it.

To please the god by following his advice. Not because they understood or wanted machines—or needed them—but to fulfill the god's inscrutable plan. They'd sicken with the bewilderment in their hearts and lose their smiles in the smelter's heat. The canoes would rot on the beaches, and the fishing spears would break. The houses would crumble on the ocean's edge until the sea reached up and swept the village clean, and the *lhoni* eggs would hatch out in the warming sun. The village would be gone, and its people slaving far away, lonesome for their ancestors.

He had to do it. Somehow, within these two weeks, he had to give them a chance of some kind.

It would be his last chance, too. Twenty-six years of life and all of it blunted. He was failing here, with the taste of the

Corporation bitter in his mouth. He'd found nothing in the TSN but brutal officers and cynical men waiting for a war to start somewhere, so the promotions and bonuses would come, and meanwhile making the best they could out of what police actions and minor skirmishes there were with weak alien races. Before that, school, and a thousand time-markers and campus wheels for everyone who thought that some day, if he was good enough, he'd have something to contribute to Mankind.

The god had to prove to be human after all. And the human could talk to these other men, as just another man, and then perhaps they might advance of themselves to the point where they could begin a civilization that was part of them and part of some plan of theirs, instead of some god's. And someday these people, too, would land their metal canoes on some foreign beach under a foreign sun.

He had to destroy himself. He had to tear down his own façade.

Just before he fell into his fitful sleep, he made his decision. At the first opportunity to be of help in some way they would consider more than manlike, he'd fail. The legend would crumble, and he could be a man.

He fell asleep, tense and perspiring, and the stars hung over the world, with the mother ship among them.

The chance came. He couldn't take it.

Two days had gone by, and nothing had happened to change the situation. He spent two empty days talking to Iano and as many other villagers as he could, and the only knowledge they gained was an insight into the ways of gods, who proved, after all, to be very much like men, on their own grander scale. One or two were plainly saddened by his obvious concern over something they, being unfortunately only men, could not quite grasp. Iano caught something of his mood and was upset by it until his face fell into a puzzled, concerned look that was strange to it. But it only left him and Imbry further apart. There was no bridge between them.

On the third day, the sea was flat and oily, and the air lay dankly still across the village. The tree fronds hung down limply, and the clouds thickened gradually during the night, so that Imbry woke up to the first sunless day he'd seen. He got up as quietly as he could and left Iano's house, walking slowly across the compound toward the sea. He stood on the beach, looking out across the glassy swells, thinking back to the first hour in which he'd hung above that ocean and slowly come down with the anticipation burning out the disgust in him.

He threw a shell as far out into the water as he could, and watched it skip once, skip twice, teeter in the air, and knife into the water without a splash. Then he turned around and walked slowly back into the village, where one or two women were beginning to light their cook-fires.

He greeted them listlessly, and they answered gravely, their easy smiles dying. He wandered over towards Tylus's house. And heard Pia crying.

"Hello!"

Tylus came out of the house, and for the first time Imbry saw him looking strained, his lips white at the corners. "Hello, Imbry," he said in a tired voice.

"What's wrong, Tylus?"

Tylus shrugged. "The baby's going to die."

Imbry stared up at him. "Why?"

"He cut his foot yesterday morning. I put a poultice on it. It didn't help. His foot's red today, and it hurts him to touch it. It happens."

"Oh, no, it doesn't. Not anymore. Let me look at him." Imbry came up the short ladder to Tylus's porch. "It can't be anything I can't handle."

He knew the villagers' attitude toward death. Culturally, death was the natural result of growing old, or being born weak, and, sometimes, of having a child. Sometimes, too, a healthy person could suddenly get a pain in the belly, lie in agony for a day, and then die. Culturally, it usually made the victim an ancestor, and grief for more than a short time was something the villagers were too full of living to indulge in. But sometimes it was harder to take; in this tropical climate, a moderately bad cut could infect like wildfire, and then some-one died who didn't seem to have been ready for it.

Tylus's eyes lighted up for a moment. Then they became gravely steady.

"You don't have to if you don't want to, Imbry. Suppose some other god wants him? Suppose his ancestors object to your stepping in? And—and besides—" Tylus dropped his eyes. "I don't know. Maybe you're not a god."

Imbry couldn't stop to argue. "I'd like to look at him anyway. No matter what might happen."

The hopelessness drained out of Tylus's face. He touched

Imbry's arm. "Come into my house," he said, repeating the social formula gratefully. "Pia! Imbry's here to make the baby well!"

Imbry strode into the house, pulling his medkit out of his suit. Pia turned away from the baby's mat, raising her drawn face. Then she jumped up and went to stand next to Tylus, clenching his hand.

The baby was moving his arms feverishly, and his cheeks were flushed. But he'd learned, through the night, not to move the bandaged foot.

Imbry cut the scrap of cloth away with his bandage shears, wincing at the puffy, white-lipped gash. He snapped the pencil light out of its clip and took a good look into the wound.

It was dirty as sin, packed with some kind of herb mixture that was hopelessly embedded in the tissues. Cleaning it thoroughly was out of the question. Cursing softly, he did the best he could, not daring to try the anesthetic syrette in the kit. He had no idea of what even a human child's dose might be.

He had to leave a lot of the poultice in the wound. Working as fast as he could, he spilled an envelope of antibiotics over the gash, slapped on a fresh bandage, and then stood up. Antipyretics were out. The boy'd have to have his fever. There was one gamble he had to take, but he wasn't going to take any more. He held up the ampule of Antinfect.

"Universal Antitoxin" was etched into the glass. Well, it had better be.

He broke the seal and stabbed the tip of his hyposprayer through the diaphragm. He retracted carefully. It was a three cc ampule. About half of it ought to do. He watched the dial on the sprayer with fierce concentration, inching the knob around until it read "1.5," and yanking the tip out.

Muttering a prayer, he fired the Antinfect into the boy's leg. Then he sighed, repacked his kit, and turned around.

"If I haven't killed him, he'll be all right." He gestured down at the bandage. "There's going to be a lot of stuff coming out of that wound. Let it come. Don't touch the bandage. I'll take another look at it in a few hours. Meanwhile, let me know right away if he looks like he's getting worse" He smiled harshly. "And let me know if he's getting better, too."

Pia was looking at him with an awestruck expression on her face. Tylus' glance clung to the medkit and then traveled up to Imbry's eyes.

"You are a god," he said in a whisper. "You are more than a god. You are the god of all other gods."

"I know," Imbry growled. "For good and all now, even if the boy dies. I'm a god now no matter what I do." He strode out of the house and out across the village square, walking in short, vicious strides along the beach until he was out of sight of the village. He stood for a long time, looking out across the gray sea. And then, with a crooked twist to his lips and a beaten hopelessness in his eyes, he walked back into the village because there was nothing else he could do.

Lord knew where the hurricane had been born. Somewhere down the chain of islands—or past them—the mass of air had begun to whirl. Born out of the ocean, it spun over the water for hundreds of miles, marching toward the coast.

The surf below the village sprang into life. It lashed along the strand in frothing, growling columns, and the *lhoni* eggs washed out of their nests and rolled far down the slope of the beach before the waves picked them up again and crushed them against the stones and shells.

The trees tore the edges of their fronds against each other, and the broken ends flew away on the wind. The birds in the jungle began to huddle tightly into themselves.

"Your canoe," Iano said to Imbry as they stood in front of the head man's house.

Imbry shook his head. "It'll stand."

He watched the families taking their few essential belongings out of their houses and storing them inside the overturned canoes that had been brought high inland early in the afternoon.

"What about this storm? Is it liable to be bad?"

Iano shook his head noncommittally. "There're two or three bad ones every season."

Imbry grunted and looked out over the village square. Even if the storm mashed the houses flat, they'd be up again two days afterward. The sea and the jungle gave food, and the fronded trees gave shelter. He saw no reason why these people wanted gods in the first place.

He saw a commotion at the door of Tylus's house. Tylus and Pia stood in the doorway. Pia was holding the baby.

"Look! Hey! Look!" Tylus shouted. The other villagers turned, surprised.

"Hey! Come look at my baby! Come look at the boy Imbry made well!" But Tylus himself didn't follow his own advice. As the other villagers came running, forgetting the possessions piled beside the canoes, he broke through them and ran across the square to Imbry and Iano.

"He's fine! He stopped crying! His leg isn't hot anymore, and we can touch it without hurting him!" Tylus shouted, looking up at Imbry.

Imbry didn't know whether to laugh or cry. He smiled with an agonized twist of his mouth. "I thought I told you not to touch that foot."

"But he's *fine*, Imbry! He's even laughing!" Tylus was gesturing joyfully. "Imbry—"

"Yes?"

"Imbry, I want a gift."

"A gift?"

"Yes. I want you to give him your name. When his naming day comes, I want him to call himself The Beloved of Imbry."

My God, Imbry thought, I've done it! I've saddled them with the legend of myself. He looked down at Tylus. "Are you sure?" he asked, feeling the words come out of his tight throat.

"I would like it very much," Tylus answered with sudden quietness.

And there was nothing Imbry could say but, "All right. When his naming day comes, if you still want to."

Tylus nodded. Then, obviously, he realized he'd run out of things to say and do. With Imbry the ancestor, or Imbry *the-man-with-many-powerful-ancestors;* with Imbry the demigod, he could have found something else to talk about. But this was Imbry, the god of all gods, and that was different.

"Well . . . I have to be with Pia. Thank you." He threw Imbry one more grateful smile and trotted back across the square, to where the other villagers were clustered around Pia, talking excitedly and often looking with shy smiles in Imbry's direction.

It was growing rapidly darker. Night was coming, and the hurricane was trudging westward with it. Imbry looked at Iano, with his wraparound plastered against his body by the force of the wind and his face in the darkness under the overhanging porch roof.

"What'll you do when the storm comes?" Imbry asked.

Iano gestured indefinitely. "Nothing, if it's a little one. If it's bad, we'll get close to the trees, on the side away from the wind."

"Do you think it looks like it'll get bad?"

Iano gestured in the same way. "Who knows?" he said. looking at Imbry.

Imbry looked at him steadily. "I'm only a man. I can't make it better or worse. I can't tell you what it's going to be. I'm only a man, no matter what Tylus and Pia think."

Iano gestured again. "There are men. I know that much because I am a man. There may be other men, who are our ancestors and our gods, who in their turn have gods. And those gods may have greater gods. But I am a man, and I know what I see and what I am. Later, after I die and am an ancestor, I may know other men like myself, and call them men. But these people who are not yet ancestors—" He swept his arm in a gesture that encircled the village. "—these people will call me a god, if I choose to visit them.

"To Tylus and Pia—and to many others—you are the god of all gods. To myself . . . I don't know. Perhaps I am too near to being an ancestor not to think there may be other gods above you. But," he finished, "they are not my gods. They are yours. And to me you are more than a man."

The hurricane came with the night, and the sea was coldly phosphorescent as it battered at the shore. The wind screamed invisibly at the trees. The village square was scoured clean of sand and stones, and the houses were groaning.

The villagers sat on the ground, resting their backs against the thrashing trees.

Imbry couldn't accustom himself to the constant sway. He stood motionless beside the tree that sheltered Iano, using his pressors to brace himself. He knew the villagers were looking at him through the darkness, taking it as one more proof of what he was, but that made no difference any longer. He faced into the storm, feeling the cold sting of the wind.

Lindenhoff would be overjoyed. And Maguire would grin coldly. Coogan would count his money, and Petrick would drink a solitary toast to the helpless suckers he could make do anything he wanted.

And Imbry? He let the cold spray dash against his face and didn't bother to wipe it off. Imbry was ready to quit.

The universe was made the way it was, and there was no changing it, whether to suit his ideas of what men should be or not. The legendary heroes of the human race—the brave, the brilliant, selfless men who broke the constant trail for the rest of Mankind to follow—must have been a very different breed from what the stories said they were.

A house crashed over on the far side of the village and

crushed apart. He heard a woman moan in brief fear, but
then her man must have quieted her, for there was no further
sound from any of the dim figures huddled against the trees
around him.

The storm rose higher. For a half hour, Imbry listened to
the houses tearing down, and felt the spray in his face thicken
until it was like rain. The phosphorescent wall of surf crept
higher on the beach, until he could see it plainly; a tumbling,
ghostly mass in among the trees nearest the beach. The wind
became a solid wall, and he turned up the intensity on his
pressors. He had no way of knowing whether the villagers
were making any sound or not.

He felt a tug at his leg, and bent down, turning off his pressors. Iano was looking up at him, his face distorted by the
wind, his hair standing away from one side of his head. Imbry
closed one arm around the tree.

"What?" Imbry bellowed into the translator, and the
translator tried to bellow into Iano's ear.

"It . . . very . . . very bad . . . very . . . rain . . . no rain . . ."

The translator struggled to get the message through to Imbry, but the wind tore it to tatters.

"Yes, it's bad," Imbry shouted. "What was that about rain?"

"Imbry . . . when . . . rain . . ."

Clearly and distinctly, he heard a woman scream. There
was a second's death for the wind. And then the rain and the
sea came in among the trees together.

White, furious water tore at his legs and pushed around his
waist. He gagged on salt. Coughing and choking, he tried to
see what was happening to the villagers.

But he was cut off in a furious, pounding, sluicing mass of
water pouring out of the sky at last, blind and isolated as he
tried to find air to breathe. He felt it washing into his suit,
filling its legs, weighing his feet down. He closed his helmet in
a panic, spilling its water down over his head, and as he
snapped it tight another wave raced through the trees to break
far inland, and he lost his footing.

He tumbled over and over in the churning water, fumbling
for his pressor controls. Finally he got to them and snapped
erect, with the field on full. The water broke against his face
plate, flew away, and he was left standing in a bubble of emptiness that exactly outlined the field. Sea water walled it from
the ground to the height of his face, and the rain roofed it
from above.

Blind inside his bubble, he waited for the morning.

He awoke to a dim light filtering through to him, and he looked up to see layer after layer of debris piled atop his bubble. It was still raining, but the solid cloudburst was over. There was still water on the ground, but it was only a few inches deep. He collapsed his field, and the pulped sticks and chips of wood fell in a shower on him. He threw back his helmet and looked around.

The water had carried him into the jungle at the extreme edge of the clearing where the village had stood, and from where he was he could see out to the heaving ocean.

The trees were splintered and bent. They lay across the clearing, pinning down a few slight bits of wreckage. But almost all traces of the village were gone. Where the canoes with their household possessions had lain in an anchored row, there was nothing left.

Only a small knot of villagers stood in the clearing. Imbry tried to count them; tried to compare them to the size of the crowd that had welcomed him into the village, and stopped. He came slowly forward, and the villagers shrank back. Iano stepped out to meet him and, slowly, Tylus.

"Iano, I'm sorry," Imbry said in a dull voice, looking around the ravaged clearing again. If he'd had any idea the hurricane could possibly be that bad, he would have called the mother ship for help. Lindenhoff would have fired into the storm and disrupted it, to save his potential slaves.

"Why did this happen, Imbry?" Iano demanded. "Why was this done to us?"

Imbry shook his head. "I don't know. A storm . . . Nobody can blame anything."

Iano clenched his fists.

"I did not ask during the whole day beforehand, though I knew what would happen. I did not even ask in the beginning of the storm. But when I knew the rain must come, when the sea growled and the wind stopped, *then*, at last, I asked you to make the storm die. Imbry, you did nothing. You made yourself safe, and you did nothing. *Why was this done?*"

Iano's torso quivered with bunched muscles. His eyes blazed. "If you were who we believed you to be, if you made Tylus's boy well, why did you do this? *Why did you send the storm?*"

It was the final irony: Apparently, if Iano had accepted Imbry as a man, he would have told him in advance how bad the storm was likely to be. . . .

Imbry shook his head. "I'm not a god, Iano," he repeated

dully. He looked at Tylus, who was standing pale and bitter eyed behind Iano.

"Are they safe, Tylus?"

Tylus looked silently over Imbry's shoulder, and Imbry turned his head to follow his glance. He saw the paler shape crushed around the trunk of a tree, one arm still gripping the boy.

"I must make a canoe," Tylus said in a dead voice. "I'll go on a long *journey-to-leave-the-sadness-behind*. I'll go where there aren't any gods like you."

"Tylus!"

But Iano clutched Imbry's arm, and he had to turn back toward the head man.

"We'll all have to go. We can't ever stay here again." The grip tightened on Imbry's arm, and the suit automatically pressed it off. Iano jerked his arm away.

"The storm came because of you. It came to teach us something. We have learned it." Iano stepped back. "You're not a great god. You tricked us. You're a bad ancestor—you're sick —you have the touch of death in your hand."

"I never said I was a god." Imbry's voice was unsteady. "I told you I was only a man."

Tylus looked at him out of his dead eyes. "How can you possibly be a man like us? If you're not a god, then you're a demon."

Imbry's face twisted. "You wouldn't listen to me. It's not my fault you expected something I couldn't deliver. Is it my fault you couldn't let me be what I am?"

"We know what you are," Tylus said.

There wasn't anything Imbry could tell him. He slowly turned away from the two natives and began the long walk back to the sub-ship.

He finished checking the board and energized his starting motors. He waited for a minute and threw in his atmospheric drive.

The rumble of jet throats shook through the hull, and throbbed in the control compartment. The ship broke free, and he retracted the landing jacks.

The throttles advanced, and Imbry fled into the stars.

He sat motionless for several minutes. The memory of Tylus's lifeless voice etched itself into the set of his jaw and the backs of his eyes. It seemed impossible that it wouldn't be there forever.

There was another thing to do. He clicked on his communicator.

"This is Imbry. Get me Lindenhoff."

"Check, Imbry. Stand by."

He lay in the piloting couch, waiting, and when the image of Lindenhoff's face built up on the screen, he couldn't quite meet its eyes.

"Yeah, Imbry?"

He forced himself to look directly into the screen. "I'm on my way in, Lindenhoff. I ran into a problem. I'm dictating a full report for the files, but I wanted to tell you first—and I think I've got the answer."

Lindenhoff grinned slowly. "Okay, Fred."

Lindenhoff was waiting for him as he berthed the sub-ship aboard the *Sainte Marie*. Imbry climbed out and looked quietly at the man.

Lindenhoff chuckled. "You look exactly like one of our real veterans," he said. "A hot bath and a good meal'll take care of that." He chuckled again. "It will, too—it takes more than once around the track before this business starts getting you."

"So you figure I'll be staying on," Imbry said, feeling tired-er and older than he ever had in his life. "How do you know I didn't make a real mess of it, down there?"

Lindenhoff chuckled. "You made it back in one piece, didn't you? That's the criterion, Fred. I hate to say so, but it is. No mess can possibly be irretrievable if it doesn't kill the man who made it. Besides—you don't know enough to tell whether you made any mistakes or not."

Imbry grunted, thinking Lindenhoff couldn't possibly know how much of an idiot he felt like and how much he had on his conscience.

"Well, let's get to this report of yours," Lindenhoff said.

Imbry nodded slowly. They walked off the *Sainte Marie*'s flight deck into the labyrinth of steel decks below.

It was three seasons after the storm, and Tylus was still on his journey. One day he came to a new island and ran his ca-noe up on the beach. Perhaps here he wouldn't find Pia and the nameless boy waiting for him in the palm groves.

He walked up the sand and triggered the alarm without knowing it.

Aboard the mother ship, Imbry heard it go off and switched the tight-beam scanner on. The intercom speaker over his head broke into a crackle.

"Fred? You got that one?"

"Uh-huh, Lindy. Right here."

"Which setup is it?"

"Eighty-eight on the B grid. It's that atoll right in the middle of the prevailing wind belt."

"I've got to hand it to you, Fred. Those little traps of yours are working like a charm."

Imbry ran his hand over his face. He knew what was going to happen to that innocent native, whoever he was. He'd come out of it a man, ready to take on the job of helping his people climb upward, with a lot of his old ideas stripped away.

Imbry's mouth jerked sideways, in the habitual gesture that was etching a deep groove in the skin of his face.

But he wouldn't be happy while he was learning. It was good for him—but there was no way for him to know that until he'd learned.

"How many this time?" Lindenhoff asked. "Coogan tells me they could use a lot of new recruits in a hurry, in that city they're building up north."

"Just one canoe," Imbry said, looking at the image on the scanner. "Small one, at that. Afraid it's only one man, Lindy." He moved the picture a little. "Yeah. Just one." He focused the controls.

"It's him! Tylus! We've got Tylus!"

There was a short pause on the other end of the intercom circuit. Then Lindenhoff said: "Okay, okay. You've finally got your pet one. Now, don't muff things in the rush." He chuckled softly and switched off.

Imbry bent closer to the scanner, though there was no real necessity for it. From here on, the process was automatic and as inevitable as an avalanche.

Lindenhoff had said it, that time last year when Imbry'd come back up from the planet: "Fred, there's a price to be paid for everything you learn about what's in the universe. It has to hurt, or it isn't a real price. There aren't any easy answers."

Certainly, for any man who had to learn this particular answer, the price could go very high. It was, in essence, the same answer Imbry himself had learned. When he had joined the Corporation, he had expected Lindenhoff, Coogan and the others to be gods—of a sort. And of course they weren't, any more than Imbry was. They were human, and had to do their job in human ways.

He had confused motive and method. Actually, the Corporation's motives were not so different from his, even though they were stated realistically instead of idealistically. To look at it another way, the Corporation simply had a clearer—more sane—knowledge of what it was doing and why.

Imbry, finding himself considered a god by the natives, had realized his own gods were only men, after all. What better way, then, to get the same natives started on the road to true civilization than to put them in exactly the same position he had been in?

Imbry watched the protoplasmic robots on the island come hesitantly through the underbrush toward the beach.

On the island, Tylus stopped. There was a crackle in the shrubbery, and a small, diffident figure stepped out. Its expression was watchful but friendly. It looked rather much like a man, except for its small size and the shade of its skin. Its eyes were intelligent. It looked trustful.

"Hello," Tylus said. "I'm Tylus."

The little native came forward. Others followed it, some more timid than the first, some smiling cordially. They kept casting glances at the magic tree-pod which could carry a man over the sea.

"Hello," the little native answered in a soft, liquid voice. "Are you an ancestor ghost or a god ghost?"

And Tylus began learning about Imbry.

BLIND LIGHTNING

By Harlan Ellison

The Budrys story depicts meek, peaceful alien beings, intelligent but simple. Now we meet a very different sort of creature: a ravenous beast out of nightmare, rippling with strength, coursing with barely repressed violence. Yet Harlan Ellison's Lad-nar and Algis Budrys' Tylus both regard the Earthmen who visit them as supernatural beings. They recognize in them the skills and powers of superior civilizations. In this story, intelligence meets brute force in a conflict that is not quite a conflict, and a strange, curiously touching relationship develops between man and monster on this rugged lightning-blasted world.

Harlan Ellison has been a professional writer since 1955, and this was one of his first published stories. It reveals the power and intensity of imagination that has since carried him to a successful career as an author of screenplays for television and motion pictures.

When Kettridge bent over to pick up the scurrying red lizard, the thing that had been waiting in shadows struck.

The thing rose nine feet on its powerfully muscled legs. It had an iridescent, glistening fur, and it resembled a gorilla and a Brahma bull and a Kodiak bear and a number of other Terran animals. But it was none of these creatures.

The comparison was as inaccurate and as brief as Kettridge's last moment of horrified awareness. He saw one of the thing's huge paws crashing down toward him. Then the brief moment ended, and Kettridge lay unconscious.

Thought: *This is the prelude to the Time of Fast. In bulk this strangely formed one will equal many cat litters. It is warm and does not lose the Essence. When the Essence-Stealer screams from the heavens, the strangely formed one will be many feastings for me. Safety and assured Essence are mine.*

O boon at last granted! To the Lord of the Heaven I turn all thought! Lad-nar's Essence is yours at Ending!

The huge creature bent sharply from the waist and scooped up the man in the form-fitting metallic suit. It brushed in annoyance at the belt of tools around the human's waist and looked over one massive shoulder at the sky.

Even as Lad-nar watched, the rolling dark clouds split, and a forked brilliance stabbed down at the jungle. Lad-nar squinted his eyes, unconsciously lowering the thin secondary lids, and filtering out the worst of the light.

He shivered as the roar screamed across the sky.

Off to his left another blast of lightning slanted down, striking a towering blue plant with a shower of sparks and a dazzling flash. A peal of thunder followed it. The jungle smoked.

Thought: *Many risings and settings of the Great Warmer it has taken this Time of Fast to build. Now it will last for many more. The Great Warmer will be hidden, and the cold will settle across the land. Lad-nar must find his way to the Place of Fasting. This strangely formed one will be many feastings.*

He shoved the man under one furry arm, clasping his unconscious burden tightly. Lad-nar's eyes were frightened. He knew the time of Death and Forbidden Walking was at hand.

He loped off toward the mountains.

The first thing Kettridge saw when he awoke was the head of the creature. It was hanging terrifyingly suspended by the light from the storm. The roar of the rain pelting down in driving sheets and the brilliant white of the lightning heightened the dreadfulness of the huge creature's head. The wide, blunt nose had three flaring nostrils. The massive double-lidded eyes seemed to be lighted from within by fires which blazed up in them like flickering twin comets. It had a high, hairy brow, and there were black half-moons under its cheekbones.

It seemed to be snarling. Certainly its pointed teeth could not have been bared more maliciously.

Kettridge was a man past the high tide of youth. He was not a strong man. At the beast's snort, he lost consciousness for the second time.

There followed a short stretch of half-slumber, confused, tormenting. Finally Kettridge blinked several times and raised himself on his elbows.

Lad-nar was still sitting with his powerfully muscled legs

crossed—sitting just inside the mouth of the small cave regarding Kettridge steadily.

"What—what *are* you?" Kettridge groaned. "We weren't expecting anything so large. The survey said . . ." Kettridge's voice quavered into silence.

Thought: *What is this? The strangely formed one speaks in my head! He is not one with the cat litters. They cannot speak! Is he a symbol, an omen—from the Lord of the Heaven?*

What is it you ask, strangely formed one?

Kettridge felt the surge of thoughts in his mind. He felt it smash against one nerve after another, sliding down in his head as the questions reverberated like an echo from far away.

My God, the thing is *telepathic!* . . . "You're telepathic!" he murmured, hardly daring to believe it could be true.

Thought: *What does he mean? What do you bring to me, strangely formed one? What is it that you say to me and that I hear as a Reading of the Essence? How do you speak? Are you from the Lord of the Heaven?*

Lad-nar's thick, leathery lips had not moved. The fanged mouth had not even twisted in speech. But to Kettridge it seemed that there must be a third being in the cave. A speaker who roared in his mind, in a voice sharp and alert.

Thought: *There is no one else here. This is the Place of Fasting. Lad-nar has cleansed it of all previous Fasting Ones. You do not answer. There is fear blended into your Essence, as it has always been with the cat litters. Yet you are not one with them. Speak! Are you an omen?*

Kettridge's lips began to tremble. He stared up in awe at the startlingly bright, double-lidded eyes, suddenly realizing that the creature was more than telepathic. It was two-way receptive. It could not only direct thoughts into Kettridge's mind. It could just as easily pluck the ideas from his reeling brain.

"I—I am from earth," whispered Kettridge, sliding up against the warm stone wall of the cave.

Thought: *The Heaven Home! I might have known. The Lord of the Heaven has sent you to me as many feastings.*

In the space of a few short seconds, as Lad-nar spoke deep in his mind, Kettridge received a complete mental picture of the being's incredible life. He had known there were living creatures on Blestone—many animal oddities in a barbaric hiding state. But the preliminary survey had not prepared him for any life of so complex a nature. Obviously Lad-nar's race was dying off.

Kettridge tried to blank out his thoughts but was terrifyingly unsuccessful.

Thought: *You cannot hide the speaking in my head.*

Kettridge became frantic. He knew exactly what the thing planned to do. He had received a cold mental image of the creature crouched mercilessly above him, ripping his right arm loose from its socket with a cruel purposefulness. The picture was hideously clear.

Thought: *You have seen the feasting. Yet you are not like the cat litters that squeal in fear every moment that I feast on them. If you are not to eat, an omen from the Heaven Lord— what are you?*

Kettridge felt his throat muscles tighten. His hands inside the heat-resistance gloves clenched. He felt his age settle around him like a heavy mantle.

"I'm an alien ecologist," he said, knowing he would not be understood.

Thought: *That has no meaning for me.*

"I'm from Earth. I'm from one of the other—" He stopped, drawing in his breath quickly and pulling the resilient hood of the suit against his mouth with an effort. The being could not possibly know about the other planets. It could not see a single one of the stars. Only occasionally could it see the sun. The dense cloud blanket of Blestone hid space forever from its gaze.

Thought: *Urth! The Heaven Home! I knew! I knew!*

There was a jubilation, a soaring happiness in the thought —an emotion at once incongruous and terrifying. But blending with it was a humanness, a strange warmth.

Thought: *Now I will sleep. Later I will feast.*

With the single-minded simplicity of the aborigine, the creature put from its mind this revelation of its religion and obeyed the commands of its body. Tired from hunting, Lad-nar began to sleep.

The thoughts dimmed and faded out of Kettridge's mind like dwindling smoke wraiths as the huge creature slipped over onto its side and sprawled out in the gloom, completely blocking the open mouth of the cave.

Kettridge's hand closed over the service revolver at his belt. It was reassuring to realize that the charges in the weapon were powerful enough to stop a good-sized animal.

Grimly he looked at the nine feet of corded muscle and

thick hide that lay directly in his path. Then his gaze swept the narrow confines of the cave. It was just possible that he could kill before it could rip him to shreds. But did he really *want* to kill Lad-nar?

The thought bothered him. He knew he had to kill—or be killed himself. And yet . . .

Outside the lightning flamed and crashed all around the cave. The long storm had begun.

Through the thin slit between the rocks and the creature Kettridge could see the sky darkening as the storm grew. Every moment there was a new cataclysm as streamers of fire flung themselves through the air.

Blestone's atmosphere was an uncomfortable-to-humans 150 degrees Fahrenheit, and the creature's body heat was almost certainly as high. The very nearness of the creature would have effectively ruined the aging career of Benjamin Kettridge had not the Earthman's insulated suit protected him.

He hunched up small against the wall, uncomfortably aware of the rough stone through the suit.

He knew that the beam from the *Jeremy Bentham* was tuned to a suit-sensitive level, but he knew also that they wouldn't come to pick him up until his search time expired. He wasn't the only ecologist from the study ship on Blestone. But they were a low-pay outfit and secured the most for their money by leaving the searchers in solitude for the full time.

The full time had another six hours to run.

In six hours Lad-nar would almost certainly get hungry.

Kettridge ran the whole thing through his mind, sifting the facts, gauging the information, calculating the outcome. It didn't look good. Not good at all.

He knew more about Lad-nar than the creature could have told him, though, and that at least was a factor in his favor. He knew about its religion, its taboos, its—and here he felt his throat go dry again—eating habits, its level of intelligence and culture. The being had kept nothing back, and Kettridge had some astonishingly accurate data to draw upon.

Not quite what you signed up for, is it, Ben? Startled by his own mental speech, he answered himself wearily, *No, not at all.*

Kettridge wondered what Lad-nar would think were he to tell the Blestonian he wasn't a blue-plate special, but a washed-out, run-down representative of a civilization that didn't give one hoot about Lad-nar or his religion.

He'll probably chew me up and swallow me, thought Kettridge. A more bitterly ironic thought followed: *which is exactly what he'll do anyhow. It would take a powerful weapon to stop him.*

It seemed so strange. Two days before he had been aboard the study-ship *Jeremy Bentham,* one year out of Capital City, and now he was the main course at a Blestonian aborigine's feast.

The laughter wouldn't come.

It wouldn't come because Kettridge was old and tired, and knew how right it was that he should die here, with all hope cut off. Lad-nar was simply following his natural instincts. He was protecting himself. He was surviving.

Which is more than you've been doing for the last ten years, Ben, he told himself.

Benjamin Kettridge had long since stopped surviving. He knew it as clearly as he knew he would die here on this hot and steaming world far from the sight of men.

Think about it, Ben. Think it over. Now that it's finished and you tumble out of things at sixty-six years of age. Think about the waste and the crying and the bit of conviction that could have saved you. Think about it all.

Then the story unfurled on a fleeting banner. It rolled out for Ben Kettridge there in a twilight universe. In the course of a few minutes he had found life in that shadowy mind-world preferable to his entire previous existence.

He saw himself again as a prominent scientist, engaged with others of his kind on a project of great consequence to mankind. He recalled his own secret misgivings as he had boldly embarked on the experiment.

He heard again the sonorous overtones and the pith and substance of his talk with Fenimore. He heard it more clearly than the blast and rush of the thunder outside. . . .

"Charles, I don't think we should do it this way. If something were to happen—"

"Ben, nothing whatever can possibly happen—unless we become careless. The compound is safe, and you know it. First we demonstrate its applicability. Then we let the dunderheads scream about it. After they know its worth, they'll be the first to acclaim us."

"But you don't seem to understand, Fenimore. There are too many random factors in the formulae. There's a fundamental flaw in them. If I could only put my finger on it—"

"Get this, Ben. I don't like to pull seniority on you, but I have no choice. I'm not a harsh man, but this is a dream I've had for twenty years, and no unjustified timidity on your part is going to put it off. We test the compound Thursday!"

And Fenimore's dream had overnight turned into a nightmare of twenty-five thousand dead, and hospitals filled to overflowing with screaming patients.

The nightmare had reached out thready tentacles and dragged in Kettridge, too. In a manner of days a reputation built on years of dedicated work had been reduced to rubble. But he had not escaped the inquests. What little reputation he had left had saved him—and a few others—from the gas chamber. But life was at an end for him.

Ten years of struggling for mere survival—no one would hire him even for the most menial of jobs—had sunk Kettridge lower and lower. There was still a common decency about him that prevented utter disintegration, just as there was an inner desire to continue living.

Kettridge never became—as did some of the others who escaped—a flophouse derelict or a suicide. He just became—anonymous.

His fortunes ebbed until there was nothing left except slashed wrists or the bottle.

Kettridge had been too old by then for either. And always there had been the knowledge that he could have stopped the project had he voiced his doubts instead of brooding in silence.

Finally the study-ship post had saved him. Ben Kettridge, using another name, had signed on for three years. He had actually welcomed the cramp and the squalor of shipboard. Studying and cataloging under the stars had enabled him to regain his self-respect and to keep a firm grip on his sanity.

Ben Kettridge had become an alien ecologist. And now, one year out from Capital City, his sanity was threatened again.

He wanted to scream desperately. His throat muscles drew up and tightened, and his mouth, inside the flexible hood, opened until the corners stretched in pain.

The pictures had stopped. He had withdrawn in terror from the shadowed mind-world and was back in a stone prison with a hungry aborigine for keeper.

Lad-nar stirred.

The huge furred body twisted, sighed softly, and sank back into sleep again. Kettridge wondered momentarily if the strength of his thoughts had disturbed the beast.

What a fantastic creature, thought Kettridge, *It lives on a world where the heat will fry a human and shivers in fear at lightning storms.*

A strange compassion came over Kettridge. How very much like a native of Earth this alien creature was. Governed by its stomach and will to survive, and dominated by a religion founded in fear and nurtured on terror! Lightning the beast thought of as a Screamer from the Skies. The occasionally glimpsed sun was the Great Warmer.

Kettridge pondered on the simplicity and primitive common sense of Lad-nar's religion.

When the storms gathered, when they finally built up sufficient potential to generate the lightning and thunder, Lad-nar knew that the cold would set in. Cold was anathema to him. He knew that the cold sapped him of strength, and that the lightning struck him down.

So he stole a cat litter and hid himself for weeks—until the gigantic storms abated. The high body heat of the creature dictated that it must have a great deal of food to keep it alive when the temperature went down. When a cat litter wasn't available, the logical alternative was to *kill and eat an alien ecologist.*

This was no stupid being, Kettridge reminded himself.

Its religion was a sound combination of animal wisdom and native observation. The lightning killed. Don't go abroad in the storms. The storms brought cold. Get food and stay alive.

It was indeed strange how a terrifying situation could bring a man to a realization of himself.

Here is a chance, he thought. The words came unbidden.

Just four words. *Here is a chance.* An opportunity not only to survive—something he had long since stopped doing consciously—but a chance to redeem himself, if only in his own mind. Before him was an aborigine, a member of a dying race, a cowering creature of the caves. Before him was a creature afraid to walk in the storms for fear of the lightning, shackled by a primitive religion and doomed never to see the sky.

In that split moment Ben Kettridge devised a plan to save Lad-nar's soul.

There are times when men sum up their lives, take accounting, and find themselves wanting. Lad-nar suddenly became a symbol of all the people who had been lost in the Mass Death.

In the mind of an old and tired man, many things are possible.

I must get out of here! Ben Kettridge told himself, over and over. But more than that, he knew that he must save the poor hulk before him. And in saving the creature he would save himself. Lad-nar had no idea what a star was. Well, Ben Kettridge would tell him. Here was a chance!

Kettridge moved up flat against the wall, his back straining with his effort to sink into the stone. Watching the Blestonian come to wakefulness was an ordeal of pure horror.

The huge body tossed and heaved as it rose. It sat erect from the thin, pinched waist and raised the massive wedge-shaped chest, the hideous head, the powerful neck and arms. A thin trickle of moisture dripped from a corner of its fanged mouth. It sat up and thought: *Lad-nar hungers.*

"Oh, God in Heaven, please let me have time! Please allow me this one *little* thing!"

Kettridge found himself with his hands clasped on his chest, his face raised to the roof of the cave. For the first time in his life he felt tears of appeal on his cheeks.

Thought: *You speak to the Lord of the Heaven.* Lad-nar seemed awed. He watched, his huge, brilliant eyes suddenly grown wide.

Kettridge thought at the beast: *Lad-nar! I come from the Lord of Heaven, I can show you how to walk in the storms! I can show you how to—*

The creature's roar deafened Kettridge. Accompanying it came a mental scream! Kettridge felt himself lifted off the floor by the force of the blow to his mind and hurled violently back against the rocks.

The aborigine leaped to his feet, threw his taloned hands upward, and bellowed in rage.

Thought: *You speak that which is Forbidden! You say that which is Untrue. No human walks when the Essence-Stealer speaks in the night. You are a fearful thing! Lad-nar is afraid!*

"Heresy, I've spoken heresy!" Kettridge wanted to rip off the metal-plastic hood and tear his tongue from his mouth.

Thought: *Yes, you have spoken that which is Unclean and Untrue!*

Kettridge cowered in fear. The creature was truly enraged now. How could it be afraid when it stood there so powerful and so massive?

Thought: *Yes, Lad-nar is afraid! Afraid!*

Then the waves of fear hit Kettridge. He felt his head begin to throb. The tender fiber of his mind was being twisted and seared and buffeted. Burned and scarred forever with Lad-nar's terrible all-consuming fear.

Stop, stop, Lad-nar! I speak the truth! I will show you how to walk in the storm as I do.

He spoke then—softly, persuasively, trying to convince a being that had never known any god but a deity that howled and slashed in streamers of electricity. He spoke of himself, and of his powers. He spoke of them as though he truly believed in them. He built himself a glory on two levels.

Slowly Lad-nar became calmer, and the waves of fear diminished to ripples. The awe and trembling remained, but there was a sliver of belief in the creature's mind now.

Kettridge knew he must work on that.

"I come from the Heaven-Home, Lad-nar. I speak as a messenger from the sky. I am stronger than the puny Essence-Stealer you fear!" As if to punctuate his words, a flash of lightning struck just outside the cave, filling the hollow with fury and light.

Kettridge continued, speaking faster and faster, "I can walk abroad in the storm, and the Essence-Stealer will not harm me. Let me go out, and I will show you, Lad-nar."

He was playing a dangerous hand; at any moment the creature might leap. It might dare to venture upon a leap, hoping that Kettridge was speaking falsely and preferring not to incur the wrath of a god he *knew* to be dangerous.

Thought: *Stop!*

"Why, Lad-nar? I can show you how to walk in the night, when the Essence-Stealer screams. I can show you how to scream back at him and to laugh at him too."

Kettridge reminded himself that the creature was indeed clever. Not only did it fear the wrath of the Lord of the Heaven and his screaming death. It knew that if it let the man go, it would have nothing to eat during the coming cold days.

"Let me go, Lad-nar. I will bring you back a cat litter for your feasting. I will show you that I can walk in the night, and I will bring you food. I will bring back a cat litter, Lad-nar!"

Thought: *If you are what you say, why do you speak to the Lord of the Heaven?*

Kettridge bit his lip. He kept forgetting . . .

"Because I want the Lord of the Heaven to know that I am as great as he," he said. "I want him to know I am not afraid of him and that my prayers to him are only to convince him that I am as great as he." It was gibberish, but he hoped that if he kept talking the creature would shuck off the thoughts rather than try to fathom them.

The Earthman knew he had one factor in his favor: Lad-nar had never before heard anyone speak against his own god and to do so with impunity immeasurably strengthened Kettridge's hand.

Kettridge hit Lad-nar with the appeal again, before the creature had time to wonder.

"I'll get you a cat litter, Lad-nar. Let me go! Let me show you! Let me show you that you can walk in the storms as I do!"

Thought: *You will go away.*

There was a petulance, a little child sound, to the objection, and Kettridge knew the first step had been achieved.

"No, Lad-nar. Here is a rope." He drew a thin cord of tough metal-plastic from his utility belt. His hand brushed against his service revolver, and he laughed deep in his mind once more as he thought of how useless it had become.

He would not have used the gun in any case. Only by his wits could he hope to win through to victory. There was more at stake now than mere self-preservation.

"Here is a rope," he repeated, extending the coiled cord. "I will tie it about myself. See—like this. You take the other end. If you hold it tightly I can't escape. It is long enough to enable me to go out and seek a cat litter, and to convince you that I can walk abroad."

At first Lad-nar refused, eyeing the glistening, silvery cord with fear in his heavily lidded eyes. But Kettridge spoke on two levels, and soon the creature touched the cord.

It drew back its seven-taloned hand quickly. It tried again. The third time it grasped the cord.

You have just lost your religion, Kettridge thought.

Lad-nar had "smelled" with his mind. He had sensed a cat litter fairly close to the cave. But he did not know where the living food supply had taken refuge.

Kettridge emerged from the dark mouth of the cave into the roaring maelstrom of a Blestonian electrical storm.

The sky was a tumult of heavy black clouds, steel and ebony and ripped dirty cloth. The clouds revolved in dark masses and were split apart by the lightning. The very air was charged, and blast after blast sheared away the atmosphere in zigzagging streamers.

Kettridge stood there with the pelting rain washing over

ward against the pull of the cord. He was forced to shade his eyes against the almost continuous glare of the lightning.

He was a small, thin man, and had it not been for the cord he might easily have been swept away by the winds and rain that sand-papered the rocky ledge.

Ketteridge stood there with the pelting rain washing over him, obscuring his vision through the hood, and leaving only the glare of the storm to guide him.

He took a short step forward.

A bolt slashed at him through a rift in the mountains and roared straight toward him. It materialized out of nowhere and everywhere—shattering a massive slab of granite almost at his feet. Kettridge fell flat on his stomach, and the crack of thunder rolled on past him.

The effect on his body was terrifying.

Immediately he went deaf. His legs and hips became numb, and his eyes reflected coruscating pinwheels of brilliance.

Thought: *The Essence-Stealer has screamed, and you have fallen!*

The rope tightened and Kettridge felt himself being drawn back into the cave.

"No!" he protested desperately. The pressure eased. "No, Lad-nar. That was the Essence-Stealer's scream. Now I shall make my power felt. Let me show you, Lad-nar!"

Kettridge seized on the lightning blast for his own purpose. "See, Lad-nar! The Essence-Stealer has struck me, but I am still whole. I will rise and walk again."

Everywhere the lightning burned and crashed. The whole world seemed filled with the noise of crashing trees and screaming elements.

He arose shakily to his knees. His legs were weak and numb. But his eyes were starting to focus again. At least he could see now. He half rose, sank back to one knee, and rose again. His head felt terribly heavy and unanchored.

Finally he stood erect.

And he walked.

The storm raged about him. Lightning struck and struck again, but his courage did not desert him.

Soon he came back to the cave.

Thought: *You are a god! This I believe. But the Lord of the Heaven has sent his Essence-Stealers. They, too, are mighty, and Lad-nar will lose his Essence if he walks there.*

"No, Lad-nar. I will show you how to protect yourself." Kettridge was sweating and weak from his walk, and the numbness extended through his entire body. He could hear nothing, but the words came clearly to him.

Very deliberately he began to unseal the form-fitting suit. In a few minutes he had it off, and it had shrunk back to a pocket-sized replica of the full-sized garment. The storm had lowered the temperature almost to freezing point.

"Lad-nar, take this," Kettridge said. "Here, give me your hand."

The creature looked at him with huge, uncomprehending eyes. The Earthman felt closer, somehow, to this strange creature than to anyone he had ever known in all the lonely years of his exile. Kettridge pulled his glove on tighter and reached for Lad-nar's seven-taloned hand. He pulled at the arm of the form-fit suit, and it elastically expanded, stretching to twice its original width.

After much stretching and fitting, the creature was encased in the insulating metal-plastic.

Kettridge had an impulse to laugh at the bunched fur and awkward stance of the massive animal. But again, the laughter would not come.

"Now, Lad-nar, put on the gloves. Never take them off, except when the storms are gone. You must always put this suit on when the Essence-Stealers scream. Then you will be safe."

Thought: *Now I can walk in the night?*

"Yes, come." They moved together toward the cave's mouth. "Now you can get a cat litter for yourself. I did not bring one, because I knew you would believe me and get your own. Come, Lad-nar." He motioned him forward.

Thought: *How will you walk without the suit?*

Kettridge ran a seamed hand through his white hair. He was glad Lad-nar had thought the question. The multiple flashes of a many-stroked blast filled the air with glare and noise.

Kettridge could not hear the noise.

"I have brothers who wait for me in the Great House from across the Skies that will take me back to the heaven Home. They will hurry to me, and they will protect me."

He did not bother to tell Lad-nar that his search time was almost up and that the *Jeremy Bentham's* flitter would home in on his suit beam.

"Go! Walk, Lad-nar!" he said, throwing his arms out. "And tell your brothers you have screamed at the Essence-Stealers!"

Thought: *I have done this.*

Lad-nar stepped cautiously toward the rocky ledge, fearful

and hesitant. Then he bunched his huge muscles and leaped out into the full agony of the storm which crashed in futility about his massive form.

"One day Man will come and make friends with you, Lad-nar," said Kettridge softly. "He will come down out of the sky and show you how to live on this world of yours so that you won't have to hide."

Kettridge sank down against the inner wall of the cave, suddenly too exhausted to stand.

He had won. He had redeemed himself—if only in his own mind. He had helped take away life from a race, but now—he had given life to a race.

He closed his eyes peacefully. Even the great blasts of blind lightning did not bother him as he rested. He knew Lad-nar had told his brothers.

He knew the ship would be coming for him.

Lad-nar came up the incline and saw the flitter streaking down, with lightning playing along its sides in phosphorescent glimmers.

Thought: *Your brothers come for you!*

He bounded across the scarred and seared rocks toward the cave.

Kettridge rose and stepped out into the rain and wind.

He ran a few steps, waving his arms in a signaling gesture. The flitter altered its course and headed for him, its speed increasing with great rapidity.

The lightning struck.

It seemed as though the bolt knew its target. It raced the flitter, sizzling and burning as it came. In a roar of light and fire it tore at Kettridge, lifting him high into the air and carrying him far from Lad-nar.

His body landed just outside the cave, blistered and charred but still struggling.

Thought: *You have fallen! Rise, rise, rise! The Essence-Stealers* . . .

The thoughts were hysterical, tearful, torn, and wanting. Had Lad-nar been able to shed tears, Kettridge knew he would have wept unashamedly. The old man lay sightless, his eyes gone, his senses altogether torn from him. The Essence ebbed.

He thought: *Lad-nar. Others will come. They will come to you, and you must think to them. You must think these words, Lad-nar. Think to them,* SHOW ME A STAR. *Do you hear me, Lad-nar? Do you* . . .

Even as Lad-nar watched, the Essence flickered and died. In the creature's mind there was a lack, an abyss of emptiness. Yet there was also contentment, a strange peace. And Lad-nar knew the Essence of the God Who Walked in the Night was strong and unafraid at Ending.

The aborigine stood on the rocks below the cave and watched the flitter sink to the stone ledge. He watched as the other Gods from the Skies emerged and ran to the charred body on the stones.

Through his head, like the blind lightning streaking everywhere, the words remained, and repeated. . . .

Thought: *Show me a star.*

OUT OF THE SUN

By Arthur C. Clarke

Arthur C. Clarke is a true citizen of the world. Where he is at any given moment only his travel agent is likely to know: perhaps in New York conferring with his publishers, perhaps excavating sunken treasure off the coast of Ceylon, perhaps supervising the filming of a movie in London, perhaps studying the coral formations of Australia's Great Barrier Reef, perhaps watching a rocket blasting moonward from Cape Kennedy. He was born in England, but he is at home on any continent, and probably will be found sightseeing on Mars and Venus as soon as commercial service to those ports of call is inaugurated.

As an acknowledged master of science fiction, Clarke's presence in any anthology is almost mandatory. He works within the great tradition of H. G. Wells, combining literary artistry with scientific accuracy to create stories of stirring wonder and breathtaking provocativeness. Here Clarke offers a fitting epilogue for this collection of stories of alien life: a glimpse of a life-form so incredibly strange that we poor mortals can barely begin to comprehend its nature.

If you have only lived on Earth, you have never seen the sun. Of course, we could not look at it directly, but only through dense filters that cut its rays down to endurable brilliance. It hung there forever above the low, jagged hills to the west of the Observatory, neither rising nor setting, yet moving around a small circle in the sky during the eighty-eight-day year of our little world. For it is not quite true to say that Mercury keeps the same face always turned toward the sun; it wobbles slightly on its axis, and there is a narrow twilight belt which knows such terrestrial commonplaces as dawn and sunset.

We were on the edge of the twilight zone, so that we could take advantage of the cool shadows yet could keep the sun under continuous surveillance as it hovered there above the hills. It was a full-time job for fifty astronomers and other assorted scientists; when we've kept it up for a hundred years or so, we may know something about the small star that brought life to Earth.

There wasn't a single band of solar radiation that someone at the Observatory had not made a life's study and was watching like a hawk. From the far X-rays to the longest of radio waves, we had set our traps and snares; as soon as the sun thought of something new, we were ready for it. So we imagined. . . .

The sun's flaming heart beats in a slow, eleven-year rhythm, and we were near the peak of the cycle. Two of the greatest spots ever recorded—each of them large enough to swallow a hundred Earths—had drifted across the disk like great black funnels piercing deeply into the turbulent outer layers of the sun. They were black, of course, only by contrast with the brilliance all around them; even their dark, cool cores were hotter and brighter than an electric arc. We had just watched the second of them disappear around the edge of the disk, wondering if it would survive to reappear two weeks later, when something blew up on the equator.

It was not too spectacular at first, partly because it was almost exactly beneath us—at the precise center of the sun's disk—and so was merged into all the activity around it. If it had been near the edge of the sun, and thus projected against the background of space, it would have been truly awe-inspiring.

Imagine the simultaneous explosion of a million H-bombs. You can't? Nor can anyone else—but that was the sort of thing we were watching climb up toward us at hundreds of miles a second, straight out of the sun's spinning equator. At first it formed a narrow jet, but it was quickly frayed around the edges by the magnetic and gravitational forces that were fighting against it. The central core kept right on, and it was soon obvious that it had escaped from the sun completely and was headed out into space—with us as its first target.

Though this had happened half a dozen times before, it was always exciting. It meant that we could capture some of the very substance of the sun as it went hurtling past in a great cloud of electrified gas. There was no danger; by the time it reached us it would be far too tenuous to do any damage, and, indeed, it would take sensitive instruments to detect it at all.

One of those instruments was the Observatory's radar, which was in continual use to map the invisible ionized layers that surround the sun for millions of miles. This was my department; as soon as there was any hope of picking up the on-coming cloud against the solar background, I aimed my giant radio mirror toward it.

It came in sharp and clear on the long-range screen—a vast, luminous island still moving outward from the sun at hundreds of miles a second. At this distance it was impossible to see its finer details, for my radar waves were taking minutes to make the round trip and to bring me back the information they were presenting on the screen. Even at its speed of not far short of a million miles an hour, it would be almost two days before the escaping prominence reached the orbit of Mercury and swept past us toward the outer planets. But neither Venus nor Earth would record its passing, for they were nowhere near its line of flight.

The hours drifted by; the sun had settled down after the immense convulsions that had shot so many millions of tons of its substance into space, never to return. The aftermath of that eruption was now a slowly twisting and turning cloud a hundred times the size of Earth, and soon it would be close enough for the short-range radar to reveal its finer structure.

Despite all the years I have been in the business, it still gives me a thrill to watch that line of light paint its picture on the screen as its spins in synchronism with the narrow beam of radio waves from the transmitter. I sometimes think of myself as a blind man exploring the space around him with a stick that may be a hundred million miles in length. For man is truly blind to the things I study; these great clouds of ionized gas moving far out from the sun are completely invisible to the eye and even to the most sensitive of photographic plates. They are ghosts that briefly haunt the solar system during the few hours of their existence; if they did not reflect our radar waves or disturb our magnetometers, we should never know that they were there.

The picture on the screen looked not unlike a photograph of a spiral nebula, for as the cloud slowly rotated it trailed ragged arms of gas for ten thousand miles around it. Or it might have been a terrestrial hurricane that I was watching from above as it spun through the atmosphere of Earth. The internal structure was extremely complicated and was changing minute by minute beneath the action of forces which we have never fully understood. Rivers of fire were flowing in curious paths under what could only be the influence of electric fields; but why were they appearing from nowhere and disappearing again as if matter was being created and destroyed? And what were those gleaming nodules, larger than the moon, that were being swept along like boulders before a flood?

Now it was less than a million miles away; it would be upon us in little more than an hour. The automatic cameras were recording every complete sweep of the radar scan, storing up evidence which was to keep us arguing for years. The magnetic disturbance riding ahead of the cloud had already reached us; indeed, there was hardly an instrument in the Observatory that was not reacting in some way to the onrushing apparition.

I switched to the short-range scanner, and the image of the cloud expanded so enormously that only its central portion was on the screen. At the same time I began to change frequency, turning across the spectrum to differentiate among the various levels. The shorter the wave length, the farther you can penetrate into a layer of ionized gas; by this technique I hoped to get a kind of X-ray picture of the cloud's interior.

It seemed to change before my eyes as I sliced down through the tenuous outer envelope with its trailing arms and approached the denser core. "Denser," of course, was a purely relative word; by terrestrial standards even its most closely packed regions were still a fairly good vacuum. I had almost reached the limit of my frequency band, and could shorten the wave length no farther, when I noticed the curious, tight little echo not far from the center of the screen.

It was oval and much more sharp-edged than the knots of gas we had watched adrift in the cloud's fiery streams. Even in that first glimpse, I knew that here was something very strange and outside all previous records of solar phenomena. I watched it for a dozen scans of the radar beam, then called my assistant away from the radiospectrograph, with which he was analyzing the velocities of the swirling gas as it spun toward us.

"Look, Don," I asked him, "have you ever seen anything like that?"

"No," he answered after a careful examination. "What holds it together? It hasn't changed its shape for the last two minutes."

"That's what puzzles me. Whatever it is, it should have started to break up by now, with all that disturbance going on around it. But it seems as stable as ever."

"How big would you say it is?"

I switched on the calibration grid and took a quick reading.

"It's about five hundred miles long, and half that in width."

"Is this the largest picture you can get?"

"I'm afraid so. We'll have to wait until it's closer before we can see what makes it tick."

Don gave a nervous little laugh.

"This is crazy," he said, "but do you know something? I feel as if I'm looking at an amoeba under a microscope."

I did not answer; for, with what I can only describe as a sensation of intellectual vertigo, exactly the same thought had entered my mind.

We forgot about the rest of the cloud, but luckily the automatic cameras kept up their work, and no important observations were lost. From now on we had eyes only for that sharp-edged lens of gas that was growing minute by minute as it raced toward us. When it was no farther away than is the moon from Earth, it began to show the first signs of its internal structure, revealing a curious mottled appearance that was never quite the same on two successive sweeps of the scanner.

By now, half the Observatory staff had joined us in the radar room, yet there was complete silence as the oncoming enigma grew swiftly across the screen. It was coming straight toward us; in a few minutes it would hit Mercury somewhere in the center of the daylight side, and that would be the end of it —whatever it was. From the moment we obtained our first really detailed view until the screen became blank again could not have been more than five minutes; for every one of us, that five minutes will haunt us all our lives.

We were looking at what seemed to be a translucent oval, its interior laced with a network of almost invisible lines. Where the lines crossed, there appeared to be tiny, pulsing nodes of light; we could never be quite sure of their existence because the radar took almost a minute to paint the complete picture on the screen—and between each sweep the object moved several thousand miles. There was no doubt, however, that the network itself existed; the cameras settled any arguments about that.

So strong was the impression that we were looking at a solid object that I took a few moments off from the radar screen and hastily focused one of the optical telescopes on the sky. Of course, there was nothing to be seen—no sign of anything silhouetted against the sun's pock-marked disk. This was a case where vision failed completely and only the electrical senses of the radar were of any use. The thing that was coming toward us out of the sun was as transparent as air—and far more tenuous.

As those last moments ebbed away, I am quite sure that every one of us had reached the same conclusion—and was waiting for someone to say it first. What we were seeing was impossible, yet the evidence was there before our eyes. We were looking at life, where no life could exist. . . .

The eruption had hurled the thing out of its normal environment, deep down in the flaming atmosphere of the sun. It was a miracle that it had survived its journey through space; already it must be dying, as the forces that controlled its huge, invisible body lost their hold over the electrified gas which was the only substance it possessed.

Today, now that I have run through those films a hundred times, the idea no longer seems so strange to me. For what is life but organized energy? Does it matter *what* form that energy takes—whether it is chemical, as we know it on Earth, or purely electrical, as it seemed to be here? Only the pattern is important; the substance itself is of no significance. But at the time I did not think of this; I was conscious only of a vast and overwhelming wonder as I watched this creature of the sun live out the final moments of its existence.

Was it intelligent? Could it understand the strange doom that had befallen it? There are a thousand such questions that may never be answered. It is hard to see how a creature born in the fires of the sun itself could know anything of the external universe, or could even sense the existence of something as unutterably cold as rigid nongaseous matter. The living island that was falling upon us from space could never have conceived, however intelligent it might be, of the world it was so swiftly approaching.

Now it filled our sky—and perhaps, in those last few seconds, it knew that something strange was ahead of it. It may have sensed the far-flung magnetic field of Mercury or felt the tug of our little world's gravitational pull. For it had begun to change; the luminous lines that must have been what passed for its nervous system were clumping together in new patterns, and I would have given much to know their meaning. It may be that I was looking into the brain of a mindless beast in its last convulsion of fear—or of a godlike being making its peace with the universe.

Then the radar screen was empty, wiped clean during a single scan of the beam. The creature had fallen below our horizon, and was hidden from us now by the curve of the planet. Far out in the burning dayside of Mercury, in the inferno where only a dozen men have ever ventured and fewer still come back alive, it smashed silently and invisibly against the seas of molten metal, the hills of slowly moving lava. The mere impact could have meant nothing to such an entity; what it could not endure was its first contact with the inconceivable cold of solid matter.

Yes, *cold*. It had descended upon the hottest spot in the solar system, where the temperature never falls below seven hundred degrees Fahrenheit and sometimes approaches a thousand. And that was far, far colder to it than the antarctic winter would be to a naked man.

We did not see it die, out there in the freezing fire; it was beyond the reach of our instruments now, and none of them recorded its end. Yet every one of us knew when that moment came, and that is why we are not interested when those who have seen only the films and tapes tell us that we were watching some purely natural phenomenon.

How can one explain what we felt, in that last moment when half our little world was enmeshed in the dissolving tendrils of that huge but immaterial brain? I can only say that it was a soundless cry of anguish, a death pang that seeped into our minds without passing through the gateways of the senses. Not one of us doubted then, or has ever doubted since, that he had witnessed the passing of a giant.

We may have been both the first and the last of all men to see so mighty a fall. Whatever *they* may be, in their unimaginable world within the sun, our paths and theirs may never cross again. It is hard to see how we can ever make contact with them, even if their intelligence matches ours.

And does it? It may be well for us if we never know the answer. Perhaps they have been living there inside the sun since the universe was born and have climbed to peaks of wisdom that we shall never scale. The future may be theirs, not ours; already they may be talking across the light-years to their cousins in other stars.

One day they may discover us, by whatever strange senses they possess, as we circle around their mighty, ancient home,

proud of our knowledge and thinking ourselves lords of creation. They may not like what they find, for to them we should
be no more than maggots, crawling upon the skins of worlds
too cold to cleanse themselves from the corruption of organic
life.

And then, if they have the power, they will do what they
consider necessary. The sun will put forth its strength and lick
the faces of its children; and thereafter the planets will go
their way once more as they were in the beginning—clean and
bright . . . and sterile.

The smash bestseller the whole country is talking about!

Rosemary's Baby

by Ira Levin

SUPPOSE you were a young housewife who moved
into an old and elegant apartment house with
a strange past. SUPPOSE that only after you
became pregnant did you suspect that the
building harbored a group of devil worshippers
who had mastered the art of black magic.
SUPPOSE that this satanic conspiracy set out
to claim not only your husband but your baby.
Well, this is what happened to Rosemary.
Or did it?

DON'T REVEAL THE ENDING

**"The climax is an icy shock which no one
will ever quite forget."** —*Providence Journal*

Watch for the Paramount movie starring Mia Farrow

A DELL BOOK   95¢